A MONSTROUS SCHEME FOR
WORLD CONQUEST

The United States and the Soviet Union are tied together in the race to stop a top Russian general from assuming leadership of a small group of men who are ready to start a Third World War.

Broom College would seem an unlikely setting, but its Board of Directors has more than university problems on its agenda. The board consists of power hungry men who plan to rule the world.

Can a student convince the CIA that a mysterious stranger on campus threatens our very existence? Can a KGB agent find and kill the general before the buttons are pushed? The answers come only in . . .

THE HAMMER STRIKE SOLUTION

THE
HAMMER
STRIKE
SOLUTION

Also by Vincent Fields

DIAMONDS

THE HAMMER STRIKE SOLUTION

Vincent Fields

PaperJacks LTD.

TORONTO   NEW YORK

AN ORIGINAL

PaperJacks

THE HAMMER STRIKE SOLUTION

PaperJacks LTD.

330 STEELCASE RD. E., MARKHAM, ONT. L3R 2M1
210 FIFTH AVE., NEW YORK, N.Y. 10010

First edition published August 1988

THE
HAMMER
STRIKE
SOLUTION

[1]

The driver brought the cab to an abrupt stop in front of the terminal at Rome's da Vinci airport. He pointed to one of the numerous doors with American Airlines printed in big red letters and in broken English said, "There, you go there."

The man in the rear seat paid the amount shown on the meter and, without tipping the driver, he left the cab. He went through one of the automatic doors, walked several steps and stopped in front of an Italian, French, German and English information panel, where he spent a few minutes reading the English section. Then he turned right and walked casually toward the American Airlines's First Class check-in counter.

He wore light-sensitive sun glasses, a gray Stetson hat with the brim turned down in front. A dark blue alpaca coat was draped across his shoulders. In his right hand, he carried a black leather attaché case.

There were two people in front of him: a man and young woman. He examined the woman, whose age he guessed to be somewhere between twenty-five and thirty, with the critical eye of a ponce. Though she was slender, she had well-developed breasts and good hips. She wore her black hair short.

When the man left the counter, the clerk said to the woman, "I will be with you in a few minutes." Then he busied himself at a computer terminal.

Though the woman looked annoyed, she said nothing.

Despite the fact he had been warned not to speak to anyone on the flight over, he could not turn away from what he sensed might become his first sexual adventure with an American woman.

"You could complain," the man said, speaking English with a slight eastern European accent. "After all, this is first class."

The woman turned. "If I really thought it would do any good, I would," she answered.

The man smiled. "A written complaint to the president of the company might have an effect. I would be more than willing to help you compose it on the flight to New York . . . you are going to New York, aren't you?"

"Yes," she replied. "But only for a night. Tomorrow I fly to St. Louis."

"Would you think me impertinent if I asked you to join me for a drink in the lounge aboard the plane?" the man asked.

She flashed him a smile. "I'd like that," she said, just as the clerk returned.

The man nodded.

During the time that it took the woman to have her ticket validated and her flight from New York to St. Louis confirmed, the man imagined how she would look nude.

When the woman finished, she turned. "See you."

"See you," the man responded and handed the clerk his ticket and passport.

"Mister Noonan," the clerk said, reading the name off the passport and at the same time typing it into the computer.

"Noonan is the name, and business is my game," he said as he watched the woman walk toward the waiting area.

The clerk smiled. "There is an hour layover at Heathrow in London."

"I thought this was a direct flight to New York," Noonan said, the tone of his voice changing.

"I'm sorry, sir, American does not have a direct flight from Rome to New York. You might consider trying another airline."

"It's too late to change airlines," Noonan growled.

"Has your baggage been checked in?"

"Yes," Noonan answered.

The clerk handed him his ticket and passport. "Seat number six."

"Would it be possible to sit next to the woman who checked in before me?"

"I'm sorry, sir," the clerk said, "but each seat is reserved. Perhaps the person occupying the seat next to her would be willing to change with you."

"Yes, perhaps," Noonan snapped, now even more annoyed than he had been a few minutes ago.

The clerk looked at his watch. "The complimentary lounge for American's first class passengers will open in five minutes."

"At least *that* will be available," Noonan responded. He walked into the waiting area and went straight to where the woman was seated.

Detective Lieutenant Sergio Petraioija looked down at the body of a white male, whom the chambermaid had found less than an hour before when she opened the door to clean the room. The body was sprawled out on the unmade bed closest to the door.

Petraioija, a tall raw-boned man with thinning brown hair, lit a cigarette and waited until the coroner finished his preliminary examination before he asked, "How long has he been dead?"

"Between three and five hours," Doctor Cusati replied.

"Any guesses about the cause of death?"

"Maybe a stroke."

"Looks kind of young for that," Petraioija commented.

Cusati shrugged. "Might have happened while he was with a woman."

"The manager said that all the records in and out of the computer for the people occupying this room are gone," Petraioija said.

Cusati, a small, wizened man, squinted up at the detective. "Surely there must be something? In your files?"

Petraioija shook his head. "This morning we received the usual information on everyone who checked in last night."

"Then you must have names."

"Nothing."

"But it's the law —"

"The passports were removed before the information on them was transferred to the proper forms," Petraioija explained.

The coroner made a low humming sound, then he commented, "The newspapers are going to have a ball with this one."

"The only thing I have to go on," Petraioija said, "is that the other man, according to the chambermaid and the manager, had a large brown moustache and spoke English with a Polish accent."

"How did they know it was Polish?"

"Since the new Pope, anyone from Eastern Europe speaks with a Polish accent," Petraioija answered with a smile.

"I'll be able to tell you a lot more about him," Cusati said, "after I finish my tests."

Petraioija nodded. "I have the feeling that your results are only going to make me ask more questions."

"Sorry about that," the coroner said as he moved aside to let the police technicians photograph the body. "As soon as they're done, my people will wrap him up and bring him to the police morgue."

Petraioija walked to the window, pulled up the venetian blind and looked down at the Via Porta Pinciana, a narrow street that for a short distance ran parallel to the Borghese gardens. Of all the hotels in Rome, the Eliseo, because it was so close to the gardens, was his favorite. He even took his wife to its rooftop restaurant during the summer because they could dine al fresco there and have a lovely view of the gardens.

He turned to look at the body. Whoever killed the man — or was with him at the time of his death

— removed all of his clothing, the ring he wore on his right pinky, and a chain of some sort from his neck. No doubt it was a gold chain. Petraioija pursed his lips. If the man died while humping some woman, he probably died in a moment of supreme ecstasy, or so Petraioija would have liked to think. But the more pragmatic part of him, coupled with his twenty years' experience, told him that man didn't die at the height of passion, but rather, death came so quickly he didn't even know he was being murdered.

The photographers finished and the men from the forensic laboratory put the body in a green canvas bag and carried it out of the room.

Petraioija followed and took the elevator down to the lobby with them. "Remind your boss that I want the report on this one as soon as possible."

"Will do," one of the men answered.

Petraioija went into the manager's office. "Tell me anything you can about either of the men," he said, looking down at the portly man behind the desk.

The manager made an open gesture with his hands. "They had reservations. They were made two weeks ago by phone from the United States. Five days later we received a bank draft for the amount."

"What bank was the draft drawn on?"

"The Bank of Rome."

Petraioija nodded. He would have one of his subordinates get a copy of the draft. "Did you have a number for them in the United States?" he asked.

"No," the manager said, shaking his head.

"In whose name was the room reserved?"

The manager opened a large black ledger. "This is our advance reservation book," he explained.

"Here you can see where one line has been whited out."

Petraioija looked at the white space. "Neat," he commented, then asked, "Beside the brown moustache, is there anything else you could tell me about the other man?"

"I only remember that one of them had a moustache," the manager said, "because I was at the desk when they came in."

"Was he the one who registered?"

"No, the other one did."

"Was he left- or right-handed?"

The manager shook his head. "This is not going to do the hotel any good," he said quietly.

Petraioija shrugged. "There's nothing I can do about that."

"It's been five years since we had a death here. Can't you just say that you're doing a routine investigation when you make it public?"

"The man didn't just die; he was murdered," Petraioija said tersely, then turned and walked quickly out of the office.

Two windows in the room filtered the gray light of the early afternoon. Standing at one of the windows, Vladimir Palovich, Deputy Director of the KGB's Second Directorate, looked down on Dzerzhinsky Square from the fifth floor of Lubianka and for several moments watched a workforce of men and women shovel the previous night's snow into mounds, which in turn were lifted into trucks by standard earth-moving equipment.

"The problem, gentlemen," he said, approaching the long, highly polished table where his aides, Boris Gargarin and Alexei Komarov, were seated, "is that we don't know what happened to

Comrade General Anatole Gorsky and his aide, Comrade Colonel Peter Lenov."

"How long has it been since the Comrade General was last seen?" Gargarin asked, holding a pencil between his hands.

Palovich, a heavyset man with wispy blond hair and wearing the same dark gray business suit as his aides, sat down in a black, leather-backed chair that squeaked under his weight. He glanced up at the digital clock on the wall just below the large colored print of Lenin and said, "Thirty-six hours and twenty-five minutes. He was last seen getting into a light plane at the Kabul airport. Comrade Colonel Lenov usually flew the Comrade General. There weren't any radio messages from the pilot after the plane took off."

"I assume the Comrade General was returning to Russia," Komarov said.

Palovich nodded. "At least, according to the flight plans that Lenov filed," he said.

"If the plane entered Russian air space, shouldn't it have been picked up by our radar net?" Gargarin asked.

"Only if it was above three hundred meters," Palovich answered. "Nothing came up on our radar and as yet, no one has reported a plane crash, though that still could happen. The Director thinks, and I concur, that something went wrong with the aircraft, forcing Lenov to land in a remote area. A bleaker possibility is that the plane crashed. Presently we have choppers flying over the route laid out in Lenov's flight plans." He paused to light a cigarette and inhaled, then leaned back in his chair and released the smoke, which drifted into a blue-gray cloud above the table. "But there are other possibilities that the Director and I agree might have happened," he said.

Gargarin and Komarov remained silent.

"Because Comrade General Gorsky is commander of our military operations in Afghanistan, he is a target for terrorists operating in that country and, perhaps, even dissidents in our own country."

Gargarin sucked in his breath and slowly let it out before he said, "Of all our senior officers, Comrade General Gorsky is the one most often mentioned to become Field Marshal of the Army."

"That's precisely why the Premier wants immediate action on this," Palovich said. "We have been given full authority to draw on the resources of any and all other departments." He took another drag on the cigarette and this time let the smoke out through his nostrils. "Because our jurisdiction is Russia, we will assume that the Comrade General and his aide are somewhere inside our borders."

"Isn't it possible that he might have been kidnapped by Western agents?" Komarov suggested, moving his thin frame forward and planting his elbows on the table.

"Yes," Palovich agreed, "but it's also possible his plane never got out of Afghanistan, though for reasons I am not privy to, the Comrade Director is certain that it did. We know that Comrade General Gorsky was given permission to spend part of his leave in Paris."

"But his flight plans were for Moscow," Gargarin said.

Palovich nodded. "The Comrade General has a reputation for changing his mind," he answered.

"We will conduct our investigation on the assumption that the Comrade General and his aide have either been killed inside Russia in a plane crash, or are still alive and are unable to contact the authorities because they are being held prisoner by dissidents, by foreign agents, or —"

"We can't rule out the possibility that only one of them survived," Komarov said.

"Or that the one or both are suffering from psychological difficulties, as well as physical injuries," Gargarin added.

"None of those possibilities can be overlooked," Palovich responded.

"Suppose the Comrade General managed to get to Paris?" Gargarin suggested.

Palovich's brow was furrowed.

"He might have been killed or kidnapped there," Gargarin ventured.

"Our responsibility," Palovich declared, "is to discover if the Comrade General and his aide are in Russia and to take whatever measures are necessary to recover them."

"Yes, Comrade Director," Gargarin responded.

"Comrade General Gorsky," Palovich said, "is one of those who distinguished himself very early in his career. He was an adviser to Comrade General Giap at Dien Bien Phu and later he helped organize the Tet Offensive, as it is referred to in the West, in Viet Nam. He's a staunch party member and as was already pointed out, he is the general most often mentioned to be in line for appointment to the rank of Field Marshal of the Army — not at all a bad position to be in at the age of fifty-five."

"I heard rumors," Komarov said, "that he has on several occasions commented that our status in

Afghanistan is no better than America's was in Viet Nam."

"I have been informed of that," Palovich answered. "The Comrade General has two excesses — women and vodka. He has a reputation for being a hard drinker, but he has never been known to drink himself into insensibility. The several occasions wherein he compared our position in Afghanistan to that of the United States's in Viet Nam have been either to other senior officers during staff meetings, or at meetings with members of the Politburo."

"Three months ago," Gargarin commented, "the Comrade General was divorced for a third time."

Palovich smiled. "There's an old expression: 'Lucky in war, lucky in bed'."

The two aides laughed, then Komarov said, "A man like that has to have enemies."

"Not as many as you might think," Palovich answered. "According to our reports from the political officers under his command, he is the most respected officer in the army. His commanders and their subordinates are completely loyal to him to the degree that our Comrade Director and several others in our organization are concerned that such intense loyalty on the part of his subordinates might surpass their loyalty to the State."

"May I ask, Comrade Director," Gargarin said, "if you share that view?"

"It is something I have thought about," Palovich responded, flicking the ash off his cigarette before taking another drag. "But the loyalty of Comrade General Gorsky's troops has no bearing on our investigation, though it would, of course, if their loyalty was in question."

"As I see it," Komarov said, "all we really have to go on is that he was supposed to have arrived in Moscow on a military plane that was piloted by his aide, Comrade Colonel Lenov."

"We also know that he intended to go to Paris on leave," Gargarin said, "and that means he'd have to refuel at least once along the way."

"That's assuming he *did* go to Paris," Palovich said, and paused. "Our portion of this investigation is limited to discovering what, if anything, happened to him in Russia. Should we find any evidence that the Comrade General and his aide are not in Russia, we will pass that information on to the proper Directorate. But in the meantime, I want the two of you to develop and put into immediate operation the most intensive search operation ever mounted by this department."

"Yes, Comrade Director," Komarov answered.

"You can be sure it will be absolutely thorough," Gargarin said.

Palovich smiled and stubbed out his cigarette. "Thank you, Comrades. I know I can depend on you to find our missing Comrade General and his aide."

[2]

On either side of the walkway the snow was piled knee-high in long banks stretching from Wheaten Hall, where Troy Sims had just finished his last class in advanced political theory, to the Sherman Library at the far side of campus, where he was going to meet Elly Mann, whom he had been dating for the last month.

The words of "God Rest You Merry Gentlemen" came from the library's loudspeaker system, and the intermittent flashing of the small colored lights on the huge Christmas tree created a variegated pattern on the snow in the center of the campus.

Troy was less bothered by the tree, which he already had described to Elly as garish, than by the constant repetition of a dozen carols. He resented being subjected to music that he considered substantially less than third-rate and to sentiments that, in his opinion, were nothing more than religious twaddle. If there was a way for him to avoid "the season of good will toward men and peace on earth," he would have gladly taken it. But he knew there wasn't and that the hypocrites of the Western world must reenact the origin of their religious myth.

Troy was long-legged, thin and muscular, with large hands and a strong chin covered by a beard slightly darker than his curly brown hair. His breath steamed in the cold air and as he passed the tree, the wind, picking up swirls of snow now, had just enough of an edge to make him pull up the collar of his tan corduroy jacket.

Troy had a more personal reason to justify his reaction to Christmas this year. He was going to have to decide whether he should stay at school over the holidays to finish a paper, already two weeks past due, for his advanced political theory class, or go down to the city to spend time with either of his parents.

"It's a three-way split," he said to himself. The paper had to be done; it counted for fifty percent of his grade. And while he was batting between a "B" and an "A", he did not want to give Professor Petorious a reason for cutting him to a "C", or perhaps even failing him. Troy had frequently voiced his objection to the way Petorious slanted his lectures in favor of Western political theory.

But both of his parents had said they wanted to see him. His father, Michael, was a very successful film and TV script writer, who, just a month before, had married for a third time. Troy had not yet met Randy, his stepmother, and he really had no inclination to.

And staying with his mother didn't rate high on the list of things Troy really wanted to do either. His mother, Victoria, ran a small but highly successful art gallery just off Madison Avenue on Sixty-Eighth Street. This was her busy season and from past experience he knew that she would be running around like a chicken without a head. Besides, he wasn't exactly crazy about Jake Forest, the man with whom she had been living for the past couple of years. The last time he saw her they had argued over it and he didn't want a repeat performance.

Suddenly Troy felt torn between Michael and Victoria. He broke his stride and kicked the snowbank, sending a shower of snow into the walkway. Then he sighed deeply. The idea of staying at school, even though he lived off campus and had a car, was a real bummer.

Troy had just about made up his mind to start jogging when a voice asked, "Mind if I join you, Mr. Sims?"

Troy glanced over his shoulder and he was surprised to see Professor Petorious. Considering their relationship in the classroom, Troy was even more surprised that the professor had spoken to him.

"This will be the last Christmas you spend at Broom," Petorious commented, as he came up alongside Troy.

"I'll be out of here in June," Troy answered laconically. Petorious, in his eyes, was an arch conservative.

Petorious chuckled, "And into the real world."

"That's right."

"And I suppose you have a job waiting for you?"

"I have one or two possibilities," Troy answered, then almost shook his head. What an asshole! Almost everyone on campus knew about his two-million-dollar trust fund left to him by his paternal grandfather, who had been the founder and owner of the Sims Corporation, a huge conglomerate whose thousands of shares of stock he and his father still owned. But despite this wealth, he actually looked forward to working in the real world. He had a deep understanding of why certain countries had to, and other countries will still have to, undergo violent political and social revolutions.

"I'm looking forward to reading your paper," Petorious commented.

I bet, Troy thought. But to Petorious he answered, "I was just trying to decide whether or not to work on it now, or go down to the city and do the work toward the end of the holiday."

"If you decide to stay up here," Petorious said, "and you've had enough of work on Christmas Day, why don't you join me and my sister for dinner? She's coming up here for the holidays. I'm sure there are a few local places that will serve the proverbial Christmas goose with all the trimmings."

"What?" Troy asked, caught completely off guard.

"We'd be delighted to have you and anyone you want to bring," Petorious said.

"Thank you, but —"

"Ah, this is where we part company," Petorious interrupted as they came up to a crosswalk and stopped.

"In case I don't see you, have a happy," Petorious said, extending his hand.

Still somewhat confused, Troy shook it.

"And if I do see you," Petorious continued, "I'm sure we'll manage to have a happy time together. Good night."

"Good night," Troy answered, releasing Petorious's hand and looking after him. The man was somewhere in his forties, compactly built, with a round face and a somewhat grizzled beard. He wore a three-quarter-length, russet-colored down coat, a long red scarf twisted around his neck several times, and a gray, heavy woolen stocking hat pulled down over his ears.

Troy continued on his way to the library. According to the biographical data in the school catalog, Petorious had been a captain in the Marines and had seen service in Viet Nam. He held two doctorates: one in political science and the other in geo-political theory. He had published several books and a score of articles, a few of which had been published in the *New York Times Magazine*.

Petorious had the reputation for being the least social member of the faculty, so an invitation from him was not to be taken lightly, even if a student had a great relationship with him, which Troy certainly didn't. They were really political adversaries and the classroom was their battlefield.

Suddenly he recalled having heard from several of his friends that Petorious's sister was a singer in a cocktail lounge in a New York hotel and that she was a very beautiful woman.

Still very surprised by the invitation, Troy quickened his pace and almost immediately found himself in front of Broom's president, Dr. Leon Hale, whose reputation as the wunderkind of college administration had brought him to the college two years before Troy had gotten there. With Hale was a man he never before had seen.

The three of them stopped inside the white circle of light cast by an overhead lamp along the walkway.

"Hello, Troy," Hale said, with a broad smile.

"Hello, Leon," Troy answered, shaking Hale's hand. Because Broom was a small college, fewer than seven hundred students, everyone called Hale by his first name.

Hale turned to the man with him. "Mr. Edward Noonan, Mr. Troy Sims, one of our more politically active students."

Smiling, Noonan said, "A real pleasure. But since everyone here is on a first-name basis, why don't you call me Ed?"

"A pleasure," Troy answered, aware of Ed's firm grip on his hand and the black seal parka he wore with the hood down, despite the fifteen-degree temperature. Troy knew the parka was black seal because his mother had a coat made from it.

"A great place you have here," Noonan commented.

Hale beamed. "I've been giving Ed a cook's tour," he explained.

"We've got some good people on staff," Troy said, guessing that Noonan was a prospective contributor to the college fund. From the treatment Hale was giving him, he probably was going to make a large endowment.

"Some of the best in their respective fields," Hale added.

"I intend to bring more of the best to Broom," Noonan said.

"Are you —"

"Ed will soon be a member of the Board of Directors," Hale said, again smiling broadly.

"Doesn't the Board meet every other Monday?" Troy asked.

Hale seemed to hesitate, but Noonan, speaking very precisely, explained. "It's because of me that the Board has decided to meet over this long weekend."

"Yes," Hale said, "this time the Board will actually be in session from now until New Year's Day. We have a great deal of work that must be gotten out of the way before the beginning of the new year."

Troy nodded and looked hard at Noonan. Suddenly he had the overwhelming feeling he had seen the man before.

"Is anything wrong?" Noonan asked.

Troy shook his head. "I just remembered that I need a certain book for my report," he lied.

Noonan smiled. "Isn't it a bitch when you suddenly remember something you forgot?"

"That's for sure!" Troy answered, sensing for the first time that Noonan spoke with an accent, or else had a speech impediment.

"Are you staying at school for the holidays?" Hale asked.

"I haven't decided yet."

"If I don't see you again," Hale said, "have a merry Christmas and a happy New Year."

"Same to you," Troy answered.

"Have a good holiday," Noonan said.

"You too," Troy responded, and after shaking hands with both of them, he headed toward the library. Still unsettled by Petorious's invitation, he was equally bothered, though he couldn't define why, by his chance meeting with Hale and Noonan. Holding a Board of Directors meeting over the holidays was weird, really weird. . . .

Troy and Elly occupied the same seat in a booth close to the fireplace in John's Place, a roadside bar a mile north of Red Hook on Rt. 9. Built to look like an oversized log cabin, its main room was finished in dark, stained wood and its overhead beams looked as if they had been scavenged from a building gutted by fire. Even the bar at one end of the room had black fire scars on it that no amount of dark stain could hide.

John's Place was owned by Gretta Holmes, who did the cooking and on slow nights either sat at the bar or with one of the customers, and nursed a beer. A big woman, she was at the bar now, looking over at Troy and Elly.

"Bet Gretta pays us a visit," Troy said from behind his hand. He not only liked the woman's cooking, she made some of the best chili he had ever tasted, but he also admired Gretta's individuality enough to write a feature article about her, for which he'd received an A in his journalism class and which was bought by the local newspaper for a hundred dollars for its "Meet Your Neighbor" section.

"She's probably wondering why you're not eating your chili," Elly answered. "After all, she has a proprietary interest in you."

"Jealous?" Troy teased.

Elly made a moue.

"I want answers, not faces," Troy said.

Elly shook her head. "Just being realistic."

"You mean just because you have a bikini body, silky blond hair, bright blue eyes, only one dimple that shows when you smile and she's more than twice your age and size, you shouldn't be jealous?"

Elly lifted her glass stein and made a slight gesture with it, she said, "I think you got it." Then she drank.

"Here she comes," Troy said

"Something wrong with the chili?" Gretta asked, settling her bulk on the end of the bench opposite Troy and Elly. "I've been watching you and you're just playing with it."

"To tell the truth, Gretta, I'm really not very hungry."

"You, not hungry?"

Troy nodded.

Gretta shifted her green eyes from Troy to Elly. "Anything wrong between the two of you?" she asked.

Before Elly could answer, Troy said, "She won't go to bed with me."

Elly gagged on the beer and immediately began to cough.

"Hey," Gretta commented drily, "the world is full of fools."

"That's what I told her," Troy said.

Gretta pointed her thumb at Troy. "Get a load of him," she laughed. "He thinks he's cock of the walk."

Troy puffed up his chest and putting his thumbs in his armpits, he said, "Maybe not 'cock of the walk,' but cock of something or other."

"I'm not going to touch that one," Gretta said, easing herself off the bench and standing up. "I just don't like to have my art go unappreciated."

"Art!" Troy exclaimed looking down at the bowl of chili.

"Art." Gretta pointed a chubby, beringed finger at him. "A famous writer named Troy Sims called my chili the only real culinary masterpiece in the Hudson Valley."

"*This?*" Troy asked, pointing at the chili.

"You bet your ass *that*," Gretta answered. "And you think about the fact that you're not eating it, not eating a work of art."

"What do you have to say about this?" Troy asked, looking at Elly.

"The two of you are banana heads," Elly answered.

"Well, I know when I've been insulted," Gretta said. She turned and lumbered back to the bar.

"I refuse to be called a banana head," Troy said, "especially by some one who doesn't think I'm the cock of something or other."

"Be serious."

"I am absolutely serious."

"Please . . . is anything wrong?" she asked.

Troy leaned forward and with his forefinger he drew imaginary circles on the table. "It's one of the times of the year when my parents remember they have a son. The other is Easter. I guess it has something to do with the religious spirit, or maybe," he added sarcastically, "just plain guilt."

Elly took hold of his left hand and grasped it tightly. "What can I say?"

Troy shook his head. "There's nothing to say. My dad has a new wife I don't want to meet, and my mom is living with a guy I don't like."

Elly raised his hand to her lips and kissed it.

"That helps," Troy said, managing a smile. "You know, I guess I still miss being part of a family, especially this time of year. I remember how it was before my folks split up."

"Was it that good?"

"I didn't mean to cry in my beer," Troy said, lifting his stein.

"Everyone has to now and then," Elly said gently.

"Are you going home?" he asked.

She shook her head. "I have a painting to finish. Besides, it doesn't really pay for me to fly all the way to St. Louis for a few days."

"If you really want to go, I'll give you the airline tickets for your Christmas present."

"That's sweet of you," she said, kissing his hand again. "But I must do that painting."

Troy took another sip of beer. "Yeah, my paper for Petorious will probably be my excuse for not going to New York. By the way, just before I met you, Petorious invited me to have dinner with him and his sister on Christmas Day."

"Maybe he's holding out the olive branch . . . you know, peace in the classroom," Elly suggested.

Troy shrugged. "He knows me better than that. A dinner, even a Christmas dinner with all the trimmings, won't keep me quiet. If something has to be said and I'm in a position to say it, then I will."

"Are you going to go?"

"I also met Leon and Ed, the soon-to-be member of the college's Board of Directors," Troy said, purposely avoiding Elly's question.

"Ed?"

"Noonan."

"I didn't even know there was a vacancy," Elly commented. "Did you?"

Troy freed his hand from Elly's. "I don't remember hearing about one either. The last time a new member was appointed to the Board was during my freshman year . . . some retired general from the Air Force . . . William Strogerly."

"One of the members was killed in a freak accident in a plane," Elly said.

"I remember," Troy responded. "The plane exploded on take-off."

Elly nodded. "It happened at the Rhinebeck airfield."

Troy stabbed at the air with a finger. "I also remember there were two professors who objected to Strogerly's appointment at the time, but I can't remember who they were."

"Don't ask me," Elly said. "I wouldn't have remembered any of it if Strogerly didn't have an interesting face. He was pointed out to me by one of my friends and I recall saying, 'That's the kind of face I want to paint.' "

"Why?"

"I can't tell you *why* now," Elly answered. "Remember, I was a freshman then."

Troy ran his hand over his beard. "There had to be a reason."

"It was almost four years ago. What's so important about it now?"

"It just is. Try!"

Elly bit her lower lip.

Troy drank again.

"All right," Elly said, "now that I think about it, to me at least, that face was filled with a sense of . . . foreboding."

"Interesting," Troy said, putting the stein down. "Interesting!"

"Now if I saw it," Elly commented, "I'd probably think his was just another face in the crowd."

"Maybe, maybe not," Troy replied. "That Noonan reminded me of someone I had seen before and speaks —" Troy snapped his fingers. "I bet English is not his first language."

"You lost me," Elly declared.

"I thought he had some kind of speech impediment," Troy said. "I wasn't sure that he spoke with an accent. But he does. He not only speaks with an accent, I bet he comes from somewhere in Eastern Europe and learned to speak English after —"

"All right, you've given me an analysis of his speech," Elly laughed. "Now for the million-dollar question, tell me where you saw him?"

Troy shrugged. "I haven't the foggiest. But if I keep thinking about it, it will come to me."

"Why bother?"

"It bugs me when I can't remember something like that," Troy said. "Besides, it's good practice to jog your memory now and then."

Elly finished her beer. "My memory is perfectly content to remain a sleeping elf."

"Hale said the Board would be meeting from Christmas until New Year's Day," Troy explained. "He said they have a lot of work to do before the end of the year."

Elly laughed. "The only work the Board does is to vote themselves more money and sign checks."

"That's for sure." Troy looked at her, then said, "I'll have another beer. What about you?"

She nodded.

For several moments Troy just looked at her. "You're beautiful," he said in a low voice.

"Thank you."

"Elly, I'd stay," Troy said, "if you'd stay with me . . . I mean, really stay with me." Though they had engaged in heavy petting, they had never made love.

"I wouldn't finish my painting and you wouldn't finish your paper," she answered.

"Somehow we'd manage to do everything that has to be done."

"I know what you want done," she said. "But I don't want to be hurt again. I know you want me and, yes, I want you too. But I'm not ready to go to bed with you."

Troy let go of her hand.

"Are you going to sulk for the rest of the evening?" Elly demanded.

"If that would change your mind, I'd do it. But I know it won't, so I'm going to do what I said I would: I'm going to get us another beer."

Elly leaned over and kissed him on the cheek. "Thanks for not putting the pressure on."

Troy put his hand under Elly's chin and tilting her face up, he brought his face close to hers. "There's pressure," he told her. "There's plenty of pressure. It's just subtle. You won't know it's there until you wind up in bed with me." He kissed her. . . .

Detective Petraioija was clearing his desk. He had promised his wife that he would go Christmas shopping with her and afterwards he'd take her to dinner. The phone rang. He cast a dour look at it, then shook his head. If he answered and it was about police business, he could very well lose the opportunity to spend the evening the way he had planned. He let it ring several times before he reached over, picked it up, and gave his usual "Detective Petraioija here" opening.

"Cusati," the voice on the other end said. "I thought you'd like to know that the man found in the Eliseo yesterday was poisoned."

"With what?"

"Curare."

"That's not what I wanted to hear," Petraioija sighed.

"There's more."

"All right, tell me the 'more.'"

"He's Russian," Cusati said.

"How the hell did you find that out?"

"From the metal caps on his teeth. They're steel. The Russians still use steel and they have a particular way of working it. Naturally, our intelligence people had to be brought into the picture."

"That's using the word 'intelligence' loosely," Petraioija commented dryly.

"Well, it's out of your hands now."

"Thanks for letting me know."

"You'll get the paper work on it in a few days."

"I can't wait." Petraioija put the phone down and whispered, "Russian, eh! That's going to make a lot of people worried, especially the Russians."

Darkness had already settled over the Virginia countryside, when William Fitzhugh, Deputy Director of the CIA's Soviet Section, looked across his desk and asked the company's two experts on the Soviet Union, Frank Robin and Steven Nathan, "Is that a wrap?" Both of them had been field men and had been brought back to Langley by Fitzhugh six months before.

"It's been calm," Nathan answered. An angular man, he was the tallest of the three men. He had been with the company for ten years, eight of which he had been active in various countries in western Europe and behind the Iron Curtain, including Russia. In addition to his field expertise, he was a specialist in geo-politics.

"Let's hope it remains that way for the holidays," Fitzhugh said, filling his pipe with tobacco from an ornately carved cedar humidor. He was a short, slight man with thin lips, a bald pate and a round face. Behind simple white metal frame glasses were green, almost child-like eyes.

Robin, the Section's communications expert, commented, "For a calm week there *has* been a significant increase of internal encoded radio and phone communications."

Fitzhugh flicked on a lighter, and put the flame close to the top of the pipe bowl. "How much of an increase is significant?" he asked, before sucking air into the pipe.

"Our sensors are about eighty-nine percent accurate and they indicate a fifty percent increase. That's communications between the KGB Headquarters in Moscow and its various units."

"All of it internal?" Nathan asked.

"With the exception of a burst of activity between Moscow and Rome," Robin answered. He was boyish looking, with blond hair, blue eyes and a fair skin marked with freckles on his face and arms. He had six years with the company, five of them spent on assignments overseas. He and Nathan had worked together in Poland and in East Germany.

Fitzhugh sent a column of smoke from the pipe bowl to the ceiling. "Any ideas?" he asked.

"Usually happens when the KGB is looking for someone," Robin said. "We might have better information in a day or two."

"Has the increase continued, or has it returned to normal?" Nathan questioned. He lit a cigarette as he spoke and let it hang from between his lips.

"It stopped yesterday at twenty-three hundred our time."

Looking at Robin, Fitzhugh said, "Try to get a line on what's happening. I'd like to know who our friends are looking for. We might want to look for him — or her."

"I've already sent word to our people," Robin replied, "but it will be a while before they come up with something."

"I'll check with our people in Italy," Nathan said, releasing smoke from his nostrils. "They might be able to shed some light on the matter."

"I'd have been very concerned if the communications were still going on at that pace," Fitzhugh said, "but since they have returned to normal, I think we'll probably find that the Russkies were playing games."

"I don't think so," Robin said quietly. "This didn't follow their usual pattern of high-density transmissions."

"What was the major difference?" Fitzhugh asked, pointing at Robin with his pipe. He noted the green numbers of the digital clock on his desk went to 5:30.06. He had a dinner appointment with a senator at 6:30.

"This went on over a period of days," said Robin, "not just a few hours, the way they usually run their communications tests."

Nathan grinned. "Their communications tests become a test of our ability to monitor them."

"Then, Frank, you're telling me that something really did go down," Fitzhugh said.

Robin shook his head. "I wouldn't bet my life on it, but the Russkies follow a pattern. As soon as that pattern changes, well, it could mean —"

"That they're starting a new pattern," Fitzhugh said, putting the pipe between his lips again.

"That certainly is a possibility," Robin agreed.

"Let's hope nothing too startling happens between now and the end of the year," Fitzhugh said. Then, changing the subject, he asked, "Where are you men going to be?"

"With my family in Boston," Robin answered immediately.

"I'll be back in Staten Island with mine," Nathan said.

"Well I'm going back to my alma mater," Fitzhugh volunteered. "I'll be spending the holiday with the Old Boys."

"Never figured you for the reunion type," Nathan chuckled.

Fitzhugh smiled. "I've been going back to Broom for years."

"Broom!" Robin exclaimed. "A boyhood friend of mine teaches there — John Petorious . . . You don't happen to know him, I suppose?"

Fitzhugh shook his head.

"Teaches political theory. We grew up together. We even went to Boston Latin together."

"Interesting," Fitzhugh responded.

"Now there's a man who's a straight arrow if there ever was one," Robin said. "He was born a conservative, if you know what I mean." Then looking at Nathan, he said, "I introduced you to his sister Helen when we went up to New York during the summer."

"Helen Peters, the singer?"

"That's her," Robin responded. "She changed her name to Peters for the stage."

"A wise move," Nathan laughed. "Petorious is a fine name for your professor friend, but it would have been a disaster for his sister."

"She's very different from her brother. Seems to get a hell of a lot more out of life."

"If I run into your Professor Petorious, I'll give him your regards," Fitzhugh said.

"Thanks," Robin answered. Looking at Nathan again, he said, "We're planning to get together over the holiday. The last time I spoke to him, he was sure that Helen was coming up to visit him at Broom for Christmas."

Fitzhugh looked down and began to occupy himself with the papers on his desk.

Nathan bobbed his head toward Fitzhugh and whispered, "I think he's telling us something."

Robin smiled and nodded.

"See you, Chief," Nathan said, standing.

"See you," Robin echoed, following Nathan to the door.

"Guys?" Fitzhugh called, looking up.

Nathan and Robin stopped.

"Just cover our asses," Fitzhugh said. "See if you can get a line on what our Moscow friends are up to before we leave for Christmas."

"We'll try," Nathan answered. He opened the door and he and Robin walked out of the room.

Fitzhugh waited until the door had closed before he picked up the phone and punched out a number.

[3]

Troy awoke with an erection; he'd been dreaming of making love to Elly and just as he was about to enter her, he awoke. "Christ!" he exclaimed and then told himself, "Be patient, just be patient." And as if that inner voice belonged to someone else, he answered, "I want her, I really want her. I love her!"

He turned his head toward the window: the lower portion was covered with a graceful curve of snow that began half way up the right side of the pane and arced down to the lower left corner — a geometer's dream!

Troy threw back the quilt, put his feet down on the throw rug and hurried to the window. The ground was covered with newly fallen snow, but the sun shone and the sky was very blue. Not far from the window was a large, very old maple whose dark gray limbs were coated with snow.

Beyond the maple was a Blue Spruce that looked like a white cone. Since he started dating Elly, he had been taught to see things that he hadn't noticed before — shades of gray, flecks of red and yellow in the bark of a tree or even in the green boughs of a pine tree. The view from his window filled him with enormous pleasure and suddenly he realized that he'd rather be with Elly, even if they weren't sleeping together, than with either of his parents.

Having made the decision to remain at school for the holidays, Troy felt pleased with himself. He left the window and went into the bathroom to begin his day with a steaming hot shower. Thirty minutes later, wearing a red quilted jacket, a red woolen stocking hat, shearling gloves and high, insulated boots, he was vigorously shoveling a path between the front door and the Jeep in the driveway. His plan was to have breakfast in Red Hook and then go to the library and begin the research for the paper he had to write. The topic he had chosen, which Petorious had approved, was "The Effect of Foreign Intervention on the American Civil War." Petorious had commented that the topic was unique and not much had been written about it. Then, for no apparent reason, General Strogerly popped into his mind and then Ed Noonan.

Troy stopped, leaned on the shovel, and looked back at the house. It was an old, two-story wooden structure with a gabled roof, a front porch and far too many rooms for him to use. But he liked living there and had decided to keep it, even after he graduated from Broom and moved to New York.

Despite the cold, Troy was wet with perspiration and used his handkerchief to wipe his brow and neck. Then, because he was still sure he had seen Noonan before, he tried to remember where. And even though he drew a blank again, he was more sure than ever that he had seen the man. He started to shovel snow again, though not as vigorously as before.

It took another ten minutes for Troy to reach the Jeep and a few minutes to clear the snow and ice from the windshield, side and rear windows. That done, he switched on the ignition to let the engine warm up, then returned to the house for his notebook and pen. As he opened the door, the phone rang.

Expecting to hear one of his parents, he picked up the phone and announced, "Troy here."

"Why so angry?" Elly asked, surprised.

"I'm not," Troy protested, settling down on the stairs near the phone. "I thought it was one of my parents." He cradled the phone in the crook of his shoulder and pulled off his gloves.

"I had a dream about you," Elly said.

"Yeah, me too."

"You dreamt about yourself?" she asked, giggling.

"No, about you," he answered. "It was X-rated all the way."

Elly laughed.

"You may laugh," Troy answered, "but it's no laughing matter when Peter wakes up ready to go and there's no place to go."

"No pressure, remember?"

"I remember," he sighed.

"I love you, Troy," she said softly.

"I love you, too," he replied.

There was a moment of silence between them, then Troy said, "Tell me what your dream was about."

"You were trying to find something, but couldn't," Elly said. "Then Petorious became angry at you and Strogerly started to chase you."

"Is that it?"

"There was more, but I can't remember it."

Troy laughed. "Don't worry, even in a dream I'm faster than Strogerly." Then he asked, "Suppose I come by and we go to breakfast together?"

"I'm still in bed."

"All the more reason why I should come by."

"Lunch?" Elly asked.

"Beggars can't be choosers."

"Make it oneish."

"I'll be there," Troy said.

"Love ya —"

"Hey, before you go, you don't happen to remember what happened to the two professors who opposed Strogerly's appointment to the board?" Troy asked.

"No," Elly answered. "I don't even recall their names."

"I wonder who would," Troy said.

"Petorious?"

"He came to Broom the following year," Troy said.

"Why do you want to know?"

Troy shrugged. "Just curious. I wonder if anyone will oppose Noonan?"

"Most of the staff doesn't even know he's alive," Elly commented, "let alone that he's going to become a member of the Board."

Troy jumped up. "Hey, that's right isn't . . . I mean, yesterday was the last day of classes until

January third. And most of the classes stopped meeting on Wednesday."

"So what does that mean?" Elly pressed.

"It means, my love," Troy said, "that with the exception of Leon, Petorious, one or two more faculty members and a few of the librarians, most of the staff and practically all of the students are gone."

"C'mon, get real," Elly scoffed. "Who'd really care whether or not Noonan became a member of the Board?"

"For Christ's sake," Troy exclaimed, "everyone should care! That Board determines what happens to this college. We should be told who a candidate is and what his or her qualifications are."

"There aren't any women on the Board," Elly said.

"Now that has to say something about Leon's attitudes," Troy commented. "Yeah, I'd really like to know what happened to the guys who opposed Strogerly."

"Troy, that's ancient history," Elly said.

"Didn't someone say, 'Those who fail to learn from history are doomed to repeat its mistakes?'"

"What mistakes?"

"I don't know what mistakes," Troy answered. "But doesn't it strike you that Noonan coming here now, just at the time when most of the faculty isn't here, is just too suspect? Even the fact that the Board is meeting now, instead of the first Friday of the new year is, even you must admit, somewhat out of the ordinary."

"Okay, it's convenient," Elly admitted. "I still don't understand why it has suddenly become important."

"Because there's no one here to object."

"Maybe there's no reason to object," Elly offered.

"But maybe there is," Troy countered. "Maybe there is and because there is —"

"Troy!" Elly exclaimed.

"What?"

"You're really on a trip with this," Elly said. "Forget about Noonan, Strogerly and anyone else on the Board. Just concentrate on the paper you have to write. That's really more important than anything else right now."

"Yeah, that's for sure," Troy admitted reluctantly.

"See you for lunch," Elly said.

"See you," Troy answered and put the phone down. Then he picked up his notebook and pen, and headed out to the Jeep.

The Sherman Library was a combination of one of the oldest buildings on campus and one of the newest. The oldest part was two stories high of red brick and had large square windows. Inside, the ceilings were high, the floors were of highly polished wood, and at each end of the downstairs reading room there was a large stone fireplace, which was used during the winter months.

The newest section of the library was a single story, white brick affair, with huge, gray tinted glass panels that took the place of windows.

The entire card catalog was computerized and there were a hundred terminals for the students to use. Troy sat in front of one of the terminals and was about to ask the computer for a printout of books on the relations between the Union and Czarist Russia when he caught sight of Sally Cooms sitting at the Student Assistance Desk.

Sally, a petite woman with a generous figure, had once told him that she had come to Broom straight out of Columbia University's School of Library Science, where she had earned her master's degree. He guessed she was somewhere in her late thirties, maybe even forty. If she came to Broom right out of graduate school, she'd have been there even before Leon and certainly when Strogerly had become a Board member. If anyone remembered the names of the two professors who had opposed Strogerly's appointment, she would.

Troy asked the computer for the particular printout he wanted and within moments the computer responded with his call number; then it referred him to the Document Retrieval Room, where the books would be held until he called for them. Troy typed in his ID number, signed off, and walked over to Sally.

"Hello," she said, smiling up at him but before he could answer, she commented, "I thought you'd be gone by now."

"Have a paper to do," he answered.

Sally wagged her finger at him. "Late, I suppose?"

"Late," Troy nodded.

"And you need my help."

"I need your help," Troy said. "But not for the paper."

She cocked head to one side and said, "Tell me."

Until that moment, Troy had never realized that she was attractive.

"Well, I'm waiting," she said with mock impatience.

"It's going to be a test of your memory," Troy teased.

"If I'm right, what do I win?" Sally asked.

"My eternal gratitude."

"For that it's hardly worth my trouble," she answered. "But just to show you how magnanimous I am, I'll do it."

"I need the names of the two professors who opposed General Strogerly's Board appointment . . ." Troy said, his voice trailing off as he watched Sally's face pale and her eyes become watery.

She shook her head and took a tissue from the box on the desk, then wiped her eyes and blew her nose.

"Are you all right?" Troy asked anxiously.

"All right," she said, but tears were leaking out of the corner of her eyes.

"Look, I didn't mean —"

"Professors Martin Giddeon and Charles Platz," she said.

Troy wrote the names on the cover of his notebook.

"What are you going to do with those names?" Sally asked.

"I want to find them."

Sally closed her eyes and began to cry softly.

Troy was beginning to feel more and more exposed. Afraid that Sally's weeping would attract attention, he shifted his position to shield her from view from the Terminal Room and hoped no one would come to the desk for help.

"Dead," Sally sobbed, her eyes still closed. "Both of them are dead."

Troy put his hand on Sally's head. "I'm sorry," he said. "I didn't know."

Raising her eyes to his face, she asked, "Why are you interested in them?"

Troy took hold of her hands. "I'll tell you, but not here," he said, looking around nervously. So far everyone in the room seemed oblivious to their exchange. "Have coffee with me and I'll tell you."

Sally wiped her eyes and blew her nose again. "My break comes in half an hour."

"Will you have coffee with me?"

"I don't know," she said. "I usually stay in the back room and —"

"Sally, please . . . it's important. We'll go off campus to Fat Al's Diner. We'll be able to talk there."

Uttering a deep sigh, she nodded.

Troy looked at his watch. "About twenty minutes."

"Yes."

"Here," he asked, "or would you prefer to meet me in the parking lot?"

"The parking lot would be better, I think."

"I'll be in my Jeep," Troy said, then added, "Don't stand me up."

"I said I'd meet you."

Though he didn't really think it was appropriate, Troy managed a smile and walked away from the desk.

They sat in a booth next to a window where sunlight streamed in. Fat Al's located at the intersection of Routes 9 and 23 was an old-fashioned, somewhat disreputable-looking diner surrounded by a large parking area. Because the food was good and moderately priced and it was open twenty-four hours a day seven days a week, it was a favorite with truckers.

"I haven't been here for years," Sally commented.

Troy looked over at the counter where a half-dozen truckers were seated on stools. "I come here whenever I want to eat something that will, as the expression goes, stick to my ribs, or when I want good pie and coffee."

"Does it still have good pies?"

Troy nodded. "This time of year I recommend the apple," he said.

"Yes," she said. "I'd like that."

Troy motioned to the waitress and ordered two apple pies and two coffees when she came to the table.

The waitress wrote the check, put it down in front of Troy and then went to get the pies and coffee.

"Hardly first-class service," Troy said wryly, "but then in a first-class restaurant, you don't ever get this symphony of delicious smells. That's another reason why I come here . . . I really love the way the food smells."

"It reminds me a lot of my mother's kitchen, God rest her soul," Sally said.

"I can't say the same," Troy said. "I just like the way it smells."

The waitress returned with the order and Troy waited until she was out of earshot before he said, "Do you want to tell me about Giddeon and Platz now, or would you rather wait until —"

"Martin and I were going to announce our engagement," Sally broke in.

"I had no idea," Troy said, and busied himself with cutting his pie.

"No one did," Sally told him. "We wanted to surprise everyone. But then he and Charles were brought up before the Board on charges."

"Charges?" Troy asked, his voice rising. "What charges?"

"Please, people are looking at us," Sally whispered.

Troy nodded. He hadn't remembered ever hearing anything about that. "What charges?" he asked again.

"It was all very hush-hush," Sally explained. "Martin and Charles were good friends. They rented a small house together and they were charged with enticing young men from the town to the house for immoral purposes," Sally said, her eyes filling again.

"Christ, I can't believe that!" Troy reached across the table and took hold of her hands. "Tell me how they died."

"Martin's car went out of control," she answered, trying hard not to weep openly, "and smashed into a telephone pole. He was dead by the time the state troopers arrived."

"And Platz?"

"Mugged in the city," Sally said. "The mugger stabbed him to death. I have the newspaper stories on both deaths."

"Will you let me see them?" he asked, letting go of her hands.

"Yes."

Troy began to eat his pie again, then stopped to ask, "Did anyone know about your relationship with Martin?"

"A few people did — Leon did. He was very sympathetic."

Troy took a sip of the coffee. Leon would be good at being sympathetic.

"But I still don't know why you're interested in

all of this," Sally said. "It happened almost four years ago."

"The Board is getting a new member —"

"Yes, I know. I met him yesterday. Leon was showing him around. From what I understand, he's a very successful industrialist. Something to do with high-speed computers, or lasers. The man has several patents to his credit."

Troy rubbed his hand over his beard. "Who told you that — Leon?"

"No," Sally replied. "He gave me a biog sheet for our records in the library."

"I want to see that when we go back," Troy said, draining his cup and signaling the waitress for another.

"Mr. Noonan is such a gallant man," Sally commented. "You know, he even kissed my hand when Leon introduced us."

"Maybe," Troy said, "but I wouldn't want to be on his shit list, if you know what I mean. My guess is that he's not the kind of person to forget or forgive." Then he added, "Speaking about forgetting, I've seen our Mr. Noonan before."

"Where?"

Troy shrugged. "That's just the trouble, I can't remember where. But I know I've seen him."

"If you don't remember, how can you be so sure?"

"I'm sure," Troy said. "I'm damned sure."

Sally broke off a piece of pie crust. "You're right, the pie and coffee are very good. Thank you for—"

Troy held up his hand. "Not necessary."

"Now will you tell me why you're interested in what happened to Martin and Charles?" she asked.

"Maybe we can finish what they started," Troy told her.

Sally put down her fork. "I don't understand."

"I don't either. Not yet anyway. But I'd also like to see the biog sheets on all of the other Board members. Maybe it's time to rock the boat a bit."

"You're not going to do anything crazy, are you?" she asked, her voice rising and the expression on her face changing to fear. "Because if you are, I don't want any part of it. I don't want any trouble."

Troy shook his head and raised his right hand. "Nothing crazy, Scout's honor."

Sally opened her shoulder bag and took out a cigarette and put it between her lips. "I really hope not. I like working at Broom." Using a yellow Bic lighter, she lit the cigarette. "I went through a very hard time when Martin was dismissed and then after the accident. It's four years later and I'm just beginning to feel like a person again, not a zombie."

Troy nodded sympathetically, then said, "Maybe this isn't the right time to ask you, but no time will really be the right time."

"Ask me what?" Sally, took a deep drag on the cigarette.

"I need a straight answer," Troy said.

She held the smoke for a moment and then let it spill out of her mouth. "What's your question?"

Troy shifted his position on the bench, picked up the fork and tapped it on the edge of the pie plate.

"Well?"

He put the fork down and looked straight at Sally. "Don't be embarrassed by what I'm going to ask."

Color flooded Sally's face.

"I have to know."

"Go ahead," she said, taking another drag.

"Were you and Martin lovers?" Troy asked. "I mean, were you sleeping with him?"

Sally began to cough. The smoke came out of her mouth in small bursts.

"I have to know," Troy pressed. "Did you sleep with him?"

"Yes . . . yes, oh God, yes!" Sally sobbed. She stubbed out the cigarette in the metal ash tray, took a napkin and wiped her eyes. "This seems to be my morning for the weeps."

"I'm sorry," Troy said, not knowing what else to say.

She blew her nose. "Is there anything else you want to know?"

"Yes, but I don't want to upset you any more."

Sally sighed deeply. "It doesn't matter. Go ahead and ask."

"Do you think Martin preferred boys to you?"

She shook her head. "Martin was a passionate man, very passionate."

"What about Charles?"

"He had a relationship with Mrs. Hobe in town," Sally said.

"A married woman?"

"Her husband was and is the president of the Valley Bank."

"Besides you and Martin, did anyone know about the affair?" Troy asked.

"No. Charles was very careful," Sally explained. "He never met Laura anywhere around here. They always went down to the city. He was killed on his way to meet her."

"Are you sure about that?"

"Yes. Charles had once told Martin that he and Laura went to the Hotel Seville. He was killed only a few blocks from there."

Troy took a sip of the second cup of coffee. It was tepid, so he put it down and reached across the table to take hold of Sally's hands. "Thanks," he said. "Really, thanks. I know this wasn't at all easy for you."

"Just don't do anything crazy," Sally said, putting the pack of cigarettes and the yellow lighter back into her shoulder bag. "And if you do, I don't want to be part of it. Remember that."

"I'll remember."

Troy drove back to the library and as he and Sally entered the building, she said, "It will take me a few minutes to gather everything together for you."

"No problem."

"I'd feel better if you didn't wait at the Student Information desk," Sally told him.

Troy nodded. "I'll be in the reading room of the old building."

Troy made a pit stop at the men's room and then went to the reading room. Counting himself, there were four people in the room. He chose a table opposite a window through which the sun silvered slanting columns of darting motes before it touched the edge of the table.

Troy draped his pea jacket over the back of the chair, placed his hat and notebook on the polished oak wood table and then sat down, bathed in the warm sunlight. He found the information that Sally had given him about Charles and Martin interesting, but there wasn't any way he could link their deaths to any cause other than the mechanical failure that had killed Martin and the mugger who had stabbed Charles. That they had died within a month of each other had certainly been a coincidence — a very large one — but still a *coincidence*. He wondered if Leon had attended their funerals? Probably did and probably took part in the eulogy.

Sally handed him several folders. "These have the names of the Board members on them. Inside are their biog sheets and other information about them. And this book has the newspaper articles about Martin and Charles. I marked the pages with yellow paper." It was a green leatherette photograph book.

"Thanks, Sally," Troy said gratefully.

She nodded and without saying anything more, she turned and walked away.

Troy opened Strogerly's folder first. Strogerly graduated from the Air Force Academy, was a fighter pilot in Viet Nam and had held various command positions before retiring — about the time he became a member of the Board. There wasn't the slightest indication of anything unusual; Strogerly was a professional soldier.

Troy noted that the Board currently consisted of eleven members, including Leon, who was its chairman. Noonan would make it an even dozen. Seven members had military backgrounds. Four had been generals in the Army, one in the Marine Corps, and Strogerly and another had come out of the Air Force. The other members, including Noonan, were either industrialists, bankers, or brokers.

Troy read each biog sheet twice, and the only thing that struck him as being in any way peculiar was that the name and address of Noonan's company wasn't on the biog sheet, but that could have been an oversight. He gathered the folders and put them off to one side, then he opened the scrapbook to the first marked page.

The article was headlined *Accident Kills Former Broom College Professor*. The story never mentioned that Martin had been dismissed from the college — Leon probably had seen to that. The accident had occurred three miles from school. According to the police and the state trooper who had arrived on the scene minutes after the crash, Martin's brakes failed and his car slammed into a telephone pole. The day was clear and the road was dry. In a follow-up story covering Martin's funeral, Troy discovered he'd guessed right: Leon had been one of the people to deliver a eulogy.

Pursing his lips, Troy looked at the two stories again. There was absolutely nothing in either about Martin's professional life. He turned to the second marked page and read *Former Broom College Professor Stabbed To Death*. Charles's murder was treated in the same perfunctory manner as Martin's accidental death had been. An unknown assailant had struck Charlie down on Lexington Avenue and Twenty-Ninth Street at about eight o'clock at night. There wasn't even a *hint* of conjecture about why he happened to be there, and nothing was mentioned about his recent termination from Broom. Again there was a follow-up story covering his funeral, and again Leon participated in the eulogy.

Troy closed the book, leaned back and rubbed his beard. There wasn't any doubt in his mind that the deaths were convenient — at least as far as Leon was concerned. He stood up, put on his pea jacket and picked up the folders and the photograph book. Then he left the reading room and headed for the Student Information desk.

Sally looked up.

"Thanks again," Troy said, putting the folders and the book down on the desk.

"Did you find anything?" she whispered.

Troy shook his head. "But I have a question." He bent over the desk.

"What is it?"

"Did Martin or Charles plan to appeal the dismissal?"

"Yes. They had already met with a lawyer. Leon knew they intended to take the matter to court."

"Interesting," Troy mused.

"I think Leon was really showing his true feelings when he came forward and offered to take part in the eulogy," Sally said.

Troy nodded, then asked, "Are you going to be around for the Christmas vacation?"

"Probably, though I might go to the city for a day to see a show."

"How would you like to spend Christmas Day with me, Elly, Professor Petorious and his sister?" Troy asked.

"I didn't realize you were that friendly with Professor Petorious."

Troy smiled. "I'm not."

"I don't understand," Sally said.

"I'm not sure I do either. He invited me and anyone else I want to bring. You and Elly will be my guests."

"Are you sure I would be —"

"The five of us will have a good time."

"Who's the fifth person?"

"His sister, Helen. She's coming up from New York. Is it a date?"

"Well, I'm not —"

"C'mon!"

"If you're sure it will be all right —"

"It will be all right," Troy said. "I'll drop by and let you know what time."

Sally flashed him a big smile.

"And thanks again," Troy said. He left the desk, put on his Greek fisherman's cap and walked out of the library, feeling strangely exhilarated. "Leon," he said, pausing to look in the direction of the President's house, "you don't know it yet, but you've got a fight ahead of you."

Ed Noonan had awakened late, shaved, showered and then had eaten a huge stack of pancakes drowned in melted butter and maple syrup and four hefty sausages. Now, wearing his black seal parka and high boots, he was out for his constitutional, with some vague thought of visiting Ms. Cooms. The woman he had met on the flight from Rome to New York, though pleasant enough, had not been willing to delay her flight to St. Louis in order to spend the night with him. And another woman — a singer in the cocktail lounge of the hotel in which he had stayed — also declined his invitation to share his bed. But when Leon had introduced him to Ms. Cooms, he had sensed that ineffable something — a smoldering sexuality, he hoped — and the more he thought about it, the more he wanted to explore the possibility.

As Noonan neared the library, he saw Troy Sims, the young man who had acted so peculiarly when Leon had introduced them the previous evening. Noonan halted, grateful that some snow-covered pines hid him from view. The kid was looking at Leon's house! Then as Troy turned and got into his Jeep, Noonan stepped out from behind the trees, but remained where he was until Troy drove out of the parking lot.

Noonan went straight to where Ms. Cooms had been the previous evening and was pleased to see her at the same desk. She was busy reading something and didn't look up.

Noonan walked over to her and smiled broadly. "Good morning, Ms. Cooms. It is a pleasure to see you again."

For a moment she looked startled, then she smiled and said, "Please call me Sally; everyone does."

"Sally it is then," he responded with a nod, noting how the color rose in her cheeks and feeling that same indefinable quality he had sensed earlier emanate from her. She wasn't nearly as voluptuous as his ex-wife Galena, but then, few women were. However, she had lovely white skin, and breasts that would fit in his hand with room to spare. He concentrated on making her feel naked under his unrelenting scrutiny.

She looked down at her desk.

"I came by to tell you how impressed I am by the library's collection," he said.

Her head bobbed up and she smiled. "Two million volumes, and twice that number of articles in our computer files."

"And Leon told me about your remarkable Elizabethan collection," Noonan said.

"Yes. It's used by Elizabethan scholars from all over the world," she said proudly, then added, "Our collection of books on filmmaking and the history of film is probably the best in this section of the country."

"I'm impressed," Noonan said. "I bet that young man I met last evening when Leon was showing me around the campus is probably an aspiring filmwriter, or director."

"You mean Troy?" she asked, then flushed.

"Ah, he must have told you about our meeting," Noonan said with a benevolent smile.

"Yes."

"I hope he was as impressed with me as I was with him," Noonan commented.

"He —" She hesitated.

"I didn't mean to put you on the spot," he said. "But I *was* impressed with him."

"He thought you were interesting," Sally responded.

"Is he studying film?" Noonan asked.

"He's a journalism major, but he probably has enough credits in political science to graduate with a double major."

"Now that's what I'd call interesting. By the way, I thought I saw him leave here just as I was crossing the parking lot."

"He was here," she answered, color coming into her cheeks again.

"Just out of curiosity, could you tell me what he was reading?" Noonan asked. "I'd like to become familiar with the books that our students read."

Sally dropped her eyes.

"I promise not to tell anyone else," Noonan said, bending over the desk.

"I really —"

"Suppose I offer you a bribe," Noonan said.

Sally looked at up at him, her eyes wide.

He smiled. "I can offer you cocktails, dinner and good company in exchange for your help."

"My help?"

Noonan detected more than a hint of interest in the tone of her voice. "I want to get to know our students," he said. "College librarians probably know more about various students — from what they read — than their professors."

"That's an interesting way of looking at it," Sally responded. "Some students come here for information and are willing to settle for secondary sources because it's easier to digest, while others want only primary sources."

"Take Troy, for example," Noonan said, "I'd be willing to bet he's a primary-source man and that his interests are very broad."

Sally laughed. "You have him pegged. He reads everything and anything he can get his hands on. Just a short while ago he spent hours reading about the Soviet Army and the structure of its command."

This time Noonan forced himself to smile. "You have books on that subject?" he asked.

"In our Military Section."

"Interesting," Noonan commented, then asked, "Would it be possible for me to borrow that book on the Soviet Army?"

Sally shook her head. "I'm afraid not. It's for reference only. It's one of those books that has photographs, maps and charts."

"Couldn't you make an exception?" Noonan pressed, finding the role of supplicant difficult.

"It's a library rule."

"You're a hard woman, Sally Cooms," Noonan chided. "But I hope not so hard that you'll reject my offer of cocktails and dinner?"

"Not as hard as all that," Sally said gaily.

"Does that mean that you'll go?"

"Yes."

"Do you want me to call for you here, or —"

"At my place," Sally said. "I have an apartment in a large house just north of the college. It's the second house on the right, about a hundred yards beyond Troy's house —" She broke off, flustered. "Oh, but of course that wouldn't mean anything to you."

Though he already knew about Troy's house, he feigned innocence. "I didn't know he rented a house."

"He owns it," Sally said.

"Owns it," Noonan repeated. "The more I hear about Troy, the more I find myself wanting to know."

"Dull he is not!"

"I don't doubt that, and I don't doubt that once he's interested in something he'll pursue it until he's found out all about it."

"That's Troy," Sally said enthusiastically.

"What's he pursuing now?"

"Something that happened four years —" She stopped.

"Oh? What was that?" Noonan asked casually.

She shook her head and sighed deeply. "Old clippings about two men who once taught here."

Noonan sensed that there was a personal connection between Sally and the clippings that was making it difficult for her to speak about the matter. Rather than force her into an uncomfortable position, he smiled and opted for another route. "I feel that I'm beginning to get a handle on Troy. Now you tell me if I'm wrong," he said, playfully shaking a finger at her. He had to know if his intuition about Troy was right. "Tell me if I'm way off base."

"About what?"

"I'd be willing to wager that Troy came here this morning to read about me," Noonan said.

Sally turned very red.

"We'll discuss it this evening," he said. Why was Troy interested in him?

She nodded.

Kissing the back of her hand, Noonan said, "I'll see you at six."

[4]

Noonan flung open the door to Leon's study without knocking. "I want —" He stopped. A young woman was seated across the desk from Leon. She looked at Noonan her eyes wide with astonishment.

"Yes?" Leon asked, completely in control.

"I'm sorry," Noonan said. "I didn't realize that you were busy."

Leon smiled. "Just finishing, Mr. Noonan," he said, looking at the young lady. "Miss Gloria Rand. Mr. Ed Noonan, soon to be the newest member of the college's Board of Directors."

Noonan interpreted the introduction as an invitation to enter the room. He stepped across the threshold and went to where the young woman sat. "It's a pleasure to meet you," he said, taking hold of her hand. She was no more than twenty.

He quickly noted how her breasts pushed at the red sweater she wore.

"My pleasure," she answered in a soft voice.

"Well, I'll speak to Professor Petorious. Perhaps we will be able to reach some sort of compromise. But in the meantime, you enjoy your holiday with your family." Leon stuck out his hand.

"Thank you, Doctor," Miss Rand said.

Noonan watched her as she stood up. She was one of those long-legged women whose every movement was sinuous . . . seductive —.

She smiled at him.

His eyes swept the length of her body and became riveted to the place where her jeans hugged her body so tightly that her mons veneris was clearly visible. And when she turned toward the door, the crack between the hemispheres of her buttocks was provocatively marked.

When the door closed behind her, Noonan turned his attention to Leon. "How the hell could you just look at that and not want it?"

"It's not that I don't *want it*," Leon answered, tamping down the tobacco in the bowl of his pipe with his thumb. "It's just that I've gotten used to it." Then lighting up, he asked, "You came in here as if the hounds of hell were after you. Anything wrong?" He drew on the pipe and let the smoke curl out of his mouth.

Noonan sat in the chair which Miss Rand had occupied. The dark leather still held her warmth. "How much do you know about Troy?" he asked.

"Did you meet him again?" Leon asked, leaning back in his swivel chair.

Noonan expected an answer; he hadn't come to trade his question for one from Leon. He stood up, circled around his chair and rested his arms on its high back. Then he said in a low, hard voice, "This is not a meeting between you and one of your pretty young female students. I *command*."

Blanching, Leon bounced forward in his chair.

"I asked a question. I expect — no, I demand — an answer, not another question."

"I —"

"The answer," Noonan snapped.

"I have his school dossier here," Leon said, getting up and walking to one of four walnut-stained file cabinets that stood along one wall.

Noonan remained standing. This was the third time he had been in the room and he was still impressed with the shelves of books that covered the walls.

"Here it is," Leon said, removing the folder from the drawer and returning to his desk with it. He sat down, opened the folder and as he read, he said, "He is, as you probably guessed, a very good student. His family is very wealthy. He himself is worth several million. He is politically active on campus, but prefers to be the power behind the throne rather than take the throne himself, if you know what I mean." Leon looked over his glasses at Noonan.

"That doesn't explain why he spent the morning reading about me and the other Board members," Noonan responded.

"He's that kind of person," Leon said. "I assure you, it means nothing, absolutely nothing."

"Don't assure me," Noonan answered sharply. "The boy is dangerous. I intend to find out just how dangerous this evening."

"I don't understand."

Noonan snorted with disdain. Ignoring Leon's question, he said, "I want you to listen to me."

Leon nodded.

"In the library there's a book which explains the structure of the Soviet Army. There are pictures of various generals. I am sure that my picture is in that book."

Leon moved as if to stand up.

"Sit down and listen!" Noonan ordered.

"He also read some clippings, something having to do with two professors who once taught here."

"Giddeon and Platz," Leon responded.

"Who are they and why would he be interested in them?"

"They — it happened four years ago," Leon said quietly.

"*What* happened?" Noonan asked, wondering how the man seated behind the desk managed to get where he was with seemingly so little intelligence.

Leon explained, "Giddeon and Platz opposed General Strogerly's appointment to the Board and had to be dealt with. But why should Troy be interested in them now?"

"Because of me."

"What?"

"There's a connection."

"I don't see it," Leon said.

"What you see or don't see," Noonan told him, "doesn't matter. Get rid of the book! That must be done."

"I'll take care of it," Leon said.

"Today."

"Yes."

"I will be using your car for a few hours this evening," Noonan said.

Leon shrugged. "My pleasure."

"We're going on an errand of mercy," Troy said, as soon as Elly settled herself in the bucket seat next to him.

"That means lunch, doesn't it?" she asked. "I'm starving."

As Troy eased the car away from the curb he glanced at her. Her face, half hidden by a hood, was red from the cold and the tip of her nose was shiny. "First, the errand of mercy," he said, placing his hand on her thigh and gently squeezing it.

She faced him. "Who's sick?"

"The body politick," he answered, putting his hand back on the steering wheel.

"C'mon, Troy, stop playing head games," Elly said.

He put his foot gently on the brake and shifted to neutral as he approached a stop sign. "I spent part of the morning with Sally."

"I hope you enjoyed yourself," Elly answered, looking out of the window.

Troy shifted again. "She was engaged to Professor Martin Giddeon," he said and before Elly could ask who Martin Giddeon was, he added, "He was one of the professors who opposed Strogerly's appointment to the Board. The other was Charles Platz."

"So?"

"So both were dismissed on the charge of luring young men from the town to their house for —"

"Was that why they were fired?"

"That was the charge," Troy said, "but not the reason. Both were dead a few weeks later, within a month of one another. Giddeon was killed in a car accident not far from the school. His brakes failed and the car smashed into a telephone pole. Platz was knifed by a mugger on Lexington Avenue in Manhattan."

"How horrible!" Elly exclaimed.

"How wonderfully coincidental for Strogerly and Leon!" Troy responded. "At the time, Charles was having an affair with a Mrs. Laura Hobe."

For several moments, Elly was quiet, then she said, "Are you trying to tell me the charges against them were false and that —"

"Sally and Giddeon were lovers."

"That doesn't mean anything. They could have gone both ways."

"Possible, but not probable," Troy answered.

"If that's the case, then you're questioning their deaths, aren't you?" Elly asked, facing him.

"Even if I was," Troy sad, "it wouldn't do any good now. No, now I'm interested in something else."

"And what's that?"

He grinned. "Getting you in bed," he answered.

"Be serious."

Troy drove up Red Hook's main street. "We're going to pay a visit to Laura Hobe."

"Troy, you can't!" Elly exclaimed. "You just can't do that."

He braked and down-shifted for a red light. "I want to know —"

"The woman was having an affair. She's not going to talk about it to a total stranger. Come back to reality!"

"It's worth the gamble," Troy answered.

"You don't know anything about her," Elly said. "Wait a minute, I know the name. Hobe —"

"Her husband is the president of the local bank."

"You know, I'm beginning to think you're certifiable."

Troy put his hand on her thigh again. "I never said I wasn't."

Elly shook her head. "Just tell me what you intend to accomplish."

"I don't really know," he said, playfully moving his hand over her thigh. "Maybe, I just want to confirm the fact that Platz was as sexually normal as I am."

Elly stopped his hand. "You're going to have the door slammed in your face for your trouble," she said.

"You buy lunch if I don't," he answered.

Elly threw up her hands. "Hey, I don't want any part of this! You can let me out now."

"Come along for the ride," he said.

"No way. This you do solo. Just let me out."

"The least you can do is wait for me, just in case I have to make a fast getaway."

"You know damn well I don't know how to drive a standard shift," she said.

Troy slowed and turned onto a mountain road. "Listen," he said, "there's something about Noonan being elected to the Board that just rubs me the wrong way."

"But why?"

"It just does. If you're not going to sleep with me, the least you can do is humor me."

Elly pouted. "You never let up, do you?"

He grinned at her and shifted into second as the grade of the road grew steeper.

"Has that sick mind of yours remembered where you saw Mr. Noonan?" she asked.

"Do I detect a note of sarcasm?"

"A whole symphony of it," Elly replied.

"To prove my love, regardless of your sarcasm, I'll answer your question with a simple *no*. There, does that satisfy you?"

"The only thing that will *satisfy* me, as you put it, will be for you to turn around and go back to —"

"See," Troy teased, "we weren't any place to go back to. I'll make you a deal: we go back to my place and make passionate love, or we go see Mrs. Hobe."

"That's blackmail!" Elly cried.

Troy shrugged. "That's reality."

"I promise," Elly said, "I'll get even for this."

"Does that mean you'll come with me?" he asked, taking hold of her hand and gently squeezing it.

"It *means* that under duress I'm accompanying you on what will probably be one of the shortest interviews on record," Elly said.

"I like your attitude," Troy responded and kissed the back of her hand. "Oh, I asked Sally to join us Christmas Day."

"I thought we might spend it with Professor Petorious and his sister," Elly said.

Troy nodded. "That's right."

"My God, you do have a pair of brass balls!"

"Hey, that's unfair. You've never even seen my balls."

"You really don't understand that you did something you shouldn't have, do you?" Elly asked.

"You mean I shouldn't have asked Sally?"

"You should have asked Professor Petorious if you could bring Sally," she told him.

"You really think so?"

"I really think it would have been the courteous thing to do," Elly answered.

After several moments of silence, Troy said, "Yeah, I guess you're right. But everyone likes Sally. Besides, I felt that I owed her something after she helped me and —"

"And what?"

"It wasn't easy for her to talk about Martin. Several times she became weepy."

"Do you think it's going to be easy for Mrs. Hobe?" Elly asked. "She might become weepy too, perhaps even hysterical."

"Listen, if I didn't feel that this has to be done," Troy said, "I wouldn't do it."

"C'mon Troy," Elly chided, "at least admit that you love doing this kind of thing."

"Yeah, maybe you're right," he said, grinning.

The Hobes' sprawling, red-brick ranch house was perched on a hill, with a clear view of the Hudson river some two miles to the west.

Troy pulled the Jeep into a parking area at the right of the house. "Remember, if we're not thrown out, you buy lunch," he said, as they started up the cleared path to the door.

"I can't believe what I see," Elly commented, looking back at the river. "The view is just spectacular."

He took hold of her hand. "Be my love and I'll build you a bigger house than this on top of that hill over there," he said.

"And you're the first to decry the evils of capitalism," she said, "and also the first to use your money to buy what you want."

"Just think of the number of people who'd be gainfully employed, if you'd agree —"

"Ring the bell, Troy," Elly told him.

He nodded and stabbed at the bell several times with his gloved hand. "Chimes," he commented.

"We can still run back to the Jeep," Elly said.

"Too late. I hear someone coming."

Elly grimaced.

"That's not your best look," Troy said.

Before Elly could answer, the door swung open and a butler asked, "May I help you?"

"Troy Sims and his associate to see Mrs. Hobe. I phoned earlier. I'm with the Kingston *Sentinel*," Troy said easily. He took out his wallet and flashed a press card.

"Mrs. Hobe is expecting you, Mr. Sims," the butler said. "Please follow me."

"Thank you." Troy stepped aside to permit Elly to enter before him.

"Mrs. Hobe will be with you shortly," the butler said, taking their coats and hats and then leading them through a spacious foyer to a small, cheerful room with a sofa, several comfortable chairs, and a fireplace with a fire going in it. "Would either of you care for something to drink? Coffee, or perhaps hot chocolate?"

Troy was about to refuse when Elly said, "I'd love hot chocolate."

"Anything for you, sir?"

"Coffee, thank you," Troy answered. For no reason he could think of, the room reminded him of the time when his mother and father were still married and he was part of a family.

The butler nodded and left the room.

As soon as the door closed, Elly hissed, "You set this up, didn't you?"

"Mea culpa. Mea culpa," Troy said, slapping his chest.

"And you lied to do it, too. That's a college press card. What if he actually looked at it? What would you have done?"

"I figured I'd have two choices: I'd either run like hell, or drop to my knees and plead to be allowed to speak to the mistress of the house."

"You are definitely certifiable."

Troy put his hands on Elly's shoulders. "Did it work?"

"That's not the point."

"That is exactly the point," he said. "Now, quickly kiss me and tell me how much you love me."

Elly touched his lips with hers. "But I'm not going to tell you how much I love you when at this moment I loathe you."

"Well, at least there's some feeling there," he said and was about to take her in his arms when he heard the doorknob being turned. "Saved," he whispered and took several steps back.

The door opened and a strikingly handsome, dark-haired woman, who Troy guessed was in her early forties entered the room. She closed the door after her and looked at him and then at Elly before she said, "On the phone you said that you were a reporter from the Kingston *Sentinel*."

Troy cleared his throat. She obviously sensed he wasn't what he had claimed to be. "I couldn't think of any other way that would —"

The door opened and the butler entered with a tray on which was a mug of hot chocolate, a cup of coffee and a plate of cookies.

"Put it down on the table, Thomas," Mrs. Hobe said.

With a nod, the butler followed her instructions and left the room.

"The cookies were my idea," she explained.

"A good one," Troy said, helping himself to one with bits of chocolate in its center.

Laura Hobe turned her attention to Troy. "Now, Mr. Sims, why did you think it necessary to pretend —"

"Because, Mrs. Hobe, I want to ask you some questions about Charles," Troy said.

For a moment it looked as if her legs would give way, but she steadied herself. "You caught me off guard," she said in a low voice.

"I'm sorry," Troy said gently.

"Please sit down," she said, going over to the couch and settling herself on it.

Troy chose an easy chair and Elly took the only high-backed one in the room.

"How do you know that I knew Charles?" she asked.

"Mrs. Hobe," Troy said, taking the plunge, "I know that you and Charles were lovers."

Her lips trembled but she managed to say, "I won't be blackmailed."

Troy leaned forward. "That's not why I'm here," he said.

Her gray eyes went from Troy to Elly and back to Troy before she asked, "Then why?"

"I want to know about Charles."

"I have nothing to say," she answered. "Absolutely nothing to say. Now if you will please leave, I —"

"Didn't it strike you — or anyone else, for that matter — as strange that Martin and Charles were dead shortly after having been dismissed from Broom?"

She nodded, then said, "Coincidence plays an enormous role in all our lives."

"One coincidence, yes," Troy answered. "But two such coincidences?"

Flushed now, she asked, "Just what are you getting at?"

Troy stood up. "I think better on my feet," he said, beginning to pace back and forth in front of the window.

"You haven't answered my question," Mrs. Hobe said.

Troy stopped. "I don't really know . . . I'm just questioning what to me is questionable, namely, the coincidence of their deaths. Did Charles ever discuss the situation at the college?"

"No," she said, folding her hands in her lap.

"Did you ever ask?"

"We didn't have that kind of a relationship," she said, looking down at her hands. "We avoided speaking about our lives, if you know what I mean."

Troy wasn't exactly sure, but to avoid looking stupid, he nodded.

"We wanted to get away from our real lives," she explained, shifting her eyes to him.

"So you never knew he was accused of having sex with boys?" Troy asked. "Young boys from town?"

She gasped. Her hand flew to her mouth and then she cried, "Oh my God!"

"He and Martin had the same charges brought against them," Troy said.

Biting her lower lip, she shook her head. "That's absurd! Absurd! He enjoyed a woman too much."

"He enjoyed you?"

"God, yes!" she exclaimed. "Yes, and I enjoyed him too!" Then suddenly her face crumpled and she began to cry softly. "There hasn't been a day since his death that I haven't thought about him."

Elly opened her shoulder bag, took out a tissue and handed it to her.

"How could they have been charged with that?" Mrs. Hobe asked.

"The college produced the boys," Troy answered.

"Neither of them was interested in boys — I'd stake my life on it."

"So would I," Troy said. "So would I."

"Tell me why you're interested in this now?" she asked. "It happened almost four years ago."

Troy sat down. "Four years ago two men tried to prevent General Strogerly from becoming a member of the Board of Directors of the college and the two men —"

"Charles and Martin?"

Troy nodded.

"Charles never said a word about it," she whispered. "Never."

"I believe you," Troy said.

"But what does that situation have to do with you?"

"Nothing really," Troy answered, "except that now a Mr. Noonan will soon become a Board member and neither the students nor the faculty have anything to say about it."

"Did they ever have anything to say about who's appointed to the Board?"

"No."

"Then why should they now?" Mrs. Hobe asked.

Troy stood up again and started to pace. Suddenly he had found what he was looking for. "I want to stop Noonan from becoming a member of the Board."

"Troy!" Elly exclaimed.

"I don't think you can do that," Mrs. Hobe said.

Ignoring both of them, Troy said, "It's time someone from the faculty is appointed, someone who understands the needs of the students and—"

"Have you anyone in mind?"

"No, but once the opportunity presents itself, there will be more than one candidate."

"But I don't understand why this is important to you?"

"Neither do I," Elly said.

Troy laughed.

"I already told him he was certifiable," Elly said.

"I don't know why it is important either," Troy said. "But it is. Maybe it's the idea of 'fighting the good fight,' or maybe it has something to do with wanting to have the 'good guys' win for a change, even though two of them are dead."

"Will you come back and tell me how it works out?" Mrs. Hobe asked.

"I'll tell you everything."

"Did you mean what you said about the faculty . . . I mean, a member of the Board being chosen from the faculty?" Elly asked.

"You don't think it's a good idea?"

Elly thought for a few moments. "Who would your choice be?"

"Someone who'd care, really care, about the school," he answered.

"It's a good idea," she said. "But it'll never happen. You're not going to be able to stop Noonan from becoming the next member of the Board."

"Maybe not," Troy admitted. "But it's the 'good fight' and maybe I *can* stop him."

"How?" she challenged.

Troy tapped the side of his head with the forefinger of his right hand. "By finding their weakness and then —" He smiled. "And then grabbing them by the balls until it hurts."

"You're wasting your time," Elly said, looking out of the side window.

Troy shifted back into third and wondered if Mrs. Hobe had a lover now.

"I wouldn't want to live like that," Elly said, as if sensing the subject shift. "The woman has everything and yet she has nothing."

"It's hard to believe that two people could have an intense physical relationship and not share anything else," Elly went on. "Would you want that kind of relationship with a woman?"

"I don't know," he answered. "I could see where it could have advantages." He found himself wondering about the kind of relationship his parents had had. Obviously, it lacked something.

"It must be hell for a woman to sleep night after night in the same bed with a man who doesn't turn her on," Elly said. "I don't think I'd be able to live that way."

Troy shrugged.

"What about you, would you be able to live with a woman who didn't turn you on?" Elly asked.

"I never thought about it," Troy admitted.

"I have. I think most women do."

"Yeah, I guess they do," Troy said. "But a lot of women marry for money and hope the turn-on will come, or at least make the best of what they've chosen." He stopped for a red light. "Still hungry?" he asked.

"Very."

"So am I," Troy said. "Are you buying?"

"You mean —"

"That was the bet."

"I never agreed to it," Elly complained.

"I'm telling you now," Troy said, "I'm not going to marry a woman who welshes on her word."

"But you would sleep with her?"

"Certainly. What kind of man do you think I am?"

"A rat-fink," Elly told him.

"I love it when you tell me how great I am," he answered, putting his hand on her thigh and squeezing it gently.

"Here I am again," Troy announced, going up to the desk where Sally was calling something up on her terminal.

"This time to do some real work, I hope," she said, looking at him.

"Sally, that's totally unfair," Troy answered. "I've been busy as hell since I saw you last." Then, before she could ask what he had done, he said, "Elly and I went to visit Laura Hobe."

"You didn't!" Sally exclaimed.

Troy nodded. "We sure as hell did."

"But why —"

Troy glanced over his shoulder, then looked to either side of him. No one was anywhere near them. He leaned over the desk. "She didn't know why Charles was dismissed," he said. "Charles never told her."

Sally's eyes went wide.

"She and Charles didn't have that kind of relationship, whatever that means," he said.

"Just sex?"

Troy nodded. "So it would seem."

Sally shook her head, but didn't say anything.

"To be sure I didn't miss anything, I want to read the newspaper clippings again," Troy said.

"What are you trying to do?" she asked.

"If I told you, you wouldn't believe me."

She stared at him. "Has it anything to do with Mr. Noonan?" she asked.

"Good guess," Troy answered with a smile.

"What have you got against that man?" she demanded.

Suddenly Troy became aware of the defensive tone in her voice. "Have you spoken to him?" he asked.

"He's taking me to dinner tonight," she replied.

Troy stood up straight. "If you don't mind my asking," he said, "how did that happen?"

"He came in here just after you left. In fact he seems to be quite interested in you."

"I bet!" Troy said sarcastically.

"He wanted to know what you were reading."

"You told him?"

"Yes. He seemed bothered by the fact that you had read his biog sheet."

"Good. I want to rattle some brains around here," Troy answered. "My guess is that he knows I'm after his ass."

"What?"

"I want to stop Noonan from becoming a member of the Board."

"But why?"

"Because Martin and Charles tried to stop Strogerly and failed," Troy said. "I want to finish what they started and then take it one step further."

7

"I don't understand. You didn't even know them."

Grinning, Troy said, "Don't you know, Sally, that all men who fight for social justice are brothers?"

"I think you're making a mistake," Sally said. "He really is a very nice man."

"But he got upset when you told him what I was doing?"

"Annoyed, rather than upset."

"What else did he want to know?" Troy asked. Troy —"

"C'mon, Sally, tell me what else did he want to know. It just might be very important."

"I'm not going to help you keep him off the Board," she said quietly.

"It was probably about me, right?"

"Wrong. He wanted to know if we have any books about the Soviet Army. That has nothing to do with you, Mr. Ego."

Troy rubbed his beard. "Now that's an area of interest I wouldn't associate with him, would you?"

With a shrug, Sally said, "People have strange interests. If I remember correctly, you recently spent hours reading a book on the Soviet Army."

"Yeah, but I'm nuts and I'm not about to become a member of this, or any other, Board of Directors."

"I'll have to agree with both statements," Sally responded.

"I need a big favor," Troy said. "No, two big favors."

"If they have anything to do with Mr. Noonan," she said, "the answer is no."

Troy leaned close to her again. "I really want to finish what Martin had started. I have nothing against Noonan. I don't even know the man. But don't you think it would be better for the college if at least one of the Board members was also a member of the faculty?"

She didn't answer.

"Wasn't that what Martin and Charles wanted?"

"Yes," Sally sighed, "that's exactly what they wanted."

"Find out the name of Noonan's company and where it's located," Troy said.

"What's the second favor?"

"Tell Noonan that I came back to reread the biog sheets," Troy said. Sensing that Sally was going to refuse him, he added quickly, "Trust me, I know all of this seems crazy to you, but I want to know more about this guy."

"You're making me feel like a traitor."

"If Martin were alive and asked you to help him, would you feel like a traitor?"

"That's unfair!" she exclaimed.

Troy shook his head. "I need your help. I can't get the information any other way. Just do these two things for me and I promise not to ask you to do anything else." Extending his hand, he asked, "A deal?"

Sally hesitated, then slowly she lifted her hand toward his. "A deal," she answered and shook his hand.

[5]

Palovich nodded and with his left hand, gestured to his aides, Gargarin and Komarov, to sit down in the chairs in front of his desk. "An hour ago," he said, "I received a phone call from the Comrade Director ending the Gorsky investigation."

Neither man commented.

Palovich reached for the humidor, opened it and pushed it toward his aides.

Gargarin helped himself to a cigar, but Komarov declined.

"Comrade Colonel Lenov's body turned up in a hotel room in Rome," Palovich said. "He had been poisoned with curare and —"

Komarov almost stood up.

"Surprised that he was in Rome?" Palovich questioned, lighting his cigar. "Well, so am I, Comrades, and I would guess so is everyone else who knows about it. His body was turned over to our people after an autopsy had been performed, which was, I was told, the way they determined he belonged to us. Some years ago he had some dental work done and it had been engraved with U.S.S.R.A. and the last four digits of his serial number."

"If Lenov was in Rome, Comrade General Gorsky —"

"Has defected to the West," Palovich said, blowing smoke toward the ceiling.

Gargarin broke into a fit of coughing. "Do we know that for sure?" he sputtered.

"One of our spotters saw him in the First-Class lounge of American Airlines at da Vinci airport."

"With Western agents?" Komarov asked.

"That's what makes it so peculiar," Palovich said. "Our spotter was sure there wasn't anyone with him. But since it is now certain he has left the country, the entire matter has been shifted to the Ninth Directorate, the Special Investigations Department, and I understand a man has already been assigned to find the Comrade General."

"Suppose it's a matter of a woman?" Gargarin asked. "The Comrade General's taste for —"

"I do not suppose anything," Palovich interrupted. "I am only pleased that the entire matter no longer be the concern of this department."

"Is the Comrade General being suspected of killing Comrade Colonel Lenov?" Komarov asked.

Palovich nodded. "It's a reasonable suspicion," he answered. "But I was not officially informed that it is the case."

"Who's being sent to find the Comrade General?" Gargarin asked.

"Comrade Major Igor Morosov," Palovich answered. "I was told that he has successfully dealt with similar assignments. But I don't know him and when I made a few inquiries about him, I was politely, but firmly told by the Comrade Director of the Special Investigations Department not to ask any more questions. But I did get the feeling the Comrade Major Morosov is already in the United States, or is en route there. But the really important news is that we don't have to deal with it."

Komarov nodded. "That will certainly make things a lot less tense around here," he said.

"The Comrade General must have been planning this for a long time," Gargarin commented.

"I would say so," Palovich answered. "But what has everyone confused is how he managed to get out without being spotted until he was leaving Rome. The consensus is that he had a great deal of help."

"Then we are not entirely free of the investigation, are we?" Komarov questioned.

Palovich smiled. "Everything has been turned over to the Ninth Directorate," he said with obvious satisfaction. "Let its men knock their heads on something that might take months, maybe even years to unravel and by then who will care what they have found? The entire incident will have been forgotten."

"Then you think Comrade Major Morosov will come up empty?" Gargarin asked.

"I do not think about it," Palovich answered.

Troy parked his Jeep in front of Leon's house, where the windows were festively decorated with large green wreaths bearing red satin bows. Through the living room window a large, beautifully decorated Christmas tree was visible.

Troy knew that Leon was deeply into the Christmas and Easter rituals. Christmas Eve he always attended Mass in the local Catholic Church and on Christmas Day he held an open house for the poor children in the area.

Troy approached the house resolutely. Earlier in the evening, he had decided to lay down the gauntlet. He walked up the four wooden steps and rang the bell. He could hear it ring.

"I'm coming!" Mrs. Forest, Leon's housekeeper, shouted, "I'm coming."

Within moments the door was opened by a middle-aged, gray-haired woman.

"I'd like to see Leon," Troy said.

Suddenly Leon called out, "Who is it, Beth?"

"One of your students," Beth answered.

"It's Troy," Troy called out.

"Bring him in here, Beth," Leon said.

Troy smiled.

"He's in the living room." Beth closed the door behind him. "Just go in."

"Thanks," Troy said, taking off his gloves, then his woolen hat and opening his coat.

She nodded, turned and marched back into the recesses of the house, while Troy headed into the living room, where he found Leon putting down track for his elaborate train set.

"Just in time to help," Leon said, smiling up at him. "Take off your coat and come on down here. You can't imagine the kick I get when I see the way the children react to the trains."

Troy hesitated. At that moment Leon looked more avuncular than usual. Perhaps it was because of the way he peered over his glasses. Or the note of genuine feeling in the tone of his voice?

"I have a special crash set," Leon said. "The children are going to go wild when they see it."

Troy slipped off his coat and squatted next to Leon.

"There's a stack of track in the box to your right," Leon said. "You hand me a piece of straight or curved when I ask for it." He went back to nailing a piece of track to the roadbed.

Troy was caught off guard by Leon.

"A straight piece," Leon said.

"A straight piece," Troy repeated, handing it to Leon.

"When I was a kid," Leon said, as he worked, "my folks were too poor to buy me electric trains. But there was one kid in the neighborhood who had a set, big old Lionel, or American Flyer, I can't remember which. Every Christmas his father set them up in the window and all the kids in the neighborhood would stand and watch the train move around a big table. The top of the table, I remember, was painted green. A piece of curved track now."

Troy handed the track to him, took a deep breath and said, "Leon, I came here to tell you that I intend to stop Noonan from becoming a member of the Board."

Leon finished putting the section of track in place before he asked, "And just how do you intend to do that?" He got to his feet, brushed his jeans off and reset the glasses on the bridge of his nose.

Troy stood up. "By asking certain questions about the men who opposed General Strogerly's appointment four years ago."

"I think it would be better if we discussed this in my study," Leon said.

"There is no need for discussion," Troy answered resolutely.

"If I've learned anything over the years," Leon said, "I've learned that there is always room for discussion. My study, please?"

"You were saying something about the men who opposed General Strogerly's appointment," Leon said, as he sat down behind his large desk.

"Questions —"

"Yes, questions," Leon repeated. "Why don't you sit down? Take any chair."

Troy chose the chair on the left.

"Tell me about the questions," Leon said, filling a pipe and lighting it.

"Questions about why Giddeon and Platz were dismissed from Broom on false charges," Troy said.

"You obviously know the situation."

"Yes."

"Then you must also know that several boys came forward —"

"Yes, I know that. But I also know that both men were sexually involved with women."

"Oh?"

"You must have known that," Troy said, sensing he had just played a royal flush.

"I knew that Martin and Sally dated sometimes," Leon responded.

"They had been living together for several months and planned to announce their engagement."

Leon puffed on his pipe. "And Charles?"

"He was involved in an affair with the wife of a prominent man in town," Troy said.

"You spoke to her?"

Troy nodded.

"And of course you won't reveal her name?"

Troy shook his head.

"Neither Martin's relationship to Sally, nor Charles's love affair with someone else's wife, eliminates the possibility that they also had a penchant for young men."

"Not entirely, I agree," Troy said. "But if the local newspapers got the story, the matter of their deaths would certainly be brought up, and of course General Strogerly's appointment would become the interesting centerpiece in all of it."

"What exactly is your reason for doing this?" Leon asked.

"I don't think the college needs another —" Troy was going to say industrialist, when he suddenly realized that every member of the Board was either a retired general, admiral, or the head of a huge industrial complex. But Noonan didn't fall into any of those categories. He was just the owner of a small electronics company, or so he said. Why was he different from the others?

"You look as if you suddenly remembered something," Leon said. "I hope it has to do with good manners."

"I'm giving you fair warning," Troy answered. "I'm going to try and stop Noonan."

"Have you anything else to say to me?" Leon asked.

Troy shook his head.

"Then if you will excuse me," Leon said, "I am having several guests for dinner tonight."

Frank Robin entered Fitzhugh's office and said, "I think I have a good line on what all that telephone and radio traffic was all about."

Fitzhugh leaned back in his chair. "I thought you were on your way to Boston by now."

"A few hours one way or another doesn't make much difference," Robin answered. "I wanted to get this business pegged down if I could."

"Sit down and tell me what you have," Fitzhugh said, relighting his pipe.

Robin dropped into the chair next to the desk. "We have unconfirmed reports that General Anatole Gorsky is missing."

"Missing? What does that mean?"

"Defected, possibly." Robin dug a pack of cigarettes out of his jacket pocket, took one out and put it between his lips. But he didn't light it. "Whoever gets him, gets a very big fish. It would probably take six to nine months to fully debrief him."

Fitzhugh leaned forward slowly. "He hasn't come to us," he said, his voice almost a growl. "And I haven't heard anything from MI-5, or the Sûreté."

"A Colonel Peter Lenov turned up dead in a hotel room in Rome," Robin said, finally lighting the cigarette with a Zippo.

Fitzhugh looked at him. "I don't know the name of every goddamned Russkie officer," he said petulantly.

"Lenov was Gorsky's aide. He was killed with curare."

Fitzhugh put his pipe down into the hammered copper ashtray. "Just how good are your sources?" he asked.

"They wouldn't pass any info to me unless it was at least eighty-five percent accurate," Robin answered defensively. "The info about Lenov is a hundred percent accurate."

Fitzhugh said nothing.

"Lenov was also Gorsky's private pilot," Robin said.

"Are you trying to tell me this Colonel Lenov flew Gorsky to Rome?"

"Maybe not all the way to Rome," Robin said. "But close enough for the two of them to get there."

"Then are you assuming Gorsky was, or may still be, in Rome?" Fitzhugh questioned.

Robin nodded and said, "Yes, he was in Rome, but I doubt if he's still there."

"Why didn't he take Lenov with him wherever he went?"

"Probably didn't need him any more," Robin said, blowing smoke off to one side.

"You're assuming that Gorsky killed him?" Fitzhugh questioned, pushing the copper ash-tray between them.

Robin nodded.

"Motive?"

"Served his purpose and could be discarded."

Fitzhugh picked up his pipe again. "Based on an unconfirmed report about Gorsky, you've made some very imaginative assumptions."

"By the time we return from our Christmas holiday, I'd be willing to bet —"

"All right," Fitzhugh said, pointing his pipe at him, "I'll bet it for now and alert our counterparts in England, France and Germany. And to be sure that no one else gets their hands on this information, put it under a Red Check Ten priority. Use your own ID. That way only you or I will be able to access the material."

Robin smiled.

"How many other people know about this besides your overseas sources?"

"No one," Robin said.

Fitzhugh nodded. "Good. I want this one kept under wraps. I don't want anyone else in on it just yet and that means keeping it away from Steve. When we know more, we'll tell him."

"You're the boss," Robin answered.

"There are times when I wish more people would remember that," Fitzhugh growled.

"Ah, the pleasures and problems of command!" Robin smiled.

Fitzhugh smiled, too. "Well, it's not as bad as all that. It does have its compensations."

Robin reached over to the copper ashtray and stubbed out his cigarette.

"Are you leaving for home tonight?" Fitzhugh asked.

Robin nodded. "I have to see my girlfriend before I go," he said. "She has some qualms about coming up and meeting the family. The usual thing, I guess."

"You're going to try and change her mind?"

"You got it."

"Good luck," Fitzhugh said. "Have a good holiday."

"You too." Robin turned and headed for the door.

Fitzhugh watched him leave. When the door was finally closed, he picked up the phone and quickly punched a number.

"Mercy Mission," a man answered.

"A new world," Fitzhugh said.

"Copying," the man replied.

"We have a red signal all the way from base two," Fitzhugh said.

"Details."

"None."

"Take your man out."

"Affirmative," Fitzhugh answered and clicked off. An instant later he punched out another number.

"Marty's Trucking," a man answered.

"Go for it," Fitzhugh said. "Make it look good."

The man laughed. "Like a work of art."

For a few moments, Fitzhugh listened to the buzz of the disconnected phone; then he dialled the Duty Officer. "I'll be gone for several days. In an emergency you'll be able to reach me at five-one-six-four-four-eight-five. That's the home number of the president of Broom College."

"Got it," the Duty Officer said. "Have a nice holiday."

"Thanks," Fitzhugh answered. "I intend to have a *very* nice holiday."

A hostess escorted Noonan and Sally to a table in the Drum and Fife Room at the 1776, an inn just outside Kingston.

Noonan helped her with the chair.

"I haven't had anyone do that for a long, long time," she said, smiling up at him gratefully.

"That is their loss," he said, seating himself opposite her.

The candlelight from the candle in the center of the table flickered across their faces and the scent of pine from the boughs decorating the walls filled the air.

"This room," Sally explained, "was once part of a house built just before the start of the Revolutionary War."

Noonan smiled and nodded appreciatively, though not because he was interested in what he had been told, but rather because Sally had just adjusted the Spanish-type shawl she was wearing and the tops of her breasts became visible.

"The rough-hewn crossbeams were part of the original structure," she said, "and so is the wall with the fireplace."

"Fascinating," Noonan answered. "American history is one of my passions."

"Mine too," she exclaimed.

A waitress wearing a black dress, white apron and a white cap, came to the table and asked if they wanted anything from the bar.

"Wine with the dinner, of course," Noonan said, "or perhaps you'd prefer champagne?"

"Wine."

He nodded. "Do you have a sommelier?" he asked the waitress.

The waitress looked at him blankly.

"A wine steward?" Sally prompted gently.

"Only a wine list," the woman said.

"Fine," Noonan said. "I'll see the wine list, and I'd like a Stolichnya on the rocks now."

"Sorry, sir, we don't serve anything Russian here," she said.

"But —" Noonan was annoyed.

Sally touched his hand. "It's because of the Russian presence in Afghanistan," she explained. "It's a way of protesting."

"Yes . . . yes, of course," he said with a smile. "Finlandia then, or Absolut on the rocks, please."

"Absolut," the waitress said.

"That will be fine," he said, and then he asked Sally if she wanted anything from the bar.

"A Bloody Mary," she answered.

8

For a few moments, Noonan looked around the room. A lot of the tables were occupied by well-dressed men and women.

"Is anything wrong?" Sally asked.

"I wanted to reaffirm my opinion," he said, engaging her eyes with his, "that we make a handsome couple." As he spoke, he slowly lowered his gaze to the tops of her breasts.

"Yes," she said, "we do."

"But why the blush?" Noonan asked.

"Because —"

"Ah," he exclaimed, patting her hand, "in this day and age when a man finds a woman who blushes it is an absolutely delightful experience!"

"If you don't stop talking that way, I'll burst into flame," she said.

"And how will I explain that to the other people here?" he asked.

She shook her head.

"A blush is as rare as a —"

"Here come our drinks," Sally said.

"Are you ready to order?" the waitress asked.

"In a little while," Sally said.

Noonan waited until the waitress left, then raised his glass. "To you."

"To *us*," Sally countered,

They touched glasses and drank.

"I hope we have a long and delightful relationship," Noonan said.

"Yes, so do I," Sally responded.

"I've been thinking about Troy," Noonan said, putting his glass down.

"Oh?"

"That young man could be a great help to me."
"I'd like to get to know him better. He could give

me an insight into the student's point of view about things."

"I'm sure he could," Sally agreed.

"You said he was reading the biog sheets of the various Board members —"

"He reread everything this afternoon," she said.

"You mean he returned to the library?"

Sally nodded. "He was specifically interested in the newspaper clippings."

Noonan picked up his glass. "Why those?" he asked.

"It's something of a story," Sally answered.

Noonan wanted to hear what she had to say. He nodded. "We have hours and hours in front of us," he said.

"Martin Giddeon and Charles Platz were professors at the college who had opposed General Strogerly's appointment to the Board. Shortly after they made their opposition known, they were called before the Board and accused of having sexual relations with several young men from town. They were fired and not long afterwards, both died. Martin was killed in a car accident not far from the college, and Charles was knifed by a mugger in New York City."

Noonan drank. "Is all of that in the newspaper articles?"

"No," Sally answered. "The charges and the reason for the dismissal were kept secret. Only the details of the accident and the mugging are in the clippings."

"How did you find out about the charges?"

"Martin and I were engaged to be married," she answered softly.

"I'm sorry, —"

"That's all right," Sally said, looking directly at him.

Noonan took her hand and kissed the back of it. "Now you look at the menu and order for the two of us. I have something I must do." He stood up. "My dinner is in your good hands."

"But I have no idea what you like or dislike," Sally protested.

"Guess," Noonan said and winked as he left the table. He went straight to the phone booth in the lobby, deposited two dimes and dialed Leon's number.

The phone rang twice. Mrs. Forest answered.

Noonan identified himself and politely asked, "May I speak with Dr. Hale?"

"Why, yes, of course," she answered.

A few moments later Leon was on the line.

"That boy is dangerous," he said gruffly.

"I'll take care of it," Leon answered.

"Before tomorrow," Noonan snapped and hung up. Men like Leon infuriated him. They never seemed to be able to act without days, weeks and sometimes months of meticulous planning. Certain situations demanded an instant response. He waited until the anger left him before he rejoined Sally.

"I ordered a rack of lamb for you," she said, as he sat down, "with all the trimmings."

"An excellent choice," Noonan responded. "And what did you choose for yourself?"

"Filet of sole amandine."

He nodded.

"And here is the wine list," she said, handing him a brown leatherette portfolio.

"A very interesting list," he commented. "I

think a Le Corton will do nicely. It's a very fine red, unless of course, you would prefer white."

"Red is fine," Sally answered.

Noonan summoned the waitress, and ordered. Then, sensing a change in Sally's mood, he smiled and asked, "Is anything wrong?"

"Everything is perfect," she answered.

"You look as if you're a thousand miles away from here," he told her.

"I am trying to make up my mind about something," she explained.

"Can I help?"

Sally laughed. "It's really two things."

"Tell me," he said, taking hold of her hands.

"You won't laugh?"

He shook his head.

"Troy —"

"He wants you to ask me a few questions," Noonan said.

"Yes. But how did you know?"

"A very lucky guess. As soon as you mentioned his name, I knew." He released her hands. "Ask whatever you want and if I can I will answer. They *are* his questions, aren't they?"

"Yes."

Noonan smiled. "Ask away," he said.

"It's really so absurd. I told him it was. But I told him I would ask and —"

"Please, ask the questions."

"He wants to know the name of your company and where it is located."

"I'll certainly tell you," Noonan responded, offering her a cigarette from a gold case.

"Not right now, thanks," Sally said softly.

"But before I tell you," Noonan continued,

inserting the cigarette into a black holder, "can you answer a question for me?"

Sally nodded. "I'll try."

Using a gold lighter, Noonan took his time lighting the cigarette. "Why is Troy so interested in me?"

Sally shrugged. "It's not you."

"I find that hard to believe," Noonan said, releasing smoke from his nostrils.

"It's what you stand for," she said.

The waitress returned with the wine and poured a bit into a glass, for Noonan to taste.

He sipped it. "Yes . . . good," he said.

Sally waited until the waitress left the table, then she said, "Troy wants to stop you from being appointed to the Board."

"But why? He doesn't even know me."

"He wants to see this appointment go to a member of the faculty," she said. "It's what he calls 'the good fight.' "

Noonan stiffened.

"It's not a personal thing," Sally said quickly.

Noonan took a deep drag, blew the smoke off to one side and said finally, "He certainly is a strange young man."

Sally smiled. "I guess he is in some ways. But he's really very sweet and considerate. It's just that he enjoys fighting for a cause."

Noonan grunted. "It's not the cause, it's the fight that interests him. I doubt if he knows what the word *cause* really means."

"You're angry," Sally remarked.

"More annoyed than angry."

"I'm sorry," she said, reaching across the table to touch his hand.

He forced himself to smile. "I'm not going to let this matter spoil our evening together," he said, taking hold of her hand. "I will answer all his questions — but on one condition."

"Oh?"

"I don't want you to tell him what the answers are," Noonan said. "I want him to come directly to me and ask the same questions."

"He won't hesitate," Sally replied.

"He shouldn't have gotten you involved," Noonan said, "and I will tell him so when I speak to him."

"I —"

Noonan put a finger across her lips. "I no longer have a company. I sold it last month to North Atlantic Industries. The information on the biog sheet wasn't updated."

Sally smiled. She was too embarrassed to ask any more questions.

"Do you think that will satisfy Troy?" Noonan asked.

"Troy is going to feel even more foolish than I do at this moment," she said.

"Promise not to tell him?"

"You never gave me a chance to say whether or not I would," Sally complained. "But I think I should tell him and then strongly suggest that he apologize to you."

At that moment the waitress arrived, carrying a tray with several plates of steaming food, and Noonan removed the cigarette from the holder and stubbed it out in the ashtray. When the rack of lamb was placed in front of him, he inhaled deeply. "This smells delicious," he said, closing his eyes.

"I really think Troy should apologize," Sally said as she began to eat.

"An apology is not needed," Noonan replied as he cut a piece of lamb. "But when you tell him to come directly to me to ask his questions, you might also suggest that he be less suspicious of strangers."

"You can be sure I will tell him that."

Noonan poured wine into Sally's glass and then into his own. Their conversation had trailed off and Noonan was glad of the respite. He was no longer sure he could depend on Leon to handle Troy. He certainly did not want to become involved in the matter any more than he was already.

"This is excellent," Sally commented, referring to her filet of sole.

"You couldn't have made a better choice for me," Noonan said.

"I'm glad you like it."

"Ah, I forgot!" Noonan exclaimed. "You said you were trying to decide two things. I hope the other one hasn't anything to do with Troy."

"I assure you," she said, "it doesn't."

"Well, are you going to tell me whether you made your decision?"

"I have," she said, laying her fork down on the rim of the plate. "I can't eat another bite."

"Well, are you going to tell me what it was you decided?"

Sally flushed, then in a low voice she said, "If you asked, whether I would go to bed with you."

Noonan stopped eating. "And what did you decide?"

Sally looked straight at him. "Yes, I would," she said.

"I was hoping you'd say that," Noonan smiled. He reached across the table and grabbed her hand. "Do you want to stay here in the inn?"

She shook her head. "I'm known here. There are motels —"

"Yes, a motel would be best," Noonan agreed, squeezing her hand.

Robin was in the right-hand, northbound lane on the New Jersey Turnpike. He glanced at the speedometer and saw he was doing sixty-five. Nathan was several car lengths in back of him. Between them were a couple of cars and a large tractor-trailer. At the last minute, he'd phoned Nathan and suggested they drive up the turnpike together. Though Nathan had planned to leave Washington early the following morning, he agreed to go.

Suddenly Robin's mobile phone rang.

"I just heard the station in Atlantic City," Nathan said. "We're going to be getting some snow."

"How far are we from New York?" Robin asked.

"About eighty miles," Nathan answered. "I saw the ninety-mile sign a couple of minutes ago."

"Put your scrambler on," Robin said. "I want to have a private conversation with you."

"Resetting," Nathan said.

Robin pressed the ON SCRAMBLER button, then he said, "I had a special reason for asking you to come up with me."

"You don't have to give me any explanation."

"Yeah, I know. But maybe you could give me some advice," Robin said. "You know I was going to go up with Deirdre."

"Is she the one with short black hair?"

"No, she has short blonde hair. I introduced you to her a few weeks ago. Last name is O'Keefe."

"I remember now, but I didn't know there was anything going on between the two of you," Nathan said. "I just thought she was another one of Frank's women."

"I wanted her to meet the family," Robin said. "But at the last minute she chickened out."

"Are you that serious about her?"

"Yeah, that's why I wanted her to go up with me for the holidays."

"The snow has started," Nathan said.

"Heavy, too," Robin commented, turning on the windshield wipers and the rear window defroster. "Anyway, Deirdre said it wouldn't be fair to meet my parents because she's not ready to make a commitment."

"But you're ready to make a commitment to her?"

"I already have. I asked her to marry me."

Nathan gave a long low whistle. "That's a commitment, all right."

"I don't really know what to do," Robin said.

"There's nothing you can do. You just have to wait until she decides whether or not she wants you."

"Hard to do," Robin answered. "Damn hard." Then he said, "We didn't part on the best of terms."

"Trouble in River City," Nathan responded flippantly.

"Don't joke. I said things I shouldn't have."

"I'm sorry," Nathan said. "I didn't mean to joke at your expense, but it probably isn't as serious as you think. Why don't you send her a dozen roses when you get to Boston with a brief note of apology?"

"You think that would work?"

"It's certainly worth a try."

"I'll do it!"

"Good," Nathan said. "Now with that out of the way, will you consider spending the night at my folks' house if this snow gets any worse?"

"Possibility."

"You can get an early start in the morning," Nathan suggested.

"I'll decide when we get closer to the city," Robin said, then added, "Thanks for helping."

"I'll send my bill in the morning," Nathan laughed.

Suddenly, Robin's rear view mirror exploded into blinding light. He squinted and adjusted the mirror for night driving, but the glare off the side view mirrors still bothered him. To put distance between him and the truck, he pressed down on the accelerator.

The truck's speed increased, too.

"You still on?" Robin asked, speaking into the phone.

"I've been waiting for you to say something," Nathan answered.

"There's a truck almost up my ass," Robin said.

"I saw the mother cut out and cut in."

"Can you ID him?"

"Not in this snow. He's too far ahead."

"I'm going to let him pass me," Robin said, as he switched lanes and slowed down.

The truck followed him.

"That mother just cut across a car to get behind you," Nathan exclaimed. "He's fucking crazy!"

"Tell me about it," Robin answered, steering back into the right lane.

"I'm putting a call into the state troopers," Nathan said.

Robin glanced into the rear view mirror. The truck was moving into the next lane, coming up fast. Within moments it was alongside him and as it passed him, it started to cut into his lane. Robin glanced up at the cab.

A man rolled down the window and pointed a gun at him.

"Holy mother of God!" Robin yelled. He felt the hot flash of pain, and the hands of a dead man pulled the wheel to the right. The car left the road, swung sideways, and smashed head-on into a concrete marker. Then it rolled over and burst into flames.

It was almost midnight when Nathan found himself seated in front of State Trooper Captain Rice's desk. The man behind it was somewhere in his fifties, gray haired and in better physical shape than most men his age. Nathan had the impression that he was the kind of man who demanded that his son — if indeed he *had* a son — address him as "sir"; anything less would not be tolerated.

"So you're the one who put out a general call for help," Rice said, looking up from the statement Nathan had written and at the same time picking up the brown coffee mug in front of him.

"About four minutes before the truck forced —"

"We questioned two other drivers at the crash site," Rice said. "None of them were as positive about what happened as you are."

"I saw it happen," Nathan said. "His last words were 'Holy Mother of God.'"

"You're telling me that someone deliberately forced your friend off the road?"

"Yes." Nathan answered, then took a cigarette out of a pack and lit it. "He was murdered by some crazy."

"Murdered is a very strong word," Rice said easily.

"You tell me what the hell else it was!" Nathan said angrily.

"For no reason? I mean your friend didn't accidentally cut him off, or do anything —"

Nathan shook his head. "What happened is there in my statement," he said, pointing to the paper on the desk.

Rice looked at Nathan's statement again. "You say here that your friend worked for the government," he said, looking hard at Nathan.

"That's right."

"Do you?"

"Yes."

"The two of you worked in the same office?"

"The same department," Nathan answered.

"You failed to name the department in your statement," Rice said.

"That information has nothing to do with what happened," Nathan replied.

"Nonetheless, we like to have a full background on anyone who makes a statement in writing."

Nathan didn't respond. He didn't like Rice's attitude.

"Too bad you couldn't ID the truck's plate, or anything about it," Rice commented. He sighed. "I'll let you know if we come up with anything. The odds are against it, you know."

"Try," Nathan snapped. "Try damned hard and when you do, contact me at the address I gave you for the next few days, or at my office in Washington."

Rice leaned back in his chair. "That almost sounds like a threat, Mr. Nathan. I hope it was not meant that way."

Nathan stood up, locked eyes with Rice, took his wallet out of his back pocket and flicking it open, thrust his ID in front of Rice's face. "It was an order, Captain Rice," he said harshly. "It was a fucking order. *Find that truck.*" Then he turned and walked out of the office.

[6]

Noonan turned in at the McKittrick Motel parking area and stopped in front of the office under the red neon sign. He smiled at Sally and kissed her lightly on the cheek. Then he got out of the car and went into the office.

"Just about gettin' ready to close for the night," the man behind the desk said. "Always close the office at midnight. After that, anyone who comes has to ring the outside bell an' wait until I come to the office. By the way, I'm McKittrick. But everyone around here calls me Donny. First name is Donald."

For a moment, Noonan forgot whether a motel room was considered a room the way a hotel room was, or was it a cabin?

"You plan on stayin' the night?" McKittrick asked, looking out the window at the car.

"Yes," Noonan answered.

"Fill out the registration and put down your license plate number," McKittrick said, pushing a white card toward Noonan and handing him a pen. "Continental breakfast starts at seven in the morning and it's on the house. But if you want a real breakfast, you can have it in our dining room for five dollars a person. My missus makes the best pancakes in this area, and all her jellies are homemade."

"That's very interesting," Noonan said, handing the card back.

McKittrick studied the card for a moment, then looked at Noonan. "All the way from Little Rock, eh!" he exclaimed. "I don't think I ever had a guest from Little Rock before."

Noonan felt beads of perspiration gather on his back. Putting down Little Rock was a mistake. He smiled. "I'm visiting some people around here," he said.

McKittrick nodded, opened a wooden file box and put the registration card in it. "Twin or double bed?" he asked.

"Double," Noonan answered.

"If you want breakfast in the dining room, that'll be an additional ten dollars in advance; otherwise the room is forty-five dollars. Cash or credit card?"

"Cash," Noonan said, taking out his wallet. He definitely didn't like the idea of that man having a registration card with his signature on it. He counted out five-twenty dollar bills and put them on top of the counter.

McKittrick looked at the bills, then at Noonan.

Noonan leaned closer to the man. "We both know why I'm here," he said, jerking his thumb toward the car. "We both know I'm not supposed to be here. Isn't that so, Donny?"

McKittrick looked confused.

"Those five twenties are yours if you give me back the registration card," Noonan said.

"But the law —"

"Make it six twenties," Noonan said.

McKittrick opened the box, took out the card and handing it to Noonan, he said, "My missus would raise the dickens if she ever found out."

"She won't," Noonan answered, pocketing the card.

McKittrick gathered the bills and then removed a key from the board. "Room forty-four."

Noonan thanked him, turned and started toward the door.

"What about breakfast?" McKittrick asked.

"No thanks," Noonan said.

"What was that all about?" Sally asked.

Noonan laughed. "The man thought I looked like someone who came from Little Rock," he said.

Noonan unlocked the door.

"The light switch is probably to the left on the wall," Sally said in a low voice.

"Yes," Noonan answered, and light from a simple overhead fixture flooded the room. He smiled at Sally and waved her inside. Then he closed the door after himself and locked it.

Sally stood between him and the bed.

"Why don't you switch on the night table lamps?" he suggested.

"Yes," she said.

He waited until both lamps were on before he switched off the overhead light; then he took off his hat and coat and put them on the chair. "Not a bad-looking room," he commented, then walked into the bathroom. "It even has a shower."

"It's really very charming," Sally called. "It doesn't have the plastic look that some motel rooms do, especially those of the big chains."

Noonan returned to the room and watched Sally take off her hat and coat, place her hat and his on the closet shelf and then put their coats on wooden hangers in the closet. "So tidy," he said, going to her.

"Habit," she replied.

Noonan drew her to him and he held her close. He could feel her press her body against his.

She raised her face.

He kissed her gently on the lips.

Her arms went around his neck.

Opening his mouth, Noonan sought her tongue.

She gave it to him without hesitation, then slowly moved her pelvis against him.

Noonan hadn't been with a woman for several weeks. His first impulse was to get her down on the bed as quickly as possible and plunge into her. But even as their tongues touched and twisted around one other, he sensed her hunger was as great, if not greater than his, and he realized she'd be a willing instrument for his sexual pleasure. He caressed the broad part of her back and gently moved his hands over her buttocks.

A soft humming sound came from deep in her throat.

"I wanted to do this all evening long," he murmured.

She could feel his warm breath on her ear. "I

know," she replied. "I could tell it from the way you looked at me."

"And how was that?"

"With eyes that stripped me naked and then devoured me."

He bent his face to the bare top of her left breast and pressed his lips to it.

Sally tilted her head back.

"Like that?" he asked and before she could answer, he kissed her neck. "Or like that?"

She answered by caressing his face with the tips of her fingers.

Noonan reached around to the back of her dress and slowly eased the zipper down.

Sally smiled and with a slight twist of her shoulders, she caused the top of the dress to fall away from her body, leaving her breasts bare.

"Lovely!" Noonan exclaimed, his hands gliding over the crescent-shaped mounds and then kissing each erect nipple.

"Oh, that feels so good!" Sally said, in a throaty voice.

"It tastes so good," Noonan responded and gently pushed the dress down over her hips, until it dropped to the floor, leaving Sally in front of him wearing only black lace panties, a black garter belt and black lacy stockings. He lowered his head and kissed her warm flat stomach.

"I think I better do the garter belt," she said, caressing the top of his head.

Noonan straightened up, stepped back and removed his jacket, tie and shirt, then watched intently as Sally stepped out of her shoes, picked up her dress and placed it over one of the chairs, and finally undid her stockings and took off the garter belt.

"You're devouring me again," she said.

"With admiration," he answered, pulling off his T-shirt.

She started to take off her panties.

"No," Noonan told her. "Let me. Come here," he beckoned, using his fingers. "Yes, come here."

She obeyed.

Noonan ran his hand over the front of her panties and gently tugged at her pubic mound. Then hooking his thumbs on either side of her panties, he began to draw them down, following until his face was level with her love mound. He glanced up.

Her lips were slightly parted, her eyes bright with expectation.

He could feel the slight increase of pressure from her hands on the back of his head. Placing his hands over her bare buttocks, he pressed his face against her love mound.

"Oh!" she gasped.

The pressure from her hands on the back of his head increased. Using his finger, Noonan deftly traced the narrow valley between the cheeks of her rump from the base of her spine to her vagina and the reversing the direction, he moved his finger back to where he'd started. He retraced the path several times. Each time a shudder passed through her body and she uttered a low, wordless moan of delight when he momentarily paused at her edge of her vagina.

Finally Noonan drew the panties all the way down, helped her step out of them and then stood up. "You're more beautiful nude than you are clothed," he said, stepping away and sitting down on the bed to remove his shoes and socks.

"Thank you," she said, her voice reduced to a whisper.

Noonan stood up and slipped off his pants and white jockey shorts.

"Here, give them to me," she said and gathering the clothes he had strewn on the bed, she placed them neatly on the chair. Then she went to the bed and as she turned it down, Noonan came up behind her. She leaned back against him.

He put his arms around her and covered her breasts with his hands. "Are you sorry —"

"God, no!" she cried, not letting him finish the question. "I would have been sorry if I had decided not to be here."

"Good!" he exclaimed and sweeping her into his arms, he placed her on the bed. A moment later he was stretched out next to her and his lips were pressed against hers.

This time she opened her mouth and sought his tongue.

Noonan caressed her breasts, rolling each nipple between his fingers until he could feel their warmth; and as he kissed them, and then sucked on each, Sally moved her hands down his chest and finally began to stroke his penis.

He kissed the hollow of her stomach and flicked his tongue over her navel.

She splayed her thighs.

Noonan fingered her warm, wet opening and then put his lips to it, using his tongue to bathe her clitoris.

She arched toward him. Breathlessly, she said, "Let me do you," and shifted her position.

Noonan felt the warm ring of her lips close around his penis and then the movement of her tongue against its head. She was doing what he wanted her to do and he knew she would do much more to please him. He said, "Do my balls."

She let go of his penis and began to use her lips on his scrotum.

"With your tongue," he told her.

Sally obeyed.

Noonan spread her vaginal lips and teased the wet, pink insides with his tongue.

Suddenly Sally tensed. "I want you inside of me," she said. "I want to come with you inside of me."

Noonan brought her around to him. "You on top?" he asked.

"No . . . no, I want you on top of me," Sally answered, spreading her thighs for him.

Noonan entered her.

She gasped with pleasure and reaching under him, she stroked his sac with her fingers.

He began thrust.

She let go of his scrotum, entwined her arms around his neck and brought his face down to hers. "Faster," she whispered. "Oh, faster!"

Noonan quickened his pace.

"I wanted this," Sally moaned, twisting her head from side to side, "I wanted to be fucked."

Noonan smiled "And I wanted to fuck you."

"Yes . . . yes. . . . Fuck me!" She cried, raking his back with her nails. Her body tensed again. "I'm there," she managed to gasp. "I'm there!" The next instant she thrust her body against his and then fell back as spasm after spasm coursed through her.

A moment later, Noonan's passion had reached its upper limit and with a low growl of satisfaction, he came.

Several minutes passed before he rolled off of her and settled by her side.

"Was it good for you?" Sally asked.

"Very. And you?"

"Tremendous," she answered.

He played with her breast. "You know," he said, "I really didn't think that I'd cause so much trouble."

"Trouble?"

"With Troy, I mean."

"Don't worry about him," she said. "Once he realizes how foolish he's been, I'm sure he'll apologize."

"Do you really think so?"

"Yes," she answered.

"I hope you're right," Noonan said. "But you know, I can't help admiring him. Maybe, if I got to know him better, we could help each other. I could even make him a student aide."

"That's really a very good idea."

"Then that's what I'll do," Noonan said. "Suppose you tell me whatever you know about him."

"Now?" she asked.

"No, silly," he said, turning to kiss her cheek. "Now, let's —"

"Make love?"

"Yes, now let's make love."

The fluid soaked through the books and dripped on to the floor. More of it was thrown along the wooden baseboards and as a parting gesture the remainder was dumped over the newspaper files. Then two windows were quickly taped; within moments they shattered noiselessly. A gust of wind rushed into the library reference section. To provide a draft, the door at the far end was purposely left open and within minutes smoke curled from those places that had been soaked. Suddenly several yellow-orange buds popped along the surfaces of the books, on top of the newspaper files and along the wooden baseboards. They, in turn, were quickly fanned into tendrils of flames that rapidly claimed large sections of the room. And then the fire roared into being as sheets of flame flung themselves over the walls of the room and burst through the exploding windows.

"There's a fire!" Mrs. Forest shouted, knocking at Leon's door. "There's a fire!"

"I'll be out in a minute," Leon yelled. He switched on the light and watched the green digital numbers change.

"Hurry!" Mrs. Forest screamed.

Leon waited until two full minutes had passed before he rushed to the door, flung it open and ran past his housekeeper.

"You can see it from the dining room windows," Mrs. Forest said, right behind him.

Suddenly the fire klaxon sounded over the campus.

Leon looked through one of the windows in the dining room. "I think it's the library," he said and ran to the hall closet for his coat and hat.

"Doctor, you can't go out like that," Mrs. Forest protested. "It's snowing and it's bitter cold. At least put a sweater on underneath the coat and wear boots."

"All right," Leon answered, grabbing a heavy sweater from the closet shelf.

The scream of sirens shredded the night.

Leon slipped the sweater over his head, pulled on a pair of insulated rubber boots, threw on his hat and coat, and ran out of the house.

Red Hook's volunteer fire company's pumper raced past Leon and went straight to the library.

Leon began to run and by the time he reached the library the firemen were laying hoses.

"We put in a call to Rhinebeck for more equipment," the Fire Chief said, as soon as Leon came up to him.

"It's that bad?" Leon asked.

"On a night like this it's bad," the Chief said. Then he looked at his men, and barked, "Get that second hose on the window!"

Leon pushed his hands into his pockets and watched. Ice was beginning to form where the water ran off the walls of the library.

"Much damage?

Leon recognized Fitzhugh's voice. "Can't tell yet," he answered, without turning.

Strogerly joined them. "Where's Noonan?" he asked.

"Out," Leon said.

"Out where?"

"Out," Leon said. "He didn't bother to tell me where he was going, or with whom."

Strogerly sighed. "I sure hope he knows what he's doing," he said.

"So do I," Leon responded.

The wail of another siren sounded above the roar of the fire. The three of them turned toward the roadway, where flashing red and yellow lights shone through the bare trees.

"This will certainly make the local papers," Fitzhugh grunted.

"That's no concern of ours," Strogerly said quickly.

The pumper from Rhinebeck arrived to help subdue the blaze and after twenty minutes, John Broderick, Chief of the Red Hook volunteers, approached Leon and said, "Some of my men think it was caused by faulty electrical wiring."

"Could well have been," Leon answered. Broderick owned the local Toyota dealership and Leon had met him several times. "Chief," he said, "I want you to meet some friends of mine." He introduced Strogerly and Fitzhugh. "We're going to be holding our Board meeting over the holidays. General Strogerly is a member of our Board of Directors and Mr. Fitzhugh is one of our advisers."

Broderick shook their hands and then turned to Leon. "Most of the damage is confined to two areas. One of them apparently had a great many newspapers in it, and the other was in the reference section beginning with the letter M and going to the letter R."

"The newspaper section and reference book section from M to R," Leon said, making a low humming sound. "That's really very interesting."

"An electrical fire can start —"

Leon shook his head. "It's not that I don't believe it was electrical," he said, "but it's almost too much of a coincidence to believe."

Broderick raised his eyebrows.

Suddenly Strogerly said, "I hope you don't mean what I think you mean?"

"He couldn't have done it," Leon said. "I mean, only a sick person would start a fire."

"Just who the hell are you talking about?" Broderick demanded.

Leon hesitated.

"For Christ's sake," Broderick exploded, "my men are out there risking their lives. If you have the slightest suspicion that someone started this fire, I sure as hell want to know."

"He should be told," Strogerly prompted.

"I have nothing to back it up with," Leon said. "It's just a suspicion."

"That's enough for me to investigate," Broderick said. He was angry now and the small pulse on the right side of his head throbbed.

"Over the last few days," Leon said, "it was brought to my attention that one of our students was inordinately interested in the library's reference section on military history and its files of old newspapers."

"What's the student's name, Dr. Hale?" Broderick asked.

Leon threw up his hands. "I really don't think that —"

"I want the student's name and place of residence," Broderick said firmly.

"If he's innocent," Fitzhugh said, "he'll suffer nothing more than having been questioned."

"Give Broderick the student's name and address," Strogerly urged.

"I want to be kept informed," Leon said. "The young man is a student in good standing at this institution and my responsibility."

"I understand that," Broderick said.

Leon nodded. "His name is Troy Sims. He owns a house a mile or so up the road from the college."

"Listen," Troy said, pointing to a large glass jar with a metal screw cap on it, "I have no idea how that got here." He was sitting in a chair at the kitchen table facing Chief Broderick. Two cops stood behind the chief.

"Why were you dressed when we came here?" Broderick asked. His shearling jacket was open and his white fire helmet was on the table next to his portable radio.

"You're repeating yourself," Troy said. He had already answered those two questions several times.

"From where?" Broderick pressed. He helped himself to a cigarette from a half-empty pack and lit it.

"I was out on a date and if push comes to shove, I can prove it."

Broderick nodded. "Didn't you hear the fire signal from the college?"

"I heard the fire signal, but I thought it was from town. The snow does things to sound."

"What about the engines?

"What about them?" Troy shot back, pointing to an ashtray on the sink counter.

"Did you hear them?" Broderick asked, standing up and walking to the sink counter to get the ashtray.

"Yeah."

"Where did you think they were going?" Broderick asked, sitting down again.

"I didn't think about it," Troy answered.

"Interesting," Broderick said, nodding. "Just why didn't you think about it?"

Troy looked straight at him. "I don't get off on fires the way some people do."

"What's that supposed to mean?"

"It means that every time I hear a fire engine," Troy said, "I don't get goose bumps and I certainly don't feel compelled to run to the fire, either to fight it or get my jollies."

"You've got quite a smart mouth, haven't you?" one of the cops said.

"You continue with this bullshit," Troy answered, first glancing at him and then looking straight at Broderick, "and you'll find out just how smart it is."

"If it's so smart, why can't you explain how this jar got here?" Broderick asked.

Troy shrugged. "I haven't got the foggiest — I never saw that before."

"And you didn't know there was carbon disulfide in it?"

"Whatever it is, it smells like rotting eggs," Troy said.

Broderick picked up his portable radio, and turned one of the switches. As he pressed the transmit button down, he said, "Badge one, this is Red Glow One, do you read me?"

"Ten by ten, Red Glow."

"I'm bringing Troy Sims in."

"On what charge, Red Glow?"

"Suspicion of arson —"

"You've got to be joking!" Troy shouted and started out of his seat.

One of the cops grasped his shoulder and pushed him back down. "Don't do that again," he growled, "or I'll make you wish you hadn't."

Troy glanced up at him. The expression on the man's face told him that he was looking forward to carrying out his threat.

"Be there in a little while," Broderick said. "Out." He released the button and put the radio down on the table again. "Better read him his rights," he said, looking at the cops behind Troy.

"Man, you damn well better know your rights," Troy fumed, "because I'm going to nail the three of you idiots to the fucking wall!"

One of the cops stepped to the side, took a small card out of his pocket and read him his rights.

"I want to make a phone call," Troy said.

"Go ahead," Broderick answered.

"The phone is in the hallway," Troy told him.

"Use it."

One of the cops started to follow Troy.

"I want some privacy," Troy said. "I'm not going to run."

"Let him go alone," Broderick told the cop. "You can keep an eye on him from the doorway."

"I'll have my gun on you all the time," the cop said.

"Did you ever think that's a fucking poor substitute for a prick?" Troy asked and without waiting to hear the man's answer, he went to the phone.

Spikes of shrill sound entered Elly's sleep, then became a ring. She reached over to the night table, lifted the phone and in a throaty voice, she asked, "Who is it?"

"Elly, it's me."

"Troy?"

"Listen, I've been arrested —"

"What?" she shouted, now fully awake and pulling herself into a sitting position. "Where are you?"

"Listen to me," Troy said. "Someone set fire to the school library and I'm being blamed."

"Oh my God!"

"Elly, listen —"

"I'll call your father," she said.

"Don't," Troy told her. "Listen to me!"

"I'm listening," she answered in a tremulous voice.

"Go to Petorious and tell him I need his help."

"Petorious?"

"Don't ask me to explain now," Troy said.

"But you're not his favorite person, and he's not yours," Elly protested.

"He's an honest man," Troy said. "First thing in the morning, go to him and tell him I need his help."

"What if he won't help you?"

"He will. If he won't, then I suppose you'll have to call my father. But I'm betting Petorious will help me."

"All right," Elly answered, unconvinced.

"I love you, Elly," Troy said.

"And I love you," Elly answered. "Troy —" The line on the other end went dead. She put the phone down, mumbling, "Troy . . . Troy . . . Troy, I love you." And hugging the pillow, she began to weep softly.

Leon stomped the snow off his boots before opening the front door. Strogerly and Fitzhugh did the same, and then the three of them trooped into the foyer, where Mrs. Forest was waiting for them.

"Is everything all right?" she asked.

"Some damage," Leon said. "But thanks to the quick response of our volunteer firemen, it was contained."

She crossed herself. "Thank the good Lord."

"A drink?" Leon suggested to his companions.

"A good idea," Strogerly answered. "It's cold out there."

"You care for one?" he asked, looking at Fitzhugh.

"Only one."

"If you gentlemen care for sandwiches, I'd be only too happy to make them," Mrs. Forest offered.

"No thanks, Beth," Leon said. "You go to bed. Some of the other Board members will be arriving tomorrow." He glanced at the grandfather clock near the steps. "I mean, later today and you'll have more than enough to do."

"Good night then," she said.

"Good night," the three of them chorused.

Leon turned toward his study. "Please, gentlemen," he said.

"Bourbon for me," Strogerly said.

"Scotch on the rocks," Fitzhugh ordered.

"First things first," Leon said. He went to the fireplace, stirred the fire to life out of the red embers, and placed a fresh log on the andirons. Then he went to the small but well-stocked bar in the far corner and poured the drinks.

"To clear sailing from here on in," Fitzhugh said, raising his glass.

The three of them touched glasses and drank.

"You handled this brilliantly," Strogerly commented, looking at Leon.

"Yes, well done," Fitzhugh said.

Leon beamed with pleasure. "Troy is, in your parlance, neutralized."

Again they touched glasses.

"Our security people will be here by morning," Fitzhugh said.

Leon nodded. "The fire will make their presence on campus much easier to explain," he said.

"How are you going to handle the local press?" Strogerly asked.

"The police have a suspect," Fitzhugh said. "Leon will tell the reporters that the damage was minimal and that whatever has to be said about the guilt or innocence of Mr. Sims will be done so in a court of law."

"The way that you say that," Strogerly said, "is very important. You want to convey to the reporters that you think Troy Sims deliberately set that fire."

"Absolutely," Leon agreed. Finishing off his drink, he asked, "Do either of you want a second?"

"Not me," Fitzhugh said, placing the empty glass on one of the end tables. "I'm off to bed."

"I'll pass," Strogerly responded, handing his to Leon. "It's been a full day."

"Seems as if it has been several days," Leon sighed.

"See you in the morning," Fitzhugh said, going to the door.

"Good night," Leon said.

Fitzhugh waved.

"Wait up," Strogerly called. "I'll go with you." Then offering his hand to Leon, he said, "That was a damn good piece of work."

"Thanks," Leon said, shaking his hand.

Strogerly let go of his hand and joined Fitzhugh, who was waiting for him at the door.

Leon put the three empty glasses on top of the bar, where Mrs. Forest would see them in the morning; then he went to the fireplace and was about to draw the bronze mesh curtain, when he paused to watch the flames lick at the wood. He was intensely pleased with himself. In a matter of days, his world would change dramatically. He was, even now, a maker of kings. Perhaps, he would be a king himself. And that, should it happen, would place him light years away from the little boy who pressed his face against a window pane to watch another boy's electric trains.

By the time Nathan came off the Goethals Bridge and on to the Staten Island Expressway, several inches of snow had already fallen and, according to the radio, more would fall until the storm moved out to sea sometime in the late morning.

He drove slowly, trying desperately hard to concentrate on the road and not think about Frank's death. But that was impossible. He and Frank had a relationship that went all the way back to the time when they were Delta Force officers and then later in the field, when they became company men. He had, on several different occasions, spent time with Frank's parents, either in Boston or at their summer home in north Truro, on Cape Cod. And Robin had been a guest at his parents' home many times. They even had made tentative plans to spend a day together, either in New York or Boston, during the holidays.

Nathan shook his head. Now he'd be attending Frank's funeral. Suddenly he found himself wondering whether he should notify Deirdre.

"The first person I have to notify is Fitzhugh," he said aloud, flicking on his directional signal to indicate a right turn. He slowed down and left the expressway at the Todt Hill/Slossen Avenue exit. At the traffic light, he turned left, went two blocks to Windsor Avenue, turned right and continued to Renwick Avenue, where he made another right that took him under the Expressway. He turned left on to Milford Drive and finally reached Hewitt Avenue.

Nathan stopped. His parents' house was half-way up the street, on the right side. But the street was a very steep hill, which when covered with snow would be an easy slide down, but would make getting up it with anything less than four-wheel drive impossible. Several cars abandoned at the bottom of the hill convinced Nathan not to even try. He parked his car on Milford Drive, took his valise and shoulder bag out of the trunk and trudged up the hill.

Because it was slippery underfoot, Nathan couldn't move with his usual big stride and by the time he reached the side door, he was breathing heavily.

He used his own keys to open the two locks and let himself in. He was hours late and didn't expect his parents to be awake. But almost as soon as he closed the door, his father called out, "That you, Steve?"

"Yes, Dad," Nathan answered, putting his valise down on the floor and the shoulder bag on a chair.

His father, a man in his late fifties with a gray beard and thinning gray hair, came into the kitchen.

"Hi, Dad."

"We were beginning to think you weren't coming until tomorrow," his father said, making sure the door was locked.

The two of them embraced.

"Your mother waited up for you until about a half hour ago, and I was just about to give up."

Nathan took off his gloves and stuck them into his coat pocket; then he removed his hat and coat.

"Give them to me," his father said, "I'll hang them up."

"How's Mom?" Nathan asked.

"Fine," his father answered.

Nathan went to the large glass sliding door that looked out on the rear deck and the small yard beyond. The snow was still falling.

"If you want something to eat, there's some cold chicken in the fridge and I can brew some coffee," his father offered.

"Coffee would be good," Nathan said.

His father moved close to him. "You all right?" he asked quietly.

"Frank was killed on the way up," Nathan said, unable to keep the tightness out of his voice.

His father's eyes went wide and his lower lip began to quiver.

"I have to call Fitzhugh," Nathan said. "I can't let you hear —"

"Use the phone in my study," his father told him.

Nathan nodded.

"I'm sorry about Frank —"

"So am I, Dad, so am I. We went through a hell of a lot together."

"The coffee will be ready and waiting for you," his father said.

Nathan left the kitchen and went down to the finished basement that his father had turned into his study. He dropped into the chair behind the computer desk, picked up the phone and punched out the Duty Officer's number at Langley. Within moments the man was on the line.

"This is agent Steven Nathan," Nathan said. "ID number one six eight dash forty-four dash two dash twenty-two dash twenty-nine."

"Number confirmed," the D.O. told him.

"I must speak to Deputy Director Fitzhugh." He paused, took a deep breath and using the code to designate the death of an agent, he said, "Black thirty."

"Black thirty," the D.O. repeated.

"That's what I said," Nathan snapped. "Now get that damn call through."

"Processing conference hookup," the D.O. said.

Nathan leaned back into the chair and looked around. There were bookshelves on all of the walls. His father, a retired professor of English, had published two novels about espionage and covert activities that were much more glamorous and exciting than anything he and Frank had experienced.

Suddenly a voice said, "Fitzhugh here."

Without any preliminaries, Nathan said, "Frank was killed on the New Jersey Turnpike at about twenty-two hundred last night."

"How?"

"Forced off the road by a truck," Nathan said. "I was driving behind him. I saw it happen."

Fitzhugh was silent.

"Frank was murdered," Nathan said. "It wasn't an accident."

"Could you ID the truck?" Fitzhugh asked.

"No, but that truck just didn't happen to be there. It was trailing him. He was its target."

"Come on, Steve, I know that you and Frank were close," Fitzhugh said. "But that's really far-fetched."

"Was there anything he was working on —"

"You're jumping to conclusions," Fitzhugh said tersely. "You know everything Robin was doing. Don't let your feelings for Frank cloud your ability to reason. It was an *accident*."

"The fuck it was!" Nathan shouted. "I was two cars behind the truck. Frank got on the radio to tell me the truck was almost up his ass!"

"Leave it to the troopers," Fitzhugh replied.

"Are you going to phone his parents?"

"Yes," Fitzhugh said.

"Will you go to the funeral?" Nathan asked.

"Certainly. We will go together. Why don't you fly up to Albany and check in at a motel or hotel? As soon as you're there, give me a call and I'll meet you for cocktails. Maybe by then the state troopers will have more information for us."

"I'll be in Albany on Saturday," Nathan said. "Give me your phone number."

"Call me through Headquarters," Fitzhugh told him and added, "Now try and relax and enjoy the time you have with your folks."

Before Nathan could respond, he heard the click on the other end.

"Your party is off the line," the D.O. said.

"I heard," Nathan answered and hung up. For several moments, he remained in his father's chair. He'd always thought that Fitzhugh was a cold fish, but now his total lack of emotion upset and puzzled him. "Goddamn it," he said, "one of his men was taken out!"

[7]

"See you, man," Troy said to Gus, the gray-haired black man with whom he shared the cell. "Remember, if you're going to beat the system, you have to know the system and the only way to do that is know Karl Marx."

"Power to the people," Gus answered.

Troy slapped his palms.

"C'mon Sims," the cop said, "I don't have all fuckin' day for your bullshit."

Troy glared at him. "What the fuck else do you do that's so fucking important?"

"If you weren't gettin' out, I'd teach you more damn respect than you've ever learned in that panty-ass college," the cop snarled, touching his night stick.

"But I *am* getting out," Troy said, "and I'll have your boss's ass and a few others on the fucking barn door."

"Are you comin'?" the cop asked impatiently.

"Yeah, yeah," he answered and moved his eyes toward the wall under the window, where he, like so many men before him, had scratched his initials into the peeling green paint. "Take care," Troy said to Gus, then he left the cell and followed the cop out of the lock-up. Petorious was waiting at the sergeant's desk.

"Sign for your belongings," the sergeant said, opening a drawer and taking out a large yellow envelope. He handed Troy a pen.

"I'll check them first," Troy answered, opening the envelope and deliberately examining every item.

"Satisfied?" the sergeant asked.

"Nothing in this shit house, including the people who run it, satisfies me," Troy answered. He picked up the pen and signed *God*.

"What the hell is that supposed to be?" the sergeant asked, his faced flushed with anger.

"My new name," Troy answered.

The sergeant looked at Petorious. "You better tell your wise-ass student to sign his right fucking name, or he isn't going to go with you."

"For God's sakes," Petorious exclaimed, "will you sign your real name!"

Troy grinned. "Get that *God* bit, Sergeant." But he picked up the pen and signed his name on the property form.

"He's all yours," the sergeant told Petorious, "and I don't envy you."

"Let's get out of here," Petorious said, walking quickly to the front door, "before you make them angry enough to change their minds."

"They don't have minds to change," Troy

retorted in a loud voice, then, in a much lower tone, he said, "Thanks for coming."

Petorious didn't answer until they were outside. "I came because of Elly. She was absolutely certain they were going to beat you."

"Where is she?" Troy asked, his breathing steaming in the cold clear air.

"Waiting for you in the car," Petorious said, gesturing toward the parking lot.

"I can cover the money you put up for bail," Troy said. "By the way, how much was it?"

"Fifty thousand," Petorious replied.

Troy whistled. "They really want to stop me, don't they?"

"What makes you think —"

Troy saw Elly getting out of the car and ran to her and took her in his arms.

She started to kiss him.

"I smell," he said. "I —"

"I don't care if you stink," Elly answered, kissing him passionately on the mouth.

"Maybe I should go to jail more often," he said, pressing her to him.

"I've never been so frightened in my life," Elly told him. "I had visions of you being raped and —"

"The guy in my cell was an old black man named Gus," Troy said. "He was busted on a vagrancy charge. I told him all about Marx."

"Tell me you love me," Elly answered, holding him tightly.

"I love you," he answered earnestly. "I love you."

Petorious reached the car. "We're going to go into Kingston to pick up my sister. She's coming in by bus."

"You're the boss," Troy answered. "I go where you go until the hearing."

"Mr. Sims, you and Elly sit up front," Petorious said as he went around to the driver's seat and slid behind the wheel, "until my sister comes."

"I think it was Jack London who said that jails have a smell all their own, and the son-of-a-bitch was right. I'll never forget that for as long as I live."

Elly pushed herself into the crook of his arm.

"Now, Mr. Sims, will you please tell me how you managed to get yourself involved in this mess?" Petorious asked, as the car bumped out of the parking lot and into the street.

"Just after I met you the other evening, I ran into Leon and Noonan, and Leon introduced Noonan to me and said that he was going to be installed on the Board of Directors."

At a red light, Petorious filled his pipe with tobacco and lit it before he said, "And you took an instant dislike to Noonan."

"After I met him, Elly and I were having something to eat when I remembered that I had seen Noonan's picture somewhere," Troy said.

"Where?" Petorious asked, putting the car in motion again.

Troy shrugged. "I can't remember."

"I still don't understand how all of that landed you in jail."

"That fire was set and some kind of chemical solution was planted in my house to make it look as if I had done it."

Petorious glanced at Troy. "Why?"

"Because," Troy said, "I put certain things together. I found out about professors Martin Giddeon and Charles Platz. They tried to stop

General Strogerly from becoming a member of the Board and were accused of having sexual relations with several boys from town."

"I had no idea —"

"I bet you didn't," Troy said. "No one did because it was all hushed up."

"How did you find out?" Petorious asked, stopping for another red light.

"Sally was sleeping with Giddeon — "

"Sally? Are you sure?" Petorious asked.

"Yeah, and Platz was making it with Laura Hobe, the wife of our local bank president. I spoke with her too. Neither Sally nor Mrs. Hobe believe that charges against Giddeon and Platz were real."

Petorious eased his foot down on the accelerator. "Where are the two professors now?"

"Dead," Troy answered quietly.

"Dead!" Petorious exclaimed, glancing sideways at Troy.

"Giddeon was killed in a car accident not far from the college, and Platz was stabbed to death in Manhattan, just a block or so away from the hotel where he had just been with Mrs. Hobe. Now you tell me whether or not you think it was coincidence or that something else was going on?"

Petorious puffed on his pipe. The smoke streamed out of the pipe's bowl and plumed toward the rear of the car.

"What do you think about all of that?" Troy pressed.

"I still don't understand what you have put together," Petorious said finally. "You haven't got any proof that there was a connection between —"

"Do you realize that every member on the Board is either a former Admiral, General or currently the president, or chairman of the board of a multinational corporation?"

"That's good for the college," Petorious remarked.

Troy shook his head. "Noonan doesn't fit into any of those categories," he said.

"I don't understand why you're so intent on —"

"Stopping him from becoming a member of the Board?"

"Yes."

"Because it's time that a member of the faculty was on the Board," Troy said. "I told Leon that I was going to try and stop Noonan from becoming a member."

"That would be enough to make Leon see red," Petorious commented, cranking down the window and slowing in order to pay the toll on the Kingston-Rhinebeck bridge. As soon as they were moving again, he asked, "Who would you accept instead of Noonan?"

"You," Troy said, noticing that ice had already begun to form along the riverbank.

"Me?"

"Why not?"

"Because —"

"You certainly would have a better grasp of what the needs of the college are than Noonan."

Placing his pipe in the pipe rest on the dashboard, Petorious said, "Let's get back to Giddeon and Platz for a few minutes."

"Sure, why not?" Troy asked, running his fingers over Elly's shoulder.

"What you're really saying," Petorious said, "is that they were framed." They came off the bridge and he turned left toward Kingston.

"Just the way I was," Troy responded. "I never even took a chem course. That solution of carbon disulfide and phosphorous was put there."

"If I understand you, you are also saying that someone purposely set fire to the library and then placed the chemicals in your house to make it look as if you did it?"

"Yes," Troy answered, nodding vigorously.

"And all because you don't want Noonan on the Board?"

"You got it."

Petorious gave a long low whistle, then he said, "That's quite a supposition on your part."

"Give me an alternate," Troy challenged.

"I can't," Petorious said, "at least not now. But give me some time and I might come up with one."

"The key to all of this is Noonan," Troy said soberly. "If only I could remember where I saw his picture, we'd have the reason I was set up."

As Petorious turned on to Main Street, he said, "Arson is a very serious charge. My advice to you is to call your parents. You're going to need a lawyer."

"Maybe. Then again, maybe not. I want to see just how far Leon plays this. He might offer me a deal."

"You're not serious?"

"One hundred and ten percent serious, and I'll tell you what I'm going to tell him."

"Let me guess," Petorious said.

"Please."

"You're going to tell him to shove it — Elly please excuse my language —"

"Say whatever you want." Elly laughed.

"You're going to tell him to shove it up his ass," Petorious said, "or words to that affect."

Troy laughed. "You're absolutely right. I'm going to push this whole business down his throat."

"Be careful, Mr. Sims," Petorious cautioned, slowing to enter the parking area next to the bus terminal, "Leon is a lot craftier and a lot smarter than you give him credit for being. He might push 'the whole thing,' as you call it, down your throat."

"I haven't underestimated him," Troy said. "But I think he has made the mistake of underestimating me and that is a serious mistake."

"Going for the jugular, eh?"

"For blood."

"There's an empty parking spot — on the right," Elly piped up.

"I would have missed it," Petorious said, maneuvering the car into the place. He shifted into neutral, turned the ignition off, and set the hand brake, then handed the keys to Troy. "Just in case the car has to be moved. I'll be back in a few minutes, or perhaps the two of you would prefer to come with me."

"No thanks," Troy said, answering for both of them. "But I'd appreciate it if you picked up some of the local newspapers."

"Want to read about yourself?" Petorious asked as he opened the door and then got out of the car.

"Isn't his ego already too big?" Elly quipped.

"Much bigger than most mortals' by a factor of at least a thousand," Petorious said, momentarily ducking his head back into the car and looking at Troy.

"No comment."

Petorious nodded and smiled. "If the bus is on time, I'll be back in five minutes and if it's late —"

"We'll wait," Troy said.

Petorious turned and walked toward the bus terminal's rear entrance.

"I really do owe him," Troy said, looking at Elly. "He really did a big one for me."

"In his own way, I think he likes you," she answered.

"Do you like me?" Troy asked, pulling Elly to him and embracing her.

"God help me, I love you," she answered. "I was so worried about you. I didn't think I'd ever see you again."

"Yeah, I was worried about me too," Troy admitted. "Those goons were just itching to work me over. But you know, there really is something about this that doesn't ring true. It's just too much for too little. I mean —"

Elly put her lips to his.

Troy caressed the back of her neck.

"I'll stay with you over the holiday," Elly whispered.

"*Really* stay with me?" Troy questioned, looking straight at her.

"In your bed."

Troy smiled broadly. "Hey," he exclaimed, "this certainly proves the yin and yang of life, doesn't it?"

"Maybe Petorious is right," Elly said, "maybe you should call your father or mother."

Troy slipped his hand inside of Elly's jacket and gently squeezed her breast. "Nah, I'd rather be doing this."

She pulled his hand out. "C'mon Troy," she

said, "this isn't the time to be funny. You're in serious trouble."

Troy rearranged himself in the seat. "The worst that can happen to me is —"

"You can go to jail for a very long time," Elly cried. "My God, years!"

Troy shook his head. "My gut feeling is that Leon won't push it that far."

"You can't be sure."

He took hold of her hands. As long as I'm out of jail," he said, "the worst is over. But I promise you that if I feel I'm in any real danger, I'll call my father. Does that satisfy you?"

"I guess it will have to," Elly answered in a low voice.

"Now come here," Troy said, gently pulling her to him.

She offered her lips.

He kissed her passionately. "Will you come back to the house with me?" he asked in a whisper.

"I said I would."

"Should I tell you what I'm going to do to you?" he asked, nuzzling her ear.

"Surprise me."

Troy smiled. "You better believe it."

Suddenly the door opened and Petorious said, "You kids have fogged up all the windows. Untangle yourselves from one another and get into the back."

"It's all right, Jamie," a woman said, "I can sit in the back."

Troy grinned. "No way," he replied and opened the door.

"Helen, meet Troy and Elly," Petorious said, handing Troy several local newspapers. "I already checked. There's a story about the fire, but no mention of you."

"Are you sure?"

"Yes," Petorious said, turning on the ignition.

Helen was a statuesque redhead with lovely blue eyes and a few freckles on the bridge of her nose. She resembled her brother, but you had to look closely at her to be aware of it. Offering her hand first to Elly and then to Troy, she said, "Jamie tells me that I have the pleasure of riding with a dangerous felon."

"Am I dangerous?" he asked, looking at Elly, but before she could answer, he said, "I'm only dangerous when I'm accused of crimes I didn't commit."

Helen threw back her head and laughed. "I'd hate to think that Jamie had finally decided to find out about the seamier side of life."

Petorious scowled at his sister.

"I'm absolutely innocent," Troy said. He instantly liked her.

Nathan was out with his father clearing the driveway of the snow that had fallen since he'd arrived. The physical work relieved some of the tension he felt. He had changed his mind several times about calling Deirdre and now as he took a few moments to rest, he changed it again and decided not to let her know that Frank was dead.

"Every year," his father said, coming close to him, "after the first snowfall, I begin to think about selling this place and moving to where there isn't any snow."

Steve grinned and shook his head. "And what would you do with all your books?"

"Get rid of them."

"Never happen," Steve said. "I took a look at your office this morning before you and Mom came down. I think you must have added a couple of hundred books since the last time I was here."

" 'Bout fifty," his father answered sheepishly.

Suddenly the front door opened and Mrs. Nathan said, "Steve, a Captain Rice on the phone for you."

"Be right there." Steve stuck the shovel into a snowbank and said, "I'll be back."

"No need," his father said easily. "There's not much left to do."

"Thanks, Dad." Steve went up the front steps, stomped the snow off his high shoes and went straight to the kitchen. "Nathan here," he said.

"The coroner just called," Rice said. "Your friend was shot in the left side of his head with .38 from a snub-nosed weapon."

Nathan felt his jaws lock.

"Did you hear what I said?" Rice asked.

"Yes," Nathan answered wearily. "Any leads?"

"None," Rice said. " But I'll let you know if we come up with anything."

"What about the drivers who witnessed the crash?"

"Checked them out," Rice said. "Both had false ID's and were driving stolen cars. Someone wanted your friend dead awfully bad."

"And they got what they wanted." Nathan put the phone back on the hook.

"About Frank?" his mother asked. She had stood in the doorway while he was on the phone.

Steve nodded and walked to the sliding door. The deck and the yard were covered with snow.

"How about some lunch?" his mother asked.

"I'm not hungry," he answered, still looking at the snow-covered yard, where several birds had landed to eat the food his father had put out for them.

His father came back into the house and walked into the kitchen. "I'm for lunch," he said. "What about you, Steve?"

"I already asked him," his mother said.

Steve turned from the sliding glass door and looked at his father, then at his mother. "Listen," he said, "I've got to go back to Washington."

"But you only just got here last night," his mother protested.

He went to her and put his hands on her shoulders. "Frank didn't have an accident," he said in a low voice.

Her eyes widened.

"He was shot in the head," Steve said.

"Oh my God!" she exclaimed, and clutched at her son.

Steve held her very tight. She smelled fresh and clean, the way she had when he was a kid. "If it were me," he told her, "he'd do the same."

His mother began to cry.

"Mom, maybe I can find something back there that will give me a clue to —"

"Then you'll go after them, won't you?"

"Yes," Steve answered. Looking at his father, he said, "I owe it to him. More than once he put his life on the line for me."

"He has to go," his father said gently, moving close to him. "He has to go."

Steve kissed his mother on the forehead and easing her away from him, he handed her to his father. "I promise I'll be home for Christmas dinner."

"I'll drive you to the airport," his father offered. "You can get the shuttle out of LaGuardia."

"Are you sure you want to?" Steve asked. "The roads are probably as slippery as hell."

His father nodded. "I'll drive you." He let go of his wife.

"Okay. I'm not taking anything with me," Steve said, looking at his mother. "If I have to stay in Washington overnight, I'll let you know."

"Do you want to leave right now?" his father asked.

"Yes, the sooner the better," Steve said. It had just occurred to him that the sudden increase in KGB radio and telephone transmissions was the only thing Robin was working on that had the potential to become something important. Then he remembered that just before they left Langley, Robin told him that he had stopped at Fitzhugh's office to tell him something that, according to Robin, was red hot.

"Are you all right?" his mother asked.

Steve nodded. But he wasn't all right; his stomach was churning the way it always did when he sensed danger.

Igor Morosov, traveling on an Irish passport under the name of Peter Callahan, sat in a window seat on the left side of an Aer Lingus 747 as it angled down over Jamaica Bay on the final leg of its landing approach to JFK airport. Through the weather-scarred pane, he could see the skyline of Manhattan, all of the city's bridges and the dark bulks of the Watchung Mountains in New Jersey, where, years before, when he was posted in New York, he had actually done some rock climbing on weekends. But that was when Tatyana, his wife,

was still well and they could lead a normal life —
that is as normal as any KGB agent could in a foreign country.

"Is that snow I see down there?" the woman
seated next to him asked. She spoke with a
brogue.

Morosov lowered his eyes to the bits of white
below them in the bay. "Yes, I think it is," he
answered in perfect English.

"And in time for the holidays too," she
commented.

He looked at her blankly.

"Christmas," she said with a broad smile. "I'm
coming here to spend it with my sister and her
family."

"Ah yes, Christmas!" he exclaimed. The celebra-
tion of the holiday meant absolutely nothing to
him. He was an atheist, not only because he was a
Communist, but because he had seen enough of
the world's pain to have come to the conclusion
that God did not exist; and if he had not reached
that viewpoint from his experiences before
Tatyana's breakdown, he certainly would have
reached it soon after.

The woman leaned closer to the window.

Morosov pressed himself back in his seat. She
smelled of perfume and her dark blond hair was
swept up in a bun.

"We're almost touching the water!" the woman
cried.

Morosov glanced out the window. With each
roll of the plane, it did seem as if the wing tip
would touch the water. Then suddenly the
wheels touched the edge of the runway.

"We're down," Morosov said.

An instant later the jet engine's roared in reverse, slowing the forward motion of the plane.

"My God, what was that?" the woman asked, her eyes round with fear.

"It's all right," Morosov assured her. "We just slowed down to taxiing speed."

The woman sat back in her seat. "You know," she said, "this is the first time I have ever flown anywhere."

Morosov nodded. "It was a good flight," he remarked, "compared to some I have had."

The stewardess came on the PA. "Ladies and gentlemen, we have landed at JFK airport. Thank you for flying Aer Lingus. In a few minutes, we will be arriving at the terminal, where you will be required to clear customs and immigration. To reach the baggage claim area, please follow the signs. For safety purposes, please keep your seat belts fastened until the aircraft has come to a complete halt and the safety belt sign goes off. Please obey the no smoking sign. Thank you again for flying Aer Lingus."

The woman smiled at him.

Morosov returned the smile and then pretended to be absorbed by the view out the window.

When the plane came to a halt, Morosov stood up. He was a tall, broad-shouldered man of forty, whose hair was ordinarily black, but had been dyed blond for the mission. His eyes, behind false glasses, were black.

"I hope you enjoy your stay," the woman said.

Morosov nodded. "I hope you enjoy your holiday with your sister and her family," he responded, waiting for the woman to leave her seat so that he could proceed into the aisle.

"My name is Peggy Ryan," the woman said, finally standing.

"Peter Callahan," he answered, helping her retrieve her coat from the storage locker above the seat, before he took his own black Burberry down. He followed her down the aisle and into the terminal, where he spotted a row of telephone stalls. "I must make a phone call," he said, "and if I don't see you again, I wish you a very good holiday."

"The very same to you," Peggy waved.

Morosov smiled and immediately headed for the phones. For a moment there, he had expected the woman to give him her sister's address. He dropped a quarter into the slot, then punched out a number.

After three rings, he hung up and immediately ran through the number sequence again.

"This is a non-working number," a woman said.

"I have arrived," he said.

"Take a cab to the Lombardy Hotel," the woman told him. "You will occupy the same room that your friend had. It has been reserved under your passport name."

Morosov hung up and took time to fill and light his pipe before he picked up his bag.

After passing through customs and immigration without any difficulty, he followed the signs to the taxi line and almost immediately found one.

"Hotel Lombardy," he told the driver, as he settled in the rear seat and automatically noted the photograph, the name and number on the ID card. The driver was a dark-skinned Caucasian. His name was Rashid Sadat and his ID number was 168-229. He was probably a recent immigrant from Egypt.

"Is there any special way you want to go?" the driver asked, speaking slowly, as if he had to hunt for each word.

"No," Morosov answered, relighting his pipe. The driver turned on to the Belt Parkway.

Morosov knew the road. While living in New York, he had driven on it countless times. For most of its length, it was ugly, but there was a small section, perhaps only two miles in length, that bordered that portion of New York's harbor known as the Narrows and passed directly beneath the Verrazano Bridge. He and Tatyana would often go there in the spring and fall and stroll along the walkway that ran parallel to the water. Whenever he returned to New York, he'd think about Tatyana more than he usually did.

He had gone to the hospital to see her the day before he left Moscow. He stood in the doorway of the room looking at her. Still a beautiful woman with lovely green eyes and cropped brown hair, she sat in front of the window oblivious to him and to the world. Later, he spoke to her doctor, a young man who seemed nervous in his presence because he probably had learned he was treating the wife of a KGB agent.

"There is almost no hope that she will ever be normal again," the doctor had said. "But you can be assured that we will continue to try. In extreme cases of catatonia, such as hers, there is nothing that can be done other than to see that the patient is comfortable."

Morosov took the pipe from his mouth and sighed. He had heard those words, or similar ones, so many times over the past ten years that he could recite them and spare himself the agony of hearing someone else pronounce Tatyana's sentence of a living death.

"One day," the driver commented, gesturing upward with his right hand, "one of them will come down on the highway." He was talking about the planes whose landing pattern took them directly over the highway, at an altitude of no more than a few hundred feet.

"It's not an impossibility," Morosov answered. Traffic forced them to slow down.

Morosov suddenly realized that the driver was looking at him through the rear view mirror and smiling to himself. Morosov wondered if they were in the same business. While he was living in New York and using the name of Allen Green, he had been a bank teller, an administrative assistant in a construction company, even a maître d' in an expensive midtown French restaurant.

"There's always something," the driver sighed.

Certain now that the man was sizing him up, Morosov answered, "It is that way in most cities."

The car rolled to a stop and the driver glanced back at him. "I have some watches," he said. "Very good watches. I sell for less than any store."

Morosov almost laughed. "Thank you," he said, "but I have a very good one." And he held up his right hand to show the Omega on his wrist.

"One for your wife or lady friend?" the driver asked.

Morosov shook his head. "No, thank you," he said pleasantly.

"Perfume?"

This time Morosov did laugh and shook his head. "No, I really don't have anyone to give the perfume to."

"You might meet a lady, and these are already gift-wrapped," the driver said.

The traffic started to move again and the driver turned his attention to the road.

When they finally stopped in front of the Hotel Lombardy, Morosov looked at his watch. It was exactly two o'clock. He had entered the West less than seventy-two hours ago and for most of that time he had been awake. Now, he looked forward to a few hours' sleep before he met with Colonel Felik Piligin, the senior KGB officer in the area. He had worked with the Colonel on various other assignments in the United States and in several other countries. Though the Colonel was presently listed by the American State Department as Dimitri Suskov, a statistician for the Russian Delegation at the United Nations, it was almost certain that the CIA, FBI and NSA knew the real nature of his work.

"Thirty-five dollars," the driver said, his eyes on the meter. "And two for the tunnel."

Morosov nodded, counted out three tens, a five and two singles and gave them to the driver. "And six more for you," he said, handing the man another five-dollar bill and a single.

"You sure you don't want a watch or perfume?"

"Yes, I'm sure," Morosov answered, grabbing his bag and leaving the cab. A few minutes later, he was alone in his room. He went to the window. Fourteen floors below was the street. Directly across was an office building. He took off his coat and dropped it over the back of a chair, then he loosened his tie and removed his jacket, and put it down on top of the coat. Finally he picked up the phone and using his middle finger, he quickly stabbed out a number.

"Suskov here," Piligin answered.

"I need a few hours to sleep," Morosov said.

"Meet me at sixteen hundred in front of the B. Dalton Bookstore on Fifth Avenue."

"I'll be there." Morosov put the phone down, walked back to the window and pulled the shade. He went to the bed, sat on the edge for the time that it took him to remove his shoes and then he stretched out. Placing his hands behind his head, he stared at the ceiling until his eyes closed and he slept.

[8]

In the deepening twilight of late afternoon, Fifth Avenue was crowded with shoppers and already ablaze with light — the thousands of colored ones that were strung across the avenue and the many Christmas displays in the store windows.

Morosov had been standing in front of the bookstore for five minutes before he spotted Piligin walking south. Piligin looked like a successful businessman, complete with a white silk scarf, a black chesterfield coat, a black bowler and a black attaché case. He was a short, stocky man, with gray eyes that made metal seem warm.

Piligin passed, gave a slight nod and stopped at the next window to look at the display of *Under Two Flags*, the season's best-seller.

Morosov moved in next to Piligin. He waited until they were the only ones standing in front of the window and without greeting Piligin said in

English, "An interesting idea that after the battle of Gettysburg neither the North or the South had much stomach left for war."

"Yes."

Then the two of them moved off.

"We have your friend's movements," Piligin said. "He spent two days at the Lombardy and rented a car, which he returned to a rental agency in Albany."

"Why Albany?" Morosov asked.

"Why not Albany?" Piligin responded. "It has as much meaning to us now as anything else he has done."

"And after Albany?"

"Nothing."

Morosov asked, "Did you find anything in the room?"

"Some doodling with what appears to be the letters HS," he said.

"What's that?"

"Something that a lot of other people beside myself would like to know," Piligin said. "Our people found it on a bit of foolscap that had fallen behind his desk." Then he asked, "Does his former wife know anything?"

"She was being questioned when I left Moscow."

"And his most recent bed companion?"

"The same. You know Comrade Colonel Lenov turned up dead in Rome on the very same day one of our people spotted my friend at the airport."

"Curare wasn't it?"

"Yes. The body had to have five bullets pumped into it so that his next of kin could be notified and told that he had been killed in action."

They reached a corner and waited for the light to turn green, when Piligin pointed to a chestnut vendor whose cart was just a few feet from them. "Care for some?"

"Yes," Morosov answered gratefully. "I haven't eaten anything since early this morning aboard the plane."

"How did you manage to find my friend?" Morosov asked, breaking the shell of a nut and taking out the smoking white meat.

"Part of it was luck," Piligin replied. "You know how much that could help or hinder you."

"There are times when it could mean the difference between success or failure of a mission."

"As soon as I received word that your friend was somewhere around this area, I gave several of my people his picture. Posing as New York City police detectives, they canvassed the better hotels and cocktail lounges — places where your friend might have gone for a few hours of diversion."

"These are very good," Morosov said, devouring another piece of chestnut.

"I remember my grandmother roasting chestnuts before the war," Piligin said. "She roasted them in the big wood-burning oven we had in the kitchen. Every time I smell roasted chestnuts I think about her. I bet you didn't know I was a farm boy, did you?"

"I didn't know," Morosov answered, somewhat surprised that Piligin had revealed anything about himself.

"All that was a million years ago . . . before the Germans came," Piligin said, his voice suddenly soft and distant.

Morosov didn't comment, he knew better.

"The past and the present sometimes meet," Piligin said finally, "at the oddest times."

"Yes, that's very true," Morosov replied.

"To return to how we got to your friend." Piligin said. "One of my men showed his picture to two waitresses in the hotel cocktail lounge and they recognized him. Each one said that he tried to date them. But it seems he was really interested in the singer. From what the two waitresses told my man, she wasn't interested in him. But you know him; he smells cunt and he can't keep away from it."

"I don't know him personally," Morosov answered. "I only know his reputation. Was the woman questioned?"

Piligin shook his head. "I thought it best to leave that to you. I have her address. She shares an apartment on York Avenue and Sixty-Fifth street with another young woman."

For several moments, Morosov was quiet. It was obvious Gorsky felt safe, or he wouldn't have risked spending time in a cocktail lounge or trying to establish a sexual relationship. A man on the run sees too many shadows, hears too many sounds. "What about the rented car?" he asked.

"The desk clerk told the same man who spoke to the waitresses that your friend asked him to arrange for the rental. Your friend was very specific about where he wanted to leave the car when he finished with it."

"Albany."

"What the hell is up there that he'd be interested in?" Piligin sounded frustrated.

"Whatever it is," Morosov replied, "it must be more important than anything else to him." He paused before he added, "Including his life!"

Piligin didn't answer and for the length of two whole blocks neither of them spoke. Then Piligin touched Morosov's arm. "You won't see anything like that in Moscow," he said, steering his companion to a window display of lingerie.

Morosov nodded. "Not too many Russian women even know these kinds of things exist," he said. He hadn't been with a woman for a month, maybe more. It wasn't that he didn't have the need, but rather that he needed more than physical satisfaction.

When they began to walk again, Piligin asked, "How is your wife?"

"Still in the hospital," Morosov answered quietly.

"Any hope —"

"I always have hope," Morosov said simply.

"Enormous progress is being made in all areas of mental illness," Piligin commented.

"Yes," Morosov said, then changed the subject. "What's the name of the singer?"

"Her real name is Helen Petorious, but for professional purposes, she uses the name Helen Peters."

"When does she work?"

"Every night, except Sunday and Wednesday. Speaking about working, in a few days it will be Christmas."

"Yes, I finally remembered. Wherever I am, I intend to celebrate it in truly American style: by treating myself to an enormous dinner."

"To tell the truth," Piligin said, "I and my family celebrate it too. Because of the children, it would be hard for me and my wife to explain why we weren't like other families. Why don't you join us?"

"I'd like that," Morosov answered, then added a smile, "and so would the FBI. I'd like to be here a while before they discover me. The longer it takes

them, the easier it will be for me to track Gorsky."
It was the first time either of them had used the
general's name.

"There's something else you should know,"
Piligin said.

"About Gorsky?"

Piligin shrugged. "Probably not, but I think you
knew the man. An agent named Frank Robin was
killed in a traffic accident on the New Jersey Turnpike. He and his partner Steve Nathan —"

"I've heard about Robin, but I know Nathan,"
Morosov said. "Was he killed, too?"

"No."

"He's good," Morosov commented, "and he's
tough. I heard he'd been pulled out of the field
and sent back to Washington."

"The information is still very sketchy about the
accident," Piligin said. "If anything else comes in
before you leave for Albany, I'll let you know."

"Robin was their communications expert, wasn't
he?"

"Yes, he and Nathan worked as a team. They
were assigned to Deputy Director Fitzhugh."

Morosov accepted the information without
comment. He was thinking about the time he and
Nathan faced each other in a small apartment in
East Berlin. Both of them were armed and Nathan
had spoken first, "I'm just as willing to kill you as
you are to kill me." Neither one of them moved.
After several minutes, Nathan said, "I'm going to
lower my gun, turn and walk out." And without
waiting for an answer, he did just that. When he
reached the door, he turned, smiled and said, "It
was a pleasure to finally meet you." Then he was
gone.

"What do you think is going on with Gorsky?" Piligin asked.

"He has given up everything for it. It has to be something big."

After a few moments of silence, Piligin said, "I wouldn't want to be him."

"Neither would I," Morosov answered with a sigh. "Neither would I."

Because of the hordes of holiday travelers, Nathan spent more time on the ground waiting for a flight to Washington than he actually spent flying. It seemed as if the entire city of New York had lined up for the shuttle to Washington. And when he finally landed, it took the better part of a half-hour for him to get a cab. By then it was five o'clock and traffic in and around the capital was moving at a crawl. To make matters worse, it had started to drizzle.

By the time Nathan arrived at Langley, it was exactly six fifteen. Five and a half hours had passed since he had left his parents' house. He went straight to Frank's office and switched on the desk lamp.

The layout of the room was exactly the same as his. A gray metal desk with a computer terminal on top of it was against one wall, a window on the right and a secured, green metal file cabinet on the left. Despite company regulations against it, he and Frank exchanged lock combinations and computer IDs. Frank had always said, "It's insurance. In this business you never know when you're going to be caught by the short hairs."

Nathan's eyes swept the desk. It was clean. He used a duplicate key to open it. A color photograph of Deirdre was in the top drawer, on the right hand side. A few pads and pencils, a calculator and a mini-chess game in a plastic box.

Nathan sat down and opened the large side drawer. It had several manila folders — for memos from Fitzhugh or from the Director, some for case histories. All were neatly labeled.

He stood up and went to the window. It was coated with droplets that blurred everything beyond the pane and gave the lights outside a yellowish-white aura. "The trouble is," he said aloud, "I don't know what I'm looking for." He looked over his shoulder at the cabinet and realized that going through all the files in it could very well take the rest of the night, if not longer.

Before tackling the file cabinet, he decided to go through the desk again. He returned to the chair and opened the center drawer. This time he spent a few moments looking at the photograph of Deirdre. She was certainly a lovely-looking woman. About twenty-five, he guessed. Because she was wearing tan short shorts and a green polo shirt, he knew that the photograph had been taken during the summer. She had short blond hair and well-shaped legs.

Nathan picked up the photo, moved it closer to the desk lamp, and felt something on its back. He turned it over. There was a small piece of masking tape on the right side. His heart suddenly began to race. There was no reason for the tape, the photograph wasn't damaged. He placed the photograph face down on the desk and carefully peeled the tape away. There was nothing under it! Still holding the piece of tape in his right hand, he found himself looking at the name *Gen. Anatole Gorsky Check Red 10 * ?*.

Nathan took a deep breath and slowly exhaled. Gorsky, he knew, was the overall commander of Russian forces in Afghanistan. Check Red 10 * ? meant that Frank was uneasy about — "But that wasn't Frank's beat," Nathan said, still looking at the name. He replaced the tape, put the photograph back in the drawer and closed and locked the drawer. But he remained seated at the desk. There *had* to be a reason why Frank put Gorsky's name on a piece of tape and then stuck the tape on the back of Deirdre's photograph.

Nathan shook his head, stood up and walked back to the window. His mind was either a blank or filled with so many thoughts that he couldn't concentrate on any one of them. Then suddenly, he wondered if there was any connection between the increase in KGB radio and telephone communications that had occurred a few days before and Gorsky. Was it possible Gorsky was planning still another all-out assault? Could that have been what Frank told Fitzhugh? If it was, why didn't he tell him? And if that was it, why the computer instructions to Check Red 10 * ?

He returned to the desk and turned on the computer. As soon as the screen turned amber, he typed in his own ID and then Check Red 10 * ?.

Not available.

Nathan typed Gorsky, Anatole Check Red 10 * ?.

All update info. on subject restricted to NEED TO KNOW I.D.

Nathan stared at the message for several moments; then he cleared the screen and typed in Frank's ID, followed by Check Red 10 * ?.

Do you want the subject's complete dossier, or the latest update?

Nathan typed in the word UPDATE.

Subject is reported missing and is believed to be some-where in the United States. No further information is available. Sub.

A red signal light began to flash in the lower right corner of the screen and then the screen went blank.

"Christ," Nathan swore, someone had just locked it under another security ID. That had never happened before. Fitzhugh was the only other person whose ID could access the data. His ID could override all other IDs.

Nathan turned off the computer and sat looking at the dark screen. He was certain that just before Frank left he gave Fitzhugh the information about Gorsky. If he told Fitzhugh, why didn't he tell me? Nathan left the chair and went back to the window. It was still raining. "Because he was told not to," he said aloud, answering his own question. Fitzhugh told him not to. He broke into a cold sweat, then suddenly realized someone was behind him. He could just barely see his reflection in the rain-streaked window. He turned. Robert Copple, Director of Internal Security, was standing in the open doorway. Nathan was absolutely certain he had shut the door.

"Thought you left for the holidays," Copple said. He was a big man with blond hair and a boyish, innocent-looking face that belied his toughness. He and Fitzhugh lunched together and often saw each other socially.

"Did," Nathan answered, his heart beating fast and loud. "Came back after Frank was killed in an accident." He purposely said nothing about Frank having been shot. "Some crazy trucker ran him off the road."

"Sorry to hear that," Copple said. "I didn't know him, but I heard he was a good man."

"One of the best," Nathan replied.

"But you still haven't told me why you're in his office," Copple said.

"Probably because you didn't ask."

"All right, I just asked," Copple said. "Now you answer."

Nathan hesitated.

"You do realize that you're in Mr. Robin's office, don't you?" Copple asked. He took a step inside the room.

"I came back to pick up some of Frank's personal things," Nathan explained. "I'll be going up to Boston with Fitzhugh, and I know Frank's family would want his things."

Copple studied him. "There was a red signal on the mainframe computer."

Nathan shook his head. "I wouldn't know about that," he responded, then asked, "Why would you get that kind of signal on the mainframe?"

"Must have been a glitch," Copple said, ignoring the question.

"Probably, if you say so." Nathan suddenly realized that he was still wearing his coat and hat.

"I was just checking the offices," Copple said. "If you're going, I'll lock this one."

"I'll be on my way as soon as I phone Frank's girlfriend," Nathan answered. "I'll only be a few more minutes."

Copple nodded and backing out of the room, he said, "Have a merry."

"You too," Nathan said. As soon as the door was closed, he uttered a deep sigh and dropping down into the chair, he used a handkerchief to wipe the sweat from his forehead and the back of his neck. Then, because he was sure Copple would check the master switchboard to see if he was really calling Deirdre, Nathan picked up the phone, called information to get her number and a few moments later was listening to the ring on the other end of the line. He hoped she would not be home.

After the third ring, a woman said, "Hello."

"Deirdre, this is Steven Nathan. I'm Frank's partner. We met a few weeks ago."

"Yes, I remember," she said. "Did Frank —"

"I have to see you," he said.

"What?"

"Meet me at the main information booth at the Washington International Airport," Nathan said. "I have something very important to tell you."

"Did Frank put you up to this?" she asked with more than a trace of anger in her voice.

"No, absolutely not," Nathan answered irritably. He was quickly becoming involved in something that no longer mattered.

"I told Frank that I wasn't going to Boston," she said. "But he was so sure that I'd change my mind that —"

"Goddamn it, meet me!" Nathan commanded.

For several moments Deirdre was silent. He could hear her breathing.

"How will I know you?" she finally asked. "I don't really remember what you look like."

"I'll find you," Nathan answered. Because he did not want to explain how he had seen her photograph, he said nothing about it.

"An hour?"

"Yes." Nathan waited until she was off the line and as he put the phone down, he heard another click. He'd guessed right: Copple had listened to the conversation. Before he left Frank's office, he unlocked the desk again, opened the middle drawer, and pocketed Deirdre's photograph.

He started to walk down the empty hallway, then stopped and walked back to his own office. Unlocking the desk, he opened the bottom drawer and removed a shoulder-holstered 9mm automatic.

Copple punched out the phone number Fitzhugh had given him.

After three rings, the phone was picked up and a woman said, "Doctor Hale's residence. Mrs. Forest speaking."

"Mrs. Forest, this is Mr. Copple. I would like to speak to Mr. Fitzhugh."

"I will see if he is available," Mrs. Forest answered.

Copple drummed impatiently with the fingers of his left hand on the top of the desk and looking at the digital clock on the opposite wall, he watched the red seconds change.

"Fitzhugh here."

"Is the line secure?"

"No."

"This is very sensitive."

"If it's that sensitive, you don't have any choice."

"Nathan came back," Copple said directly. "He was into the computer before I could stop him."

Fitzhugh uttered a ragged sigh. "How much do you think he got?"

"Less than forty seconds, maybe a full minute."

"On the update?"

"No doubt about it."

"Do you think he has made any connections?" Fitzhugh asked.

"If he hasn't, he will," Copple answered. "He's smart."

Fitzhugh uttered another sigh before he said, "Take him out. But this time don't do it in front of one of our people. Make it look as if he had connections to drug dealers, or the Mafia."

"Yes, sir."

"Do you think he knows Robin was shot?"

Copple switched the phone from his right hand to his left. "If he did, he never mentioned it."

"Put a tail on him," Fitzhugh said. "I want to know what the hell he's doing."

"But you just said you wanted him taken out?"

"When it makes sense. He's coming up to Albany to meet me," Fitzhugh said. "He's going to check into a motel and call me. If he's not taken out before, do it then."

"It'll be done," Copple said. He waited until he heard the click on the other end before he put the phone down. He was one step ahead of Fitzhugh. To hell with tailing Nathan, he already had ordered his men to kill him.

By the time Nathan was on his way to the airport, the drizzle had turned into a hard, cold rain. He sat back in the cab and tried to relax, even tried to smoke his pipe, but the tobacco wouldn't stay lit. His brain was mush. He couldn't focus on one thought before another took its place. He bit down on the pipe stem and cracked it. He realized he was sweating. There had to be a connection between Robin's murder and his knowing that Gorsky was in the States and Fitzhugh. And if there's that connection, then it had to be Fitzhugh who ordered him killed.

Though he was sweating, Nathan involuntarily shivered. He had to be next. Then he remembered having heard, though at the moment he couldn't recall from whom, that Copple was reputed to head a special hit squad on an extra-duty assignment basis. That meant he was paid for each hit and —

"We're being followed," the driver announced.

"How long?" Nathan asked. He forced himself not to look through the rear window.

"Since we turned on to the highway."

"They're probably Russians," Nathan said, unable to think of another explanation the driver would believe.

"Russkies, eh!" the driver exclaimed, glancing over his shoulder.

Nathan nodded. The man needed a shave. He wore an old sweater with two button on it. One read "Up Yours", the other, "Dirty Old Men Need Loving Too."

"How about givin' them a run for their money?" the driver suggested.

"Be my guest!"

"This is on me," the man said, switching off the meter.

The cab leaped forward and then steadily accelerated.

Nathan grabbed hold of the hand strap.

"Doin' eighty," the cabby said.

Nathan looked out of the rear window. "They're still behind us."

"Eighty-five," the driver said. "We're goin' ta turn off in a minute or two."

Nathan sucked in his breath.

"Now!" the driver exclaimed.

The wheels screamed.

Nathan was thrown forward.

The rear of the cab fishtailed.

"Son-of-a-bitch!" the driver swore, fighting to keep control of the wheel.

The cab bounced off one shoulder, then careened off the other.

Nathan forced himself back into the seat.

"Did it!" the driver exclaimed excitedly. "We ditched the fuckers, didn't we?"

"We sure as hell did," Nathan answered, attempting to settle down again.

"Now we'll take a nice leisurely ride to the airport," the man said, looking over his shoulder and grinning.

"Why the hell did you do it?" Nathan asked.

"Hell, now I can tell my friends I was being chased by some Russkies and I beat them."

"I've heard worse reasons," Nathan answered.

A half hour later, Nathan gave the driver a fifty-dollar bill. "No change. It's all for you."

The man touched the brim of his dirty cap with two fingers. "Have a good and safe trip," he said with a smile.

Nathan grinned. "Has to be after the ride I had with you." Then he turned and walked into the crowded terminal. He made his way to the main concourse, where the information desk was located.

Though Nathan immediately saw Deirdre, he did not go straight to her. Instead, he ambled over to the United Airlines ticket counter and studied the Christmas decorations, even the large tree near the information desk and the Salvation Army's Santa Claus not far from it. After several minutes passed, he crossed the concourse and stood in front of one of the windows that looked out on the rainswept airport. When he was certain he wasn't being followed, Nathan went to the information desk.

"Deirdre," he said, coming up behind her.

"Steve?" she asked, turning to face him.

He nodded and took hold of her arm.

"Where are we going?"

"To the cocktail lounge," he said, steering her through the crowds of people.

"I should tell you," she said, looking at him, "that no matter what you say, I'm not going to Boston."

Nathan didn't answer. But he found himself responding to her determination. He liked the sound of her voice and even the set of her chin. She was, as her photograph showed her to be, a long-legged woman with freckles on the bridge of her nose and on her cheeks. She wore a blue pantsuit, with a red scarf around her neck and she carried a three-quarter length black leather jacket over her arm.

"You're staring at me," she said.

"Sorry," Nathan answered easily.

They entered the crowded cocktail lounge. But Nathan spotted a table where a couple was just leaving. "That table there." He gently pulled her toward the table.

"That man is going for it," Deirdre said.

"The table is ours," Nathan called out.

The man glared at Nathan. He was taller by a half a head and he wore a shearling jacket with fringes on the sleeves, tight cowboy pants, highly polished brown boots and a dark brown Stetson.

There was a well-dressed young woman behind him. "I don't take kindly to —"

Ordinarily, Nathan would have backed off. Experience had taught him never to seek a confrontation. But nothing that had happened to him in the last twenty-four hours was in the least bit ordinary.

"I don't have time for this," Nathan growled and opening his coat, he pulled it back just enough for the man to see the automatic.

The man's eyes widened and moved from the gun to Nathan's face. "I get the message," he said and turning to the woman behind him, he told her they'd have a drink at the bar.

"My God, that man turned pale!" Deirdre, said.

Nathan gestured at the chair. "Sit down," he told her.

"I don't know if I want to."

"Please sit down," he said, his tone considerably more gentle. "*Please.*"

Deirdre hesitated. "I don't like bullies."

"Please?" he asked again.

"All right," she said defiantly. "Now what?"

"I'll order drinks." Nathan looked around for the waitress.

"Coming here was a mistake," Deirdre told him.

"You can't decide that until you know why I asked to see you," he said, catching the waitress's eye.

"I know why," Deirdre said sharply.

The waitress arrived and put down a bowl of bar nuts.

"Deirdre, what will you have to drink?" Nathan asked, then added, "Please have something."

"A glass of white wine," she said.

"Stoli on the rocks," Nathan told the waitress. When she was gone, he said, "There is no easy way of telling you what I am about to tell you."

Deirdre drew back and frowned.

"Frank is dead," Nathan said.

"Oh, my God!" Deirdre cried. "Oh, my God!"

Nathan grabbed hold of her hands. "Take it easy. Take it easy. People are staring at us."

"When? How?" Tears were already sliding down her cheeks.

"A truck ran him off the Jersey Turnpike," he lied. "I was driving a few cars behind him when it happened." Suddenly he noticed two men enter the lounge. They went directly to the bar, then one of them made a half turn and casually looked around.

"The chemistry wasn't there between us," Deirdre wept softly. "He wanted me to go up to Boston and meet his parents. But I told —"

Nathan handed her his handkerchief, his eyes on the two men at the bar. They had their backs to him, but he could just about see their reflections in the mirror behind the bar. Neither one looked the least bit familiar.

"Thanks," she said tearfully.

"You don't have to explain anything to me."

"I wanted to be his friend," she sniffled. "But he wanted a deeper, more intimate relationship."

As he watched one of the men leave his stool and walk toward the rest room, he picked up his drink, looked at Deirdre and toasted, "To Frank, May he rest in peace."

She glared at him. "My God, how could you say that so calmly?"

Nathan stopped his hand from trembling. He

drank, then said, "Look, I'll phone you in a few days." He put the glass down on the table.

"You're leaving? Just like that?"

He took a handful of bar nuts. The man was coming out of the men's room.

Deirdre looked over her shoulder, then faced Nathan. "Do you know him?"

"No."

"Are you interested in him?" she asked.

"Not the way you obviously mean it," he answered, lifting his drink again. "Have your wine." The man sat down again and his companion turned around.

Deirdre sipped her wine.

"I will call you," Nathan said. There was no longer any doubt: he'd been identified.

"You're leaving," she said dully.

He nodded. "That's why we're meeting here. I'm going to fly back to New York and spend Christmas with my parents, then go up to Boston to —"

"I want to go with you," Deirdre said.

He started to cough. "What?" During the few minutes they had spent together, she'd called him a bully, accused him of being insensitive to Frank's death and suggested he was a homosexual.

"I don't want to stay alone during Christmas," she said.

"But —"

"If your parents don't have room for me, I'll stay in a hotel. I just don't want to stay here."

Nathan rubbed his hand across his chin. "I'm not sure this is going to work."

Tears filled her eyes again. "I'd go home, but that's three thousand miles away." She looked out toward the main concourse. "What chance do you think I'd have of getting a ticket now?"

Nathan shook his head. "None," he admitted, suddenly touched by her loneliness. "How long will it take you to get the things you need for a few days?" he asked, wondering if he was making a monumental mistake.

"An hour," she said earnestly. "No more."

"Meet me at the Shuttle gate three," he told her. "If you're not there, I'll go without you."

"You would, wouldn't you?"

"Believe it," Nathan answered.

"An hour from now at the Shuttle gate three," she said standing up.

Though he enjoyed watching her walk to the door, he wondered how he was going to explain her to his parents. He was sure they would jump to the wrong conclusion.

[9]

Petorious, his sister Helen, Troy and Elly were seated around the dining room table. Eating off paper plates and with chop sticks, they finished the Chinese food that Elly had brought an hour before from Sing Bo, the only Chinese take-out restaurant in Red Hook.

"You really didn't eat much," Helen observed, looking at her brother.

"Enough for me," Petorious answered. Then with a slight, wry smile, he said, "I think there should be a law prohibiting the preparation of Chinese food outside of New York City, San Francisco, and perhaps one or two other cities."

Helen said, "That, no doubt, is your way of telling the rest of us that what we've just eaten doesn't meet with your culinary standards."

"My dear sister," Petorious answered with exaggerated dignity, "this so-called Chinese food is so far below my culinary standards, as you so correctly stated, as to have no status. On a scale of zero to ten, I would have to place this somewhere below zero."

Troy laughed. "Hey, this is the best show in town. The distinguished Professor Petorious and the world-renowned singer, Ms. Helen Peters —"

"Thank you, Mr. Sims, for that marvelous introduction," Helen said, bowing from the waist.

"I give credit where credit is due," Troy replied.

"Then please continue," Helen told him, "I can use all the credit I can get."

"As I was saying," Troy said, "these two illustrious personages —"

Petorious made a face and held up his hand. "I object to the word *illustrious*."

"I don't," Helen said.

Troy turned to Elly. "You're a neutral party. What do you think about the word *illustrious*?"

Elly put a paper napkin over her head and said, "Before I render my decision, I am going to take this opportunity to say the following: one, the illustrious professor would have to prove the validity of his culinary standards."

"Here, here!" Helen exclaimed, clapping.

"Wise beyond words," Troy commented.

"Two," Elly continued, "Mr. Sims, as usual, has taken it upon himself to speechify —"

"Speechify!" Troy shouted. "What's this *speechify*?"

"*Speechify*, to make a speech," Petorious said. "Something Mr. Sims does frequently, often on lesser occasions than having just eaten substandard Chinese food."

Troy threw up his hands and feigning hurt, he cried, "Who, me?"

"You," Petorious and swore with mock solemnity.

Troy turned to Helen and shaking his finger at her, said, "First I'm falsely accused of being an arsonist and now of *speechifying* without cause." He faced Petorious. "Of the first charge, I am innocent; of the second, I only exercise my right under the first Amendment of the Constitution."

"The matter here," Helen interposed, "is my brother's culinary snobbery, not Mr. Sims's guilt or innocence as an arsonist or a speechifyer."

"Ms. Peters, if I wasn't already in love with Elly," Troy said, "I'd certainly fall in love with you."

Helen put the back of her hand up to her forehead. "Ah, that there was no other woman in your life and that you were ten, no twenty, years older!"

"Just to bring us back to reality," Petorious said, "the phone happens to be ringing and if you will excuse me, I will answer it."

"You're excused," Helen sad.

Petorious stood up and left the table.

"Your brother is an all right guy," Troy said. "I mean he's different here than he is in the classroom."

"He told me that you have your differences with him," Helen said.

Troy nodded. "But there's no one else I'd trust."

Helen nodded. "He's that kind of a man," she said quietly.

Petorious came back into the dining room. "That was Leon," he said, standing behind his chair and looking at Troy. "He asked me to come over for a drink."

"Are you going?" Helen asked, her eyebrows arching.

"Yes. I told him I'd be over in a half-hour."

"Listen," Troy said, "if he gives you any static about me —"

Petorious shook his head. "Please, Mr. Sims, no advice. Nothing was mentioned about you by either Leon or me. I was invited for a drink and nothing more."

"Did it ever happen before?" Helen asked.

"Yes, many times," Petorious lied. "After all, Leon *is* the president of the college."

"That too might need changing," Troy said.

"I don't believe what I just heard!" Elly exclaimed. "Aren't you already in enough trouble without —"

"If he can agree to having someone like Noonan on the board," Troy said, "then maybe it's time to think about getting rid of him."

"One windmill at a time, Don Quixote," Petorious counseled, his expression one of disapproval.

Troy started to answer, but a nudge from Elly silenced him.

"I'd better get going," Petorious said, standing up.

"You have lots of time," Helen argued. "The campus is only five minutes from here."

Petorious shook his head. "If I stay," he said softly, "I almost certainly will argue with my young guest, whose idea of great fun is to dismantle what exists without having the slightest idea of what to erect in its place."

"That's not fair, or true!" Troy responded.

"Troy, shut up!" Elly snapped.

"Thank you, Elly," Petorious said and leaning over Helen, he kissed her on the forehead. "I shouldn't be home too late."

"Enjoy yourself," she told him.

"I'll certainly try," he answered and left.

Elly turned to Troy. "You upset him. Why did you have to make that dumb comment about Leon?"

"It wasn't a dumb comment," Troy said defensively. "Leon has had things his way too long."

"You know, I really think you're crazy."

"And you don't understand what power is all about," he snapped

"But you do. No one else. Only Troy Sims understands —"

"Elly?" Helen broke in.

"I'm sorry." Elly was contrite. "But sometimes he gets me so angry I could scream."

"I'm sure he does and I'm sure you could and sometimes probably do scream," Helen responded. "But my brother can handle himself. Yes, Troy's comment upset him, but he'll get over it."

"Look, I'm sorry," Troy said. "I —"

"Don't apologize to us," Helen said. "Apologize to James."

Troy nodded. "Okay, I will. As soon as he comes back." He took hold of Elly's hand. "Will that be okay with you?"

"Okay," she answered.

"Now that everything is calm again," Helen said, "let's clear the table."

Petorious drove halfway to the campus, pulled over to the side of the road and stopped the car. He was not about to arrive at Leon's house early, which might be misconstrued as a sign of anxiousness on his part. He hadn't been exactly truthful with Helen about how often he'd been invited by Leon for a friendly drink. The only other time he could remember was when he first started to teach at Broom. It was a less than successful experience. Leon was effusively charming and he was exceedingly stiff. After that, each was professionally cordial to one other. Nothing more.

Troy's statement about Leon suddenly made him realize just how far out on the proverbial limb he'd gone. "Perhaps too damn far," he told himself aloud. He enjoyed teaching at Broom and would certainly not want to jeopardize his position. But to accuse Troy of arson was totally absurd. He grimaced, shifted into first and began to roll back onto the roadway. This just wasn't going to be a friendly drink between friends. Leon was going to want an explanation of why he put up bail for Troy and he was going to have to answer that he believed him to be innocent. "And that," Petorious said aloud, "will not please Leon at all."

Minutes later, Petorious was in the foyer of Leon's house.

"Looks like we might have a white Christmas," Mrs. Forest said, taking his hat and coat.

"Yes," Petorious answered. As far as he was concerned, the snow that had already fallen was more than enough.

"Dr. Hale is in the library," she said with a smile. "You know where that is, don't you?"

Petorious nodded.

"Go right in. Dr. Hale is expecting you."

Petorious crossed the foyer and as he passed the living room, he stopped for a moment to look at the tree and the layout of Leon's trains. To his surprise, he found himself looking at a very good model of Hudson. Only one detail didn't ring true. There wasn't an airport anywhere nearby that was large enough for a 747 to land, and yet in the layout there was what appeared to be a landing strip to the north and east of the town, complete with a miniature of the 747.

Petorious turned left into a small hallway and at the very end of it he could see that the door to the library was open.

"Ah, Professor!" Leon exclaimed, coming to meet him. "It is a pleasure to have you here."

Just inside the room, Petorious stopped and they shook hands.

"Professor, I don't know if you've ever met General Strogerly," Leon said, gesturing to his left.

Strogerly, cigar jutting out of the right side of his mouth, came forward with his right hand outstretched. "Pleasure, Professor," he said. "A real pleasure."

"I've seen you on campus from time to time," Petorious said, shaking the general's hand. He hadn't expected to see anyone else.

"What would you like to drink?" Strogerly asked, going to the bar. "Eggnog?" He waved his hand over a large silver bowl on top of the bar. "Mrs. Forest swears by it."

"Scotch neat, please," Petorious answered.

"Bell's, Chivas, Glenlivet —"

"Glenlivet would be fine," Petorious said.

"Make mine Bell's," Leon said, looking toward the bar. "But put it on the rocks for me." Then he gave his attention to Petorious. "I'm really so pleased you could come on such short notice. Please sit down."

Petorious chose a wing-backed leather chair.

"If you're somewhat confused by the way the room looks," Leon said, sitting in a chair across from Petorious, "it's because I had it redone over the summer. I use it more for entertaining now.

Most of the books that were in here are now in my office."

"Drinks, gentlemen," Strogerly announced, bearing two shot glasses in his right hand and a bigger glass in his left. "Yours, Leon, is the big one. Professor, the shot glass on your right. Good, everyone has a drink."

"To a successful, healthy and happy new year," Leon toasted.

The three raised their glasses and drank.

Strogerly settled in a club chair close to Petorious.

"I think the room has a certain warmth as it is," Leon said, looking at Petorious. "Especially with a fire going."

Petorious nodded. "Yes," he said. "But as I remember, the way it was, it had warmth too and certainly the books gave it a special feeling, or at least, it gave me a special feeling."

"That's the academic in you," Leon responded.

"Speaking about being an academic," Strogerly said, "I hope Leon didn't give you any hint about why you were asked here?"

Petorious raised his glass. "To have a friendly drink."

Strogerly grinned, left his chair and went to the bar to retrieve his cigar, which he lit with a gold lighter as he sat down again. "Your work here," he said, rolling the cigar to the right side of his mouth, "has not gone unrecognized."

"That's certainly gratifying," Petorious responded before he raised the glass and drank the rest of the scotch. He was being set up. Stroked. But for what?

"You are aware, no doubt, that the Board will be meeting soon," Strogerly said.

"Yes."

"I wanted to tell you myself that you're being considered for the Chairmanship of the new department of geo-politics."

Petorious shifted his eyes to Leon.

"It's true," Leon said.

"I had no idea that formation of such a department was under consideration," Petorious said slowly.

Leon smiled. "It was one of my better-kept secrets."

"No one else in the political science department has better credentials than you do," Strogerly said.

"Your published work is well-respected," Leon added.

Petorious rolled the shot glass between his fingers.

"Then the matter is settled," Strogerly said, leaving his chair. "Suppose we have another drink on it." He collected Petorious's and Leon's glasses and went to the bar.

"Naturally, there will be a substantial increase in salary to compensate you for the added responsibility."

Petorious nodded, wondering when the other shoe would drop.

Strogerly returned with the second round of drinks. "As far as the additional responsibility is concerned," he said, "we think it would be in the best interests of the college if you took a more aloof stance in relation to your students."

Petorious laughed. "If I was any more aloof, General, I'd be in outer space."

"To your new appointment," Leon toasted.

"To your new appointment," Strogerly echoed.

Petorious thanked them and drank.

"What I mean is," Strogerly said, "it would be in

the best interests of the college if you dissociated yourself from Troy Sims."

Before Petorious could answer, Leon commented, "You really don't have much in common with him."

Petorious put the shot glass down on the end table to his right. "On the contrary, we have much in common," he said.

"Not according to the information I have."

"We share a common love for the truth," Petorious responded. "Only Mr. Sims isn't old enough yet to be wise enough to realize that there are many kinds and many different levels of truth."

"He will go to trial for —" Strogerly started to say.

"What exactly was destroyed?"

"Our military collection and newspaper files," Leon answered.

"Interesting," Petorious commented, then he said, "I don't know who set that fire, but Troy didn't. He never had a chemistry course. He wouldn't have known that carbon disulfide dissolves phosphorous."

"The Board will certainly recommend that he be dismissed from this institution." Leon cleared his throat.

"On what grounds?"

"Arson," Strogerly snapped.

Petorious snapped back, "That has yet to be proved, General."

"Suspicion of a crime is sufficient to —"

"Troy believes that he is being framed because he wants to stop Mr. Noonan from becoming a member of the Board."

"He came into my office," Leon said, "and

threatened to cause a riot if Mr. Noonan became a Board member."

Petorious picked up the shot glass and drank the remaining scotch, then he said, "Yes, he told me he did that, and I told him it was a stupid thing to do. But with all due respect to the present members of the Board, it does seem to be heavily weighted with former generals, admirals and present-day captains of industry. A member of the faculty would certainly provide an alternate viewpoint to —"

Strogerly leaped out of his chair. "Professor, are we to understand that you agree with this radical?"

"Only looking at a different truth, General," Petorious answered. "But from any perspective, except of course the Board's, Mr. Sims does seem to have a valid point."

Strogerly looked at Leon. "I can't believe you recommended this man to head a department," he said. "I can't even believe he has been allowed to teach here."

"Leon, now that we're on the subject of charges," Petorious said, "I have a question or two about professors Giddeon and Platz. Were the charges against them ever proved?"

"Not in a court of law."

"Then how?"

"We had written statements from the young men involved," Strogerly said.

Petorious looked at him. "Wasn't it your appointment they opposed?" Every time Strogerly said something, he disliked him more and more.

"Without reason," Strogerly said.

Petorious leaned forward. "You're telling me that two or more young men came forward of their own and admitted to having sexual relations with Giddeon and Platz?"

"Something like that," Leon sniffed.

"Then what it really came down to was their word against the word of two professors?"

"In a manner of speaking."

"The answer, Leon, is either *yes* or *no*; there can't be any equivocation about it."

"I'll put it to you this way," Strogerly said. "Either you abandon Troy Sims, or the Board will have to rethink its offer to you in the light of your refusal to uphold the dignity of this institution."

"It might also have to rethink its position with regard to your position at Broom," Leon added. "Of course, I hope you will not force this kind of action."

Petorious got to his feet. He looked at Strogerly. The cigar was dead. He shifted his eyes to Leon, then he said, "There is neither dignity or truth in your offer; therefore, I respectfully decline it."

"You would do this for a young man who challenged you for an entire semester, who ridiculed your politics and just about everything else you believe?" Leon asked.

Petorious rubbed his hand across his chin. "I am doing it as much for me as for him."

"Think about what you're throwing away before you throw it away!" Strogerly's face was bright red.

Petorious shook his head.

"I don't understand you," Leon told him reproachfully. "I really don't."

"Maybe this will help," Petorious said. "Once, in another life, in another time I carried a wounded North Vietnamese soldier back to our aide station, but the doctor there refused to even look at him until —"

"What has that to do with this situation?" Strogerly broke in.

"Listen!" Petorious commanded. "Listen! That NV was dying. But he wasn't an NV anymore, he was a man and I wasn't about to let him die. I pushed the muzzle of my M-16 into the doctor's stomach. He got the message. If I could do that, and I did, then I certainly could do what I'm about to do now, which is to thank you gentlemen for making the offer and then say, as I am now saying, *no thank you.*"

"So he offered you the deal," Troy said, leaving the couch to put another log on the fire.

Petorious nodded. He was standing behind the chair in which Helen sat.

"I thought Leon would offer me a deal," Troy said, going back to the couch and settling next down next to Elly.

"Do you think you'll lose your job?" Helen asked, looking up at her brother.

"More than a possibility of that happening, I'm afraid," Petorious answered, puffing on his pipe. He looked around the room. "I'd really hate to give up this house. I've really become attached to it."

"You said the fire destroyed the military section and —" Troy began.

"That's hardly important now," Helen said, cutting him off.

Troy leaped to his feet. "It's fucking important!"

"Are you off again?" Elly cried, trying to pull him back down on the couch.

"Listen to me," Troy said. "All of you listen to me. I've got it. I've got it! Everything makes sense now!"

"What are you shouting about?" Petorious asked.

"Noonan!" Troy answered. "I remember where I saw him."

"Oh, not now," Helen responded. "Not Noonan now."

"You don't fucking understand! He's the key to everything!" Troy's voice was triumphant.

"There's no need to use obscenities on my sister," Petorious said sharply.

"I'm sorry, Helen, I apologize. But everyone, please, just listen to me."

"We're listening," Elly said impatiently.

"Okay. I saw Noonan in a book about the command structure of the Soviet Army. His picture was in that book."

"Troy!" Elly exclaimed.

"Don't you see," Troy said excitedly, "that's why that section and the newspaper section was burned! Someone on campus didn't want me to remember. That's why —"

Petorious pointed his pipe at him. "A Russian general, is that what you think Noonan is?"

"It's him or his clone," Troy maintained steadfastly. "He even speaks with an accent."

"Then explain why the newspaper section was burned," Helen challenged.

Troy looked toward Petorious. "Because of Giddeon and Platz."

"I'll explain who they were later," Petorious told his sister; then to Troy, he said, "Let's get back to Noonan. Tell me why you think a Russian general would be here in Broom."

Troy began to pace. Then, stopping, he said, "Maybe he defected? Maybe Broom is his safe house? Maybe the name Noonan is his cover?"

"Do you *really* believe what you're saying?" Petorious asked.

Troy shook his head. "A defecting general wouldn't be a candidate for the Board."

Petorious nodded his agreement.

"But Noonan is a Russian general," Troy insisted, dropping down next to Elly again. "Okay, let's drive up to Albany State and check the library for the book. They must have it. Christ, we can even go down to West Point. I'm sure their library would have it. If you don't want to go with me, I'll go alone."

"You can't go anywhere," Petorious said. "You're out on bail and I'm responsible for you."

"Come on, Petorious," Troy insisted, "you know I'm not going to jump bail."

"That issue is closed," Petorious answered. "But if you could give me just one logical reason why a Russian general would be here, then maybe —"

"That's just it," Troy said. "There is no logical reason. But is there any logical reason why I was set up? Why is it so important for Noonan to become a member of the Board?"

"Perhaps Noonan isn't the issue at all," Petorious suggested. "Perhaps Leon and the other members feel that they don't want a student to dictate to them."

Troy was on his feet again. "There has to be a better reason than that for Leon to have offered you a deal. Noonan has to be more important; he *has* to be the key to something bigger than —"

"What?"

"Jamie, it wouldn't hurt to check it out," Helen said. "It would only take a couple of hours to drive down to the Point and back, less if you go up to Albany."

"Suppose Noonan and this Russian general do look alike, what have we got?" Petorious asked and before anyone could speak, he said, "We've got nothing more than a coincidence and that doesn't mean a damn thing."

"Maybe," Troy 'replied. "Sally had dinner with Noonan last night. I asked her to ask him —"

Astonished, Petorious exclaimed, "You did what?"

"The name and address of Noonan's company wasn't on his biog sheet," Troy said.

"So?"

"I asked Sally to find out the name of the company and its address."

"It's probably an oversight," Petorious said.

"Could be. But suppose he doesn't have a company and doesn't have a former address? You'd have to admit that we might be on to something, wouldn't you?"

Petorious stepped out from behind the chair and walked to the window. Then he turned around and looked straight at Troy. "You're really enjoying this, aren't you?"

"I'm enjoying the prospect of finding out what the hell is going on."

"Suppose nothing is going on?" Elly offered. "Suppose Noonan is just a look-alike?"

"I can't buy that," Troy said. "Something has to be going on, or Leon and the other Board members wouldn't be so nervous about my objection to Noonan. No, something *is* going on, or I would not have been blamed for a fire I didn't start."

"Jamie, do you think something is going on?" Helen asked.

Reluctantly, Petorious nodded. "I don't think it has anything to do with a Russian general," he said. "But I'll drive up to Albany State with Troy the day after Christmas and look at the book."

"And this," Mrs. Nathan said, turning another page in the family photograph album, "was Steve the summer he graduated from Susan Wagner High School, here on Staten Island."

"Mom, it has been a long day for all of us," Steve said, catching Deirdre's eye. They had arrived at his parents' home at eight o'clock. It was now eleven-thirty and his mother had been introducing Deirdre to his uncles, aunts, grandparents and good friends via the family photograph album. And before that, his mother had insisted they must be hungry and so they'd had to sit at the table for a late dinner. He finally reached a compromise and his mother settled for serving him and Deirdre coffee and her homemade cheesecake. By now Steve realized that his parents had made the assumption that Deirdre was that special woman in his life, that he had brought her home to meet them because he intended to marry her. Watching the two of them sitting close together with the photograph album between them gave him a funny feeling. And Deirdre actually seemed to be enjoying herself. The very best he could do was smoke his pipe and try not to think of what might come down.

"You know Steve played football in high school and in college," his father said.

"You never told me that," Deirdre said, smiling at him.

"There's a whole lot I haven't told you," he said.

"You know, Deirdre, Steve was always a good boy —" Mrs. Nathan began.

"Mom, if you tell her everything about me now," Steve said, "you won't have anything left for tomorrow, or the next day."

"It's all right," Deirdre said, patting Mrs. Nathan's hand. "I want to know whatever you want to tell me."

Steve left the chair.

"Where are you going?" his mother asked.

"Just to the kitchen for a beer," he said. Bringing Deirdre home with him was a mistake, but he couldn't do anything about it now. He went to the refrigerator, took out a bottle of beer and unscrewed the top. He walked over to the sliding door and looked out at the yard. He no longer had the slightest doubt that Fitzhugh had Frank killed because Frank knew Gorsky was in the States. Now he was in danger of being killed because he knew what Frank had known. Nathan lifted the bottle to his lips and drank. *Why* was Gorsky here?

"Steve?" his mother called from the doorway. He turned around.

"I'm so happy you brought Deirdre to meet us," she said. "I really didn't expect it. I mean, with Frank's death and —"

"I didn't expect it myself," Steve said. "It just kind of happened."

Mrs. Nathan smiled knowingly. "Yes, sometimes it does kind of happen that way. She's a darling young woman and I really think she likes us."

Steve put his arm around his mother's shoulders. "I love you," he said, kissing her gently on her cheek.

"The two of you make a good-looking couple."

"I'll tell her you said that."

"But there is something I have to speak to you about," Mrs Nathan said.

"Oh, I hope it's not serious."

"Well, it might be," his mother answered. "Whether it becomes serious or not, will depend on the way you take what I have to say."

Perplexed, Steve said, "You better tell me what's bothering you, Mom, or we'll be up all night talking in circles."

"Although I consider myself a modern woman," Mrs. Nathan said, "I still think certain proprieties should be observed, at least on the surface."

"Mom, I really don't know what you're talking about. Maybe it's the day, but you're going to have to be clearer."

"I don't think you and Deirdre should be in the same room," his mother said. "It's not that I don't realize you have been sleeping together, but —"

"Did she tell you that?" he asked.

Mrs. Nathan shook her head. "I know how things are today. Most people want to sample the merchandise before they buy. I'm not saying it's wrong or right. But until you're married, I'd feel uncomfortable knowing that you were in bed with a woman in my house."

Steve wanted to laugh.

"Well, I said what I wanted to say," his mother sighed.

"Mom, I know you're not going to believe this," Steve said, "but it's the truth. I hardly know Deirdre."

"What?"

"Today is only the second time I met her."

"It happens that way sometimes," his mother said, trying to act blasé. "Love is love."

"I have no intention of sleeping with her," he explained, then added, "at least not tonight."

"Enough!" his mother said. "She'll have the guest room."

"That's fine with me," he said, "and I'm sure it will be fine with her."

"Tomorrow, do you think you will have time to explain why you brought a strange woman home to meet your parents?"

Steve shrugged. "I'll tell you now. She was too frightened to stay alone. She knew Frank."

Mrs. Nathan gulped air. "Were they serious?"

Steve shook his head. "They weren't," he answered, telling half a lie.

Mrs. Nathan started out of the kitchen, but when she reached the doorway, she stopped and turned to face her son. "I still like her," she said.

Nathan smiled.

"That's what I thought," his mother said.

Nathan waited until everyone was asleep before he put on his coat and hat and removed his gun from its holster. Opening the front door, he stepped into the street. He walked up to the top of the hill and checked every car on either side of the street; then he did the same with the cars parked between his parents' house and the bottom of the hill. He found nothing in the least bit suspicious. All of the cars were empty.

When Nathan walked back into the house, his father was waiting for him. "I needed some fresh air," he said. The bathrobe his father was wearing looked familiar. It was faded and threadbare.

"Your gun needed it, too?" his father asked dryly.

"No questions, Dad," he said, slipping the gun back into its holster.

"Only one."

"Go ahead — ask," Nathan said, as they moved away from the hall closet and into the darkened living room.

"How much danger are you in?" Mr. Nathan switched on an end table lamp.

"What makes you think I'm in any danger?"

"An answer, Steve, not another question."

"A considerable amount."

"Has Deirdre anything to do with it?"

"No," Steve said. "She doesn't even know that I'm in danger."

"This danger, does it have something to do with Frank's death?"

"Dad, I don't want to talk about it."

Mr. Nathan nodded. "If you need me —"

Steve went to his father and hugged him. "Go to sleep, Dad. I've been in tough situations before."

"Yes, I know," his father said patiently, "but I was never there. Now I am and it makes a difference."

"I'll be okay," Steve assured him. "Really, I will be."

His father nodded, "Remember this robe?"

"I'm not sure, but didn't I give it to you for Christmas?"

"Yes, and it's about time you gave me another one. Know what I mean?"

"If that's what you want, that's what you'll get."

His father kissed him and said, "Deirdre is a nice woman. Even if you really don't know her, you might give some thought to changing that situation."

"I already have."

"And?"

"I'll let you know how it works out"

Chuckling, his father walked out of the living room and slowly climbed the stairs.

Nathan switched off the lamp, went to the window and easing the curtain back looked out on the street again.

[10]

Boris Gargarin just finished the midnight to 8 a.m. shift as the departmental duty officer. He was, in the vernacular of the department, at the wheel. From his office at the Lubianka, he could, in an emergency, immediately activate all of the considerable resources of the Second Directorate, even before he'd notified the Comrade Deputy Director, Palovich.

But the night had been routine and he had spent most of it reading a pirated edition from Hong Kong of *The Spy Who Came In From the Cold*, written by former British intelligence agent John le Carré. As a matter of routine, he had checked the huge electronic status board several times during his tour. The board was really an enormous computerized map of the Soviet Union capable of displaying, in moment-to-moment update, a variety of information, including a detailed street map of every city, town, village and hamlet in the country. It could also display the ready condition of every military base unit, missile installation, fighter and bomber aircraft and every naval vessel in port. It gave the Department instant access to information vital to its operation.

Gargarin, who had come to the Second Directorate by way of his experience as an intelligence officer with the 245th Armored Infantry Division, made a final check of the board before he left the building. The conditions were normal. And then, for no particular reason other than he was curious about where the 245th was stationed and what its assignment was, he activated the UNIT DISPOSITION MODE and typed in his name and KGB ID number. Then he typed:

Request disposition and assignment of 245th Armored Infantry Div.

The answer came up immediately: *Subject request involved in special exercises.*

Gargarin pondered the message on the screen. Whenever a unit was engaged in a special exercise within the territorial boundaries of the Soviet Union or any of the eastern bloc nations, the Second Directorate was informed, and several of its agents monitored the field exercises. But he had seen nothing about the 245th, nor had anyone mentioned the unit to him. He typed in:

Request ID of all units engaged with 245th Armored Infantry in special exercises.

The screen went blank again.

Gargarin fished out a cigarette and lit it.

Units ID only by unit number.

Gargarin took the cigarette from between his lips. "If I had the damn unit numbers, I wouldn't be asking for them," he muttered and typing in his code designation: *BG/*44/2/22/29** he signed off and left the building.

It was snowing and the square in front of the Lubianka was empty. He dropped the remains of his cigarette on the snow and ground it underfoot.

Looking forward to a good breakfast, a few hours' sleep and spending the rest of the day with Galena, he started to walk toward the entrance of the metro. Just a month ago he and Galena had become lovers. He had met her at a concert — Suddenly, he stopped thinking about Galena and thought about the message he had gotten on the computer. Something was very wrong. . . . Gargarin looked back at the Lubianka and then at the metro's kiosk. He was midway between the two. He wanted very much to be with Galena. She had, in the short time he had been with her, given him more than any woman ever had. . . . Still looking at the Lubianka, a sudden chill gripped him. He had seen something he shouldn't have, something that others had taken enormous precautions to hide.

Gargarin shook his head and started to walk. If he hadn't ID'd 245th, he wouldn't have any knowledge about the special exercise and if he hadn't known about that, he wouldn't have asked for the other units involved in it. He was sweating profusely now. The people involved in whatever was going had his ID.

Instead of going into the metro, Gargarin went to the nearest phone booth to warn Galena. But the instant he heard her voice, he knew it was too late. They were already there waiting for him. He hung up and started to walk again.

Troy had been given a room on the third floor, in what once had been an attic. The king-size bedstead was made of brass and the mattress was high and firm. But Troy was unable to sleep. The events of the last two and a half days were almost beyond his ability to believe.

He left the warmth of the bed and slipping on an old maroon velvet bathrobe he had borrowed from Petorious, he went to the window and looked out at the road. The plows had been through earlier and had banked the snow on either side of the road. He looked up at the sky, where a white half-moon appeared to be darting in and out of low, scudding clouds. He moved his eyes down to the strand of woods directly across from the house. Except for the intermittently silvered tree tops, everything else was dark.

Suddenly feeling the cold acutely, Troy shivered and hugged himself. That he could stand trial and possibly be sent to prison, sent a surge of fear through him. His mind filled with everything he had read about life in prison: the brutality of the guards, of the men toward each other, the rapes, the beatings. "I'd never survive that," he said aloud. "Never!" And running his hand over his beard, he remembered an ex-con-turned-author who had been invited to speak to the college's fiction writing seminar. He'd had the saddest brown eyes Troy had ever seen in a human being. The man, who "told it like it was," was filled with rage at himself, at society and at the men with whom he had spent so much of his life.

The man ended by saying, "After a man spends time in the joint, something happens to him; he never again looks like other men. A grayness fills his body and colors his skin and his eyes reflect the pain he has endured. On the outside, it is these differences that identify one ex-con to another." For some reason, Troy never forgot those words and now they became especially meaningful to him. His throat tightened and tears began to sneak out of the corners of his eyes.

"Christ, if I call my father," he told himself, "he'd only say, 'Don't worry, kid. I'll get you the best defense lawyer in the country.' He wouldn't even bother asking whether I was guilty or not. It wouldn't matter."

Troy sat down in the wicker rocker by the window. "Mom would be worse. She'd cry and then complain that this was her busiest season and —"

He stood up, took a deep breath and slowly exhaling, he used the right sleeve to brush the tears from his eyes. "I'm not going to feel sorry for myself," he said resolutely. "Leon and whoever else is involved knows I didn't set — What the hell am I talking about? The fire isn't the issue. The issue is Noonan. What the hell is a Soviet General doing here?" He began to pace, then stopped, looked at the door and made up his mind. He opened the door, stepped quietly into the darkened hallway and very carefully closed the door behind him.

Troy went quickly down the stairs to the floor below and slowly turned the brass knob on the door of the room Elly occupied. For several moments, he stood looking down at her. Enough light came through the window for him to clearly see her. She was sleeping in the fetal position, her back toward him. The blanket was drawn almost over the top of her head. Some of her long hair escaped from under it and was spread over the pillow. Her breathing was slow and regular. An enormous feeling of tenderness welled up inside of him. He really did love her.

He bent close to her ear. She smelled of sleep. "Elly?" he called in a low voice. "Elly?

She shifted her position and the blanket moved off her bare shoulder.

Troy put his hand on it. "Elly, it's me," he said.

She bolted up, and the blanket fell away from her bare breasts. "What —"

"Move over," Troy said. "It's cold out here."

She pulled the blanket up. "What if Petorious finds out?" she asked.

"I hope you're not expecting him," he quipped, "because if you are I'd be very disappointed. Besides, a promise is a promise." He slipped out of the robe, dropped it on the floor and removed his t-shirt and briefs. "You'll either make room for me, or take responsibility for me being frozen to death."

Lifting the blanket, Elly moved to the other side of the bed.

"Ah, nice and warm!" Troy exclaimed, taking the end of the blanket from her and drawing it over him. "Another few moments out there and my teeth would have started chattering." He put his arm around her bare shoulder and drew her to him.

"Your hands are as cold as ice," she said.

He nuzzled her ear. "I told you I was freezing out there." Then in a low voice, he said, "I love you, Elly." He moved his hand over her bare breasts.

"I love you too," she answered, caressing the side of his face.

"Elly," he whispered, delighting in the warmth

of her naked body next to his. "I watched you sleep. You sleep like a baby."

She put her lips to his, then said, "This is hardly what a baby does."

"Hardly," he answered, kissing her ardently.

Elly opened her mouth. His tongue caressed hers. As his hand moved down her body, Elly took hold of his penis. "That feels wonderful," he said, stroking her moist opening.

"Come inside of me," she told him.

Troy rolled over onto her.

Sighing with pleasure, she gently guided him into her. "You know," she admitted, "I must have dreamed about this a couple of hundred times."

"Me too," Troy said, beginning to move. "Me too."

Elly stroked his scrotum. "You feel so good," she said huskily.

Troy kissed her eyelids and the side of her face.

"Love me?" she asked in a whisper.

"Yes, very much. Very, very much."

With a circular motion she moved against him. "I'm coming," she said. "I'm coming!" She grabbed hold of his shoulders.

Troy thrusted faster.

"Yes . . . yes . . . Oh my darling, yes!" Her voice went from a whisper to a low cry, her body tensing under his.

"Troy . . . Troy . . . Troy!" she wailed, raking his back with her nails. She raised her face to his.

He kissed her hard on the lips, meeting her tongue with his and feeling the exquisite burst of heat roaring through his groin.

Several minutes passed before Troy lifted his head from her breasts and gently kissed the still erect nipples.

Elly caressed the top of his head. "Good?" she asked.

"Better than good," he said, moving so that his face was directly above hers.

She smiled up at him.

"Good for you too?" he asked.

Elly nodded. "Do I look as if it was good?"

"You look satisfied and wonderfully beautiful."

She drew his face down and kissed him.

"Elly," he said, "I think we should think about making this permanent."

"You mean live together?"

Troy rolled off of her and drawing her close to him, he said, "For now. But I was thinking of marriage when we graduate in June. I have all the money we'll ever need and —"

She put her finger over his lips. "Let's see if there's really something between us before we start talking about marriage. Let's see how things work out. I want a career and so do you."

Troy took hold of her hand and kissed each finger.

"Before we decide to do anything," Elly said, "we have to get you out of the mess you're in. I still think you should phone your parents."

Troy let go of her hand, folded the pillow against the back of the bed and then sat up and leaned against it. "They wouldn't be of any use — at least now with the new twist."

"What new twist?" Elly asked, putting her arm around Troy's middle.

"The fact that Noonan is a Russian general," Troy answered.

"Troy, you still don't know that for certain."

"I don't remember his name," Troy said, "but I'm certain he's a Russian general."

Elly rolled away from him. "Tell me, what would a Russian general be doing here at Broom?"

"There must be some kind of a secret meeting," Troy answered. "Yeah, I bet that's it. There's some kind of a secret meeting going on."

"You *must* be joking."

"Hear me out."

"Okay, I'm listening," Elly answered with a sigh.

"All the other Board members are either retired brass from the military, or top-drawer world industrialists. All of them have the same credentials, except Noonan. But in fact he has them, because he's not really Noonan, he's really a Russian general!"

"Okay, suppose you're right. I don't see what it proves."

"It has to prove something, or they wouldn't have started the fire in the library and then planted the chemicals in my house," Troy said, sliding down on his back and pulling the pillow with him.

"Tell me who *they* are and maybe I'll be able to see where you're coming from."

Troy was silent for a few moments; then he said, "*They* are them, all of the members of the Board. They don't want anyone to rock the boat."

"Over an appointment to the Board?" Elly asked incredulously. "Troy, that doesn't make sense."

"You know what happened to Giddeon and Platz when they tried to stop Strogerly from becoming a member of the Board," Troy said.

"But they didn't say that Strogerly was a Russian general. They just didn't want him on the Board."

"Holy shit!" Troy exclaimed, sitting up again.

"I didn't see it before, but now I do." He looked down at her. "You made me see it."

"What?"

"Strogerly had to become a member of the Board, but Noonan is never going to become a member of the Board."

Elly shook her head. "I don't understand."

"Everything is being done to make it seem as if he will become a member of the Board."

"You just blew away your whole argument," Elly said.

"Only the part about him being on the Board," Troy answered. "Their game is to have everyone think he will become a member of the Board."

"Come on, Troy, that doesn't make sense."

Troy slid down again and propped his head up with his hand. "Sure it does. In fact, it's absolutely brilliant if what they want is to hide his real reason for being here."

"He could be a defector," Elly offered.

Troy shook his head. "Defectors are given new identities. Noonan has a false ID. But this place isn't exactly where he's going to live. Besides, Leon took great pains to introduce him around. No, he's here for another reason."

"Three guesses?" Elly said, jokingly.

"I wish I knew," Troy answered. "I really wish I knew."

Elly put her hand on his chest. "Do you think," she whispered, "you can stop being a super-sleuth long enough to make love to me again?"

"Yes, I think I can," Troy answered, taking her into his arms.

At precisely 11:30 p.m. the doors to the conference room in the administration building were electronically disengaged and slid open, revealing a long, highly polished mahogany table, around which were placed thirty swivel chairs. In front of each chair was a white pad, a pen, a glass and a quart-size bottle of water and a simple, square, copper ash tray.

The place at the head of the table had, in addition to the writing and drinking paraphernalia, a small, gray, electronic control keyboard, similar to a remote control for a television set.

The room's oak-panelled walls were bare and the floor was covered by a light beige rug with a thick pile. There were no windows, but a constant temperature of sixty-eight degrees was maintained at all times and the air was changed and filtered every five minutes.

The thirty men who followed Leon into the room, included not only industrialists from the United States, but from Germany, France, England, Japan, Brazil and Hong Kong. These men had arrived at Broom during the last twelve hours and took up residence in two off-campus, college-owned buildings.

Leon, who had chaired the meetings ever since he arrived at Broom, took his place at the head of the table. Noonan was on his right; Strogerly sat to his left. Fitzhugh occupied the chair at the foot of the table.

As soon as everyone was seated, Leon picked up the electronic control, pointed it toward the doors, and touched one of the buttons. The doors slid closed.

"Gentlemen," he said, "before I introduce the man who will lead us into our new and brilliant future, I am going to take a few minutes to explain an unexpected development that conceivably could have an effect on our plans."

Immediately conversation erupted around the table.

"Please, gentlemen," Leon said gravely, "allow me to give you the facts."

The men became quiet and several of them began to smoke. Strogerly cut a fresh cigar and lit it.

"A senior, Troy Sims, whose politics are decidedly Marxist," Leon explained, "has suddenly become interested in the two professors who opposed General Strogerly's appointment to the Board."

"You mean Giddeon and Platz?" Mr. Schmidt, the president of I.G. Farbin, asked.

"Yes."

"Why now?"

"Because of Mr. Noonan," Leon said, then he added, "In order to conceal his real identity and purpose, he was introduced to various individuals as the new member of the Board."

"If I may say a few words on this subject Mr. Chairman," Strogerly interjected, rolling the cigar to the right side of his mouth.

"Please," Leon answered with a nod.

"This student has managed to gain the support and protection of Professor James Petorious, who has refused our attempts to convince him to abandon Mr. Sims."

"What exactly does all of this mean?" asked Mishima, the CEO of Shokia, the largest shipbuilding company in the world.

"That depends on how serious their opposition becomes," Leon answered. "I have already had

Mr. Sims accused of setting fire to the library and he is out on bail —"

"Bail," Strogerly interrupted, "furnished by Professor Petorious."

"Could they possibly stop our plans from going forward?" Mishima asked.

"Possible, but not probable," Leon answered.

"I do not think we can permit any possibility of anyone coming between us and our goal."

"I absolutely agree," Fitzhugh said. "In a moment I will tell the Board how I handled a somewhat similar, albeit more dangerous, situation, but first I want to get this one out of the way."

Leon sensed the drift of the comments and said, "There is no time to plan their deaths. They will have to be taken out at some convenient time within the next forty-eight hours."

"Why not sooner?" Schmidt asked.

"Let's not rush into this," Strogerly said. "If we kill them, the police will become involved. We don't know how many people each of them has spoken to. Involving the police might be more dangerous than having two malcontents make noise."

"I agree," said Lau, president of the International Bank of Hong Kong. "I suggest that we put the two of them under surveillance. If their moves become substantially more threatening, then we will have no other recourse."

"All in favor of Mr. Lau's position?" Leon asked. The vote was unanimous.

"Mr. Fitzhugh," Leon said, "we would now like to hear about how you dealt with a similar problem."

"One of my agents," Fitzhugh said, "through his sources in Europe, managed to learn that

General Gorsky was missing and was probably in the West."

An excited murmur rippled around the table.

"When he reported this to me," Fitzhugh continued, "I ordered him killed."

"Was he?" Leon asked.

"In what appeared to be an accident on the New Jersey Turnpike," Fitzhugh answered.

"Well done!" Strogerly exclaimed.

"Not as well done as I had hoped," Fitzhugh responded. "There was a problem. A second agent saw the accident and he too must be killed."

"But if it was an accident —"

"The men who killed the first agent made the mistake of shooting him in the head before they forced him off the road, and that started a chain of events that led the second agent back to Langley, where he was able to access the first agent's update on General Gorsky on our mainframe computer before my special security chief could block him out."

"Then he certainly knows that General Gorsky is in the United States," Mishima said.

"He knows," Fitzhugh said. "I have already given the order to kill him. He will soon be in Albany, where I have arranged to meet him on the pretext of the two of us attending the other agent's funeral. If he has not been killed before we meet, he will be killed then. It will be made to look as if he was involved in either drug dealing, or with the Mafia."

"Could you be more specific about the chain of events that led to the second agent's return to Langley?" Schmidt asked.

"The autopsy on the first agent's body revealed the bullet hole. This information was no doubt given to the other agent. A bullet hole could only mean that the first agent had been shot to death."

"But why would that make him return to Langley?" Leon asked.

"Because the improbable happened," Fitzhugh answered. "This agent was two cars behind the other one when the accident occurred. That put him in a position to be in contact with the state police and to ask himself, after he was informed about the bullet hole in the first agent's head, why was the man shot? The answer to the question could only be found at Langley."

"I'm not completely sure I understand the sequence of events," Strogerly said, "or at least a few of the details. For example, why was the second agent there?"

"They were going home for Christmas. Each was driving his own car. The first agent's parents live in Boston and the second agent's parents live in Staten Island."

Strogerly nodded and said, "As I understand it, information put into your mainframe computer by an agent under his ID at Langley can only be accessed by him, yourself and the Director."

"That's so," Fitzhugh said. "But the fact that the second agent was able to access the information makes it absolutely certain that he used the first agent's ID."

Strogerly nodded and asked, "Isn't that a breach of rules?"

"Yes," Fitzhugh admitted, "but these two were very close; they had worked together in the field."

"Then unless the second agent is killed, we must consider him a threat?"

Fitzhugh poured himself a glass of water and

drank half of it before he answered, "As I have already told you, he will be killed."

"Suppose," Leon said, "just suppose he takes the information he already has and presents it to the Director, or the FBI?"

"He can't. The information he has isn't worth anything unless he can corroborate it and even if he or anyone else tried to access it, they would discover the information no longer exists. I have instructed my security chief to eliminate it from the mainframe."

"I have one more question," Strogerly said.

Fitzhugh nodded.

"Are you certain your security people will be able to kill the second agent?"

"Absolutely," Fitzhugh answered.

Leon looked at Strogerly.

"I'm satisfied," Strogerly said.

"Does anyone else have any questions concerning either one, or both of the previous matters?" Leon asked and after waiting a few moments, he said, "Good. Now gentlemen, we will begin the business that brought us to this room at this time. It is with great pleasure that I turn the Chair over to General Anatole Gorsky." And gesturing toward Noonan, Leon joined the applause.

Gorsky stood up. Nodding, he acknowledged the approbation. He waited until it stopped before he said, "I thank you, gentlemen, for all that you have done to make it possible for me to be here and part of this extraordinary group of men. This group, like the other groups who came before it, will soon be responsible for making the most drastic geo-political change the world has ever seen." For a moment, he paused and looked down at a three-by-five index card. "Ever since the end of the American Civil War in eighteen sixty-five, a group similar to this one has determined the significant economic, political and military events in the world. Previous groups were responsible, as I am sure all of you know, for most of the minor and all of the major military conflicts, including the Russian Revolution of nineteen seventeen and, of course, World War Two, which could not have happened without the financial support that members of a group similar to this one gave to Hitler. That support unfortunately proved to be a mistake. The group lost control and Hitler proved to be the worst investment made by any group before or after."

Again, Gorsky paused, this time to take a sip of water. "This group is certainly after," he said with a smile. "Gentlemen, on your New Year's Day, Operation Hammer Strike will begin and in a matter of hours I will deliver the Soviet Union to you."

The men were on their feet and clapping.

Gorsky held up his hands.

The applause died and the men sat down.

"Dr. Hale, may I have the control module?" Gorsky asked. He accepted it with a nod and pointing it at the far wall, he pressed a button. Within moments the panels reversed themselves to form a huge screen. "Just so!" he exclaimed, touching another button. Instantly, a huge map of the Soviet Union came up on to the screen.

"Now gentlemen," Gorsky said, "please pay close attention to the map." He ran his fingers over several of the control buttons. "The four positions now circled in red on the map indicate the positions of the four divisions whose commanders are completely loyal to me. Their numbers are the Two Hundred and Forty-Fifth Armored Infantry, the Sixty-Sixth Tank, the Eighty-Second Infantry and the Forty-Fourth Air Assault. These four divisions are now in areas where they will, within the next six hours, commence extensive field exercises. These exercises were designed by me some eighteen months ago — approximately a year after we came to terms."

He touched another set of buttons and black check marks appeared within the red circles. "Those marks indicate ICBM bases at all four locations. What will begin as a military exercise, will end as an actual attack. The troops of those four divisions will kill the defending forces and all other personnel on the bases; then at my command from a plane, the officers will launch a pre-emptive strike against the United States. That strike, gentlemen, will begin the Third World War, which this group so urgently requires in order for it to consolidate its power and finally rule the world!"

The men began to beat on the table.

Smiling, Gorsky nodded and holding up his hands, he called, "There's more, much more."

The assemblage quieted down.

"In a matter of days both nations will have exhausted themselves. But because of its ballistic submarine fleet, the United States will have the edge and be in a position to dictate terms. Many of you will be involved in those negotiations in which the Soviet Union will come under the control of the United States, just as West Germany and Japan did after World War Two. As a consequence of those negotiations, I will become Supreme Commander of all the Soviets, answerable only to whomever becomes the head of the new government here. Be aware, gentlemen, that I did not use the word *president* to describe the head of state because the political structure of this country as it now exists, will no longer be intact. This group will put its own government into place."

The men leaped to their feet. Clapping, they shouted Gorsky's name over and over again.

"The time has come for this," he shouted back at the them, "for the powerful, the strong to take control. To have everything!"

Leon reached out and shook Gorsky's hand.

Finally, the shouting and clapping abated and the men sat down.

Gorsky helped himself to more water before he said, "Now that you have the broad-based scheme, I have to be assured that all the necessary arrangements on this end have been made."

Strogerly removed the cigar from his mouth and carefully placed it in the ashtray. Clearing his throat, he said, "Ten miles northeast of the campus we have prepared an airstrip from which an exact duplicate of Air Force One will take off. Over the past years that 747 has been trucked into the area part by part, each one coming from a different Air Force base. The plane is ready and waiting. It will be your command post, General."

"Excellent!" Gorsky exclaimed.

"The area is guarded by a small, select group of men who have been detached from their regular units for this assignment."

"Tell me more about my Command Post," Gorsky said.

Strogerly picked up the cigar, put it back in his mouth, relit it and rolling it to the right side of his mouth, he said, "You will be flown over the North Pole and give your signal from there. At the same time, several admirals and generals loyal to our cause will issue the necessary orders to take control of the vital centers of communications, power, water supply and transportation. We will hold sixty-five percent of all of those facilities within five hours after the first missile strike."

"Who will give the order for the retaliatory strike?" Gorsky asked.

"The stand-in for the President," Strogerly responded. "The real Air Force One will be airborne, on its way back to Washington from the President's western vacation. In the general confusion it will be destroyed. At that point in time, one of our men aboard the plane with you will order the retaliatory strike. The order will be given immediately after you send your signal."

Gorsky nodded and asked, "Are you sure about where the President's plane will be?"

"Yes. We have his flight plans, and even if there is a change, we will be told what it is before the plane takes off."

"How will the plane be downed?"

"By a fighter," Strogerly answered.

"I am satisfied," Gorsky said, looking at Leon.

De Ville, president of the multinational Dumond Industries raised his hand.

Leon acknowledged him with a nod.

"Has everything been prepared for the safety of the group?"

"The bunkers are ready," Leon responded.

"And I trust all of you have moved your families to the designated safe areas," Strogerly said.

Leon moved his eyes from man to man, each of whom nodded or said yes.

"Now," Fitzhugh said, "the only thing we have to do is wait and make ourselves visible to the students who have remained on campus."

"Ah yes, that reminds me!" Gorsky exclaimed, looking at Leon. "I almost forgot Mr. Sims and Professor Petorious. I would like to know exactly how you intend to handle those two."

"We'll let Mr. Sims stew. As far as Professor Petorious is concerned, General Strogerly and I have already indicated that his days at the college are numbered. I really don't think he'll be much trouble. Naturally, if I have to employ other methods, I'll ask Fitzhugh for help. He has twenty or so of his men on campus for security purposes."

"Twenty-five, to be exact," Fitzhugh said.

"Yes, I have seen them," Gorsky commented. "But still I think it would be to our benefit to keep the two of them under very heavy surveillance. That way, if we have to act, we will be in a position to act swiftly."

"Does that pose a problem?" Strogerly asked, looking down the length of the table.

"Absolutely not," Fitzhugh responded. "I'll activate the surveillance as soon as we're finished here."

"Good," Gorsky said, nodding appreciatively.

"Gentlemen, unless there are additional comments and or questions, this meeting is at an end. Before you leave, all of you are invited to join me at my home on New Year's Eve to welcome in the new year. In the meantime, in order to present the proper face to everyone, we will meet every day in this room at two o'clock in the afternoon, with the exception of Christmas Day, when I will be your host for the traditional dinner. And, of course, we will meet here on New Year's Day at exactly twelve noon. Are there any questions? Then this meeting is adjourned until tomorrow at two p.m."

It was almost midnight when Morosov and Piligin left Marci's Restaurant on Thirtieth Street, just off Second Avenue.

"It's one of my favorite Italian restaurants in this city," Piligin said, as they walked to the corner.

Morosov agreed and added, "I came here once with Galena toward the end," he said. "She made a scene and we had to leave."

"Had I known," Piligin said, "I would have taken you —"

"It's all right," Morosov assured him. "It's all right. Despite what happened in our pasts, our lives must go on."

Piligin nodded and when they reached the corner, he stopped and said, "I'm going to leave you here. By this time, your weapons are in your room."

"The usual?" Morosov asked.

"A Tokarev automatic, a snub-nosed .38 with a leg holster, which is in the attaché case I am holding, along with your driver's license, registration for your car and a gold shield and ID, identifying you as Detective Lieutenant James Callahan."

"That's a demotion in rank," Morosov said, taking the attaché case.

"I suggest you arm yourself at the first opportunity," Piligin responded, ignoring Morosov's comment.

"Anything else?"

"You have also been given a new one — a dart gun."

"You're joking!" Morosov exclaimed.

"It's effective at a hundred meters. When the dart enters the body, its tip explodes and releases poison. The victim is dead within ten seconds, often sooner."

"How large is it?" Morosov asked, sure that he was being given some sort of rifle.

"It is a modified Tokarev. The dart is fired by a burst of compressed air. Its main advantage is that it can do the job silently."

Morosov nodded. "I'll let you know how good it is."

"Take care of yourself," Piligin said, offering his hand.

Morosov shook it. "I'll keep in touch," he responded.

"Are you going to try to take him back?"

"He won't come."

Piligin shrugged. "Be careful. When you find him, he will be a man with his back against the wall."

Morosov let go of Piligin's hand.

The two men looked at one another a moment longer; then each turned and went in a different direction.

Morosov walked west on Thirtieth Street and when he reached Park Avenue South, he hailed a cab.

The driver rolled down the window. "Where you goin'?" he asked.

"Bedford Avenue and Glenwood Road."

"That's in Brooklyn," the driver said. "I'll be coming all the way back to the city empty."

"No you won't," Morosov answered. "You'll be taking me back."

"That's a bad place to be at night," the driver said, facing him.

Morosov handed him a fifty-dollar bill. "That plus whatever comes up on the meter," he said.

"You got it!" the driver responded, reaching into the back to open the lock.

Morosov settled into the seat and quietly opened the attaché case and placed the necessary iden-
tification papers in his wallet, pinned the gold
shield to the inside surface one of the wallet's
halves and then went about the business of arm-
ing himself. Finally, he filled his pipe and, lighting
it, savored the taste of the smoke.

All through dinner he'd thought about going
back to where he and Tatyana had lived before she
had become ill. This would probably be his last
chance to do it. After he finished with Gorsky, he
planned to enter Canada and return to Russia by
way of Paris.

"You want the tunnel or the bridge?" the driver
asked.

"The Manhattan Bridge," Morosov answered.

The driver didn't comment.

Morosov watched the streets pass. There were
few people out and when they reached the Bow-
ery, he saw several street people gathered around
a fire burning in a garbage can.

They turned on to the bridge and crossed it in
minutes.

Morosov closed his eyes. He knew exactly
where they were. He had driven the same route
hundreds of times, if not more over the years he
lived in Brooklyn.

"Not much traffic," the driver commented.

Morosov opened his eyes. "Not much," he
answered, realizing they swung around the half
circle of Grand Army Plaza, with its arch-shaped
monument to the Union Soldiers who died in the
American Civil War in the center and the large,
white marble building of the Brooklyn Public Library's central office on the southeast portion of
the circle's arc.

Within moments, they were moving south on Flatbush Avenue, between the Botanical Gardens on their left and Prospect Park on their right. He and Tatyana often visited the Botanical Gardens, especially when the cherry blossoms were in bloom in the early spring and when the roses came in to full flower. On one summer's night, even though they had been married for ten years, they made love in the park. They went to hear the New York Philharmonic and found a lovely patch of grass completely surrounded by bushes. It happened during Brahms' Fourth Symphony. Morosov bit his lower lip. "No matter what happens," Tatyana said, "I'll always remember this time between us."

"I have remembered it," Morosov whispered in Russian, "and you —"

"Did you say somethin'?" the driver asked.

"Go down Ocean and turn into Glenwood," he answered, quickly recovering control of himself.

"It's your ride," the driver said.

Morosov silently accepted the driver's comment and looked out of the window. On the left were apartment houses. Some tall enough to have elevators, others were walk-ups. On the right was the park, here and there on either side he saw a burned-out car and, though the night was cold, there were people on the street. The area had, in the years he was away, changed from white to black.

The cab rolled to a stop for a red light at Parkside Avenue.

"I used to come here years ago," Morosov couldn't help remarking, as he looked at the entrance to the park.

"Couldn't do that now," the driver said, "not

with all the niggers around. They even live where I'm taking you."

The light changed and the cab started to move.

Morosov was too familiar with American racial prejudice to even answer the man. Besides, after spending several hours talking to Piligin, he really hadn't any desire to talk to anyone. Tatyana was very much on his mind. After the last time he saw her, the sadness that was always with him seemed to become more intense, the grayness inside of him took on a luminosity it never before possessed.

"You from around here?" the driver asked.

"Used to be," Morosov answered, realizing the driver was looking at him in the rear-view mirror.

"Yeah, I thought so. That's the only reason a guy would want to come out here in the middle of the night to look around."

"That and the fact that a guy can't sleep," Morosov said.

"Try warm milk and a piece of cheese before you hit the sack. Has something to do with the calcium in the blood."

"I'll remember that," Morosov responded.

"Another couple of blocks and we'll be at Glenwood," the driver said.

"When you reach Bedford, just pull up and stop in front of the yellow brick apartment house on the corner."

"You goin' in there?" the driver asked.

"No, I just want to walk around a bit. You can keep the meter running while you wait for me."

"Listen, Mister," the driver said, "unless you're black or a Spic, you don't do what you want to do."

"Just wait for me!" Morosov snapped.

The driver turned onto Glenwood. "It's your nickel," he said again.

In less than a minute, the cab stopped in front of the apartment house and Morosov got out. He looked up at the second floor, at the left-hand corner apartment. The shades were drawn. That used to be his and Tatyana's apartment. There was no sign of the big maple that had been in front of the house. The house was shabbier than he remembered. He walked to the corner. There was a private house directly across Glenwood, another apartment house was diagonally across Bedford from where he had lived, and Midwood High School was on the other side of Bedford. He pulled up his collar and walked to the corner and turned down Bedford.

Directly behind the apartment house was a playground, where every Sunday morning during the spring, summer and fall local sandlot teams played softball. Sometimes he even went down and watched them. That memory brought a smile to his lips. He never ceased to wonder at the enthusiasm and combativeness of the players. It was as if their lives depended on — He heard a car behind him. He glanced over his shoulder — three men, including the driver.

The car was rolling closer.

It had to be right the first time, or they'd have him. He sucked in his breath and slowly exhaled, sending steam in front of him. He continued to walk. If they overshot him, he'd have a better chance. But they probably knew that too.

The car stopped behind him.

Now! He went down on his right knee, gripping the .38. It came out of the holster.

"He's got a gun!" one of the men yelled.

It was too late. He squeezed off a round. The explosion seemed to throw the man against the car.

The other man fired. The bullet sent a shower of concrete into the air in front of Morosov.

Suddenly the car raced forward, turned toward him and jumped the curb.

Morosov fired directly at the driver and leaped out of the way. The car slammed into the chain fence and tore part of it down. Another bullet pinged off the concrete.

The cab suddenly turned the corner. The third man glanced over his shoulder. Morosov squeezed off another round. The man screamed and dropped to the sidewalk.

Lights were coming on in every window of the apartment house.

Morosov ran to the cab and he jumped in next to the driver. "Get the hell out of here," he said, pointing the gun at him and breathing heavily. "Drive until I tell you to stop."

"You shot all three of them!"

"Drive."

"Where?"

Morosov took several deep breaths. "Back to the city," he said.

[11]

Nathan awakened all at once and much to his surprise found he had spent the night on the living room couch and someone — probably his mother or father — had thrown a blanket over him. He sat up, aware of the smell of coffee in the air.

"I bet you feel the kinks in your bones," his father said.

"You win," Steve answered, standing up. His father was standing in the doorway to the kitchen.

"Coffee?"

Steve nodded, picked up the automatic, clicked the safety on and stuck the gun into his belt. "Where's Mom?" he asked, moving to the window and looking out. A weak sun splashed its light over the street. His eyes moved from car to car. Those he could see hadn't been moved all night.

"Upstairs getting ready for church," Mr. Nathan answered.

"I'll get the papers," Steve said, knowing the Sunday papers would have been delivered.

"I got them and I also checked the street. It is, in your parlance, 'clean.'"

Steve nodded, left the window, walked into the kitchen and poured himself a cup of coffee. He sat down at the table and began to drink.

"Black, eh!" his father commented, sitting opposite him.

"Only the first eight cups today," Steve said.

"Is there anything I can do?" his father asked. "You know I'm a very good listener."

"The less you know, the safer you'll be," Steve said.

"How much does that young woman know?"

Steve shook his head. "Nothing."

"I think I hear your mother coming down," his father said, getting to his feet.

"Since when did you start going to church with Mom?" Steve asked. His father was a confirmed atheist.

His father smiled and with a slight shrug, he said, "I drive your mother there and sit in the car while she hears the word of God and then I drive her home. I figure by doing that I've done my weekly duty to the Lord."

Steve grinned. "I guess you have."

His mother bustled into the kitchen.

"You look lovely," Mr. Nathan told his wife.

She smiled with delight.

"You'll probably be the most beautiful woman in the church," Steve said, going to her and kissing her on both cheeks.

"I was thinking," his mother said, "of making a small party on Christmas day. Just a few members of the family and a couple of friends."

"Mom —"

"It would be a perfect time for them to meet Deirdre," his mother said.

"I'll get my coat," Steve's father announced.

"Think about it," Mrs. Nathan said, looking at Steve.

He nodded.

"If Deirdre wants breakfast before we come back, there's eggs and bacon and a package of biscuits in the refrigerator."

"I'll take care of it," Steve said, pouring more coffee into his cup.

"Want anything?" his father asked.

Steve shook his head.

"Come," Steve's father said, gently taking his wife by the arm and leading her toward the front door, "let's go and pay homage unto the Lord."

Steve followed them out of the kitchen. Standing in the open doorway, he watched them drive down the hill. When they turned the corner, he retreated into the house, returned to the kitchen and turned on the radio.

The strains of an old English Christmas carol filled the room. He turned the volume lower and sat down at the table again. He no longer had any doubt that he had blundered into something so secret it cost Frank his life for having done the same thing. Nathan put the cup of coffee down and stared at it. The question was whether that *something* had already happened, or was in the process of happening. "Perhaps," he said aloud, "a mixture of the past, present and future."

Suddenly his attention was on the radio.

"Late last night there was a shoot-out in the Flatbush section of Brooklyn that left three unidentified men dead," the newscaster said. "Witnesses from a nearby apartment house said that the gunman fled in a taxicab that was apparently waiting for him. A police spokesperson said that there are no clues and the killings do not appear to be the result of mob rivalry."

He left the table and shut off the radio. There was something he knew about the area where the killings took place but he couldn't remember what it was. He picked up the phone and was going to ask the police for more information about the killings, when he changed his mind and dialed the number of his friend in Naval Intelligence, Commander Brian Scott.

"Hey, I thought you were back in the field," Brian said, after Nathan identified himself.

"I'm sorry I haven't called," Nathan said. "But I've been up to my eyeballs in work. In fact, I'm on something now —"

"All right, tell me what you want," Brian laughed.

"Do you know of anything going down over the next few days involving a Russian defector?"

"Negative. Do you know something we should know?"

"Would I be checking with you if I did?"

Brian hesitated, then he said, "What we do have is word that a special Russian agent has come into the United States through Kennedy."

"What kind of special?"

"The eliminator kind. He was recognized by someone in National Security who was reviewing a tape of passengers waiting to pass through immigration."

"Any ID on him?"

"An old friend of yours — Igor Morosov," Scott said.

Nathan's heart raced.

"Are you still there?" Scott asked.

"He killed three men in Brooklyn last night," Nathan said, now understanding why the mention of the Flatbush section had a particular meaning for him.

"You're pulling my chain."

"It came over the radio a few minutes ago," Nathan said. "Before his wife became ill and he had to go back he lived in the Flatbush section of Brooklyn."

"Do you think that's why he came in?"

"No. That just happened. Those three were either some of my people, or —"

"Or who?"

"No questions, Brian," Nathan said.

"Okay, no questions."

"Tell me more about Morosov."

"He's traveling with an Irish passport under the name of Callahan."

"What I really need, Brian, is anything you can get me on General Anatole Gorsky."

"Where the hell are you?"

"With my parents, in Staten Island. Can you get the information down to me in the next few hours."

"That important?"

"Yes."

"Be easier if Gorsky was an admiral," Scott said.

"Can you get it?"

"Interesting name, Gorsky."

"I'm only interested in interesting people," Nathan said, forcing himself to be casual.

"You'll have it in three to four hours. At the very most, six," Scott promised.

"I owe you one, a big one," Nathan said and put the phone down. That was why Frank was killed: he knew Gorsky was here and now Morosov was here to find and kill Gorsky. "If Gorsky didn't defect, why did he come here?" he said.

"Who's Gorsky?" Deirdre asked.

Nathan turned. Dressed in blue jeans and a white shirt, she was leaning against the wall, just inside the kitchen.

"What was that all about?" she questioned.

"Business," he answered laconically.

Deirdre stepped away from the wall and pointing to the gun in his belt, she asked, "That kind of business?"

"Want breakfast?" Nathan asked, wondering how much of his conversation she had heard.

"Coffee."

He took a mug down from the cupboard shelf and poured coffee into it. "Milk or cream?"

"Milk."

"Sugar?"

"No."

He handed her the mug of coffee.

She nodded and said, "You haven't answered either of my questions."

"I don't intend to," Nathan said.

She took a sip of the coffee, then asked, "Are you in some sort of trouble?"

Nathan chuckled.

"Well, are you?"

"Sit down," he said, gesturing to the chair across from him.

"Is that an order?"

"I'm sorry if it sounded like one. Please, sit down."

"I prefer to stand, if you don't mind."

"Whatever makes you happy," he said, realizing that he found her very attractive.

"You're staring at me," she told him.

"Sorry. I was just wondering if you knew what Frank did?"

"He was always very vague about it," Deirdre answered. "Something with the government. I didn't press him for any more of an explanation."

"He was with the CIA."

She drank more of her coffee before she said, "You are too, aren't you?"

"Yes."

She pushed her hair away from the side of her face. "You know I wasn't going to marry him."

"I already told you," Nathan said, "you don't have to explain anything to me."

"It's important that you know I was not in love with him and I had no intention of going to Boston to meet his family. I tried to tell him that the chemistry wasn't right, but he wouldn't listen."

Nathan shrugged. He wasn't about to say anything against his dead partner.

"I just wanted you to know how things were between us," Deirdre said, pouring herself another cup of coffee.

"Suppose I make you breakfast," Nathan offered, getting to his feet and going to the refrigerator. "Mom said there were eggs, bacon and biscuits."

"You sit down and I'll make it," she said, coming close to him. "I'm very good at —"

Nathan put his arms around her. "My mother still thinks there's something between us. She wants to have a party on Christmas Day to introduce you to some members of the family and some friends."

"What do you think about the idea?" Deirdre asked.

"It might turn out to be a dud."

"Then again it might not," she countered. "Besides," she added with a smile, "I like parties."

Nathan gently touched her lips with his and then kissed her passionately. "Is the chemistry right?" he asked.

"Yes," Deirdre answered. "Oh yes!"

Nathan scooped her up in his arms. "We're going to test that chemistry all the way," he said, carrying her toward the stairs.

"What about your folks?"

"They're at church," he answered with a smile.

Circling his neck with her arms, she said, "You still haven't answered my questions."

Nathan kissed her nose. "For a while only we exist," he said, pushing open the door to his bedroom.

Morosov stopped at a phone booth, deposited a coin and dialed Piligin's special number.

"Where are you?" Piligin asked.

"Fifty-fifth Street and Eighth Avenue."

"You killed the three of them," Piligin said.

"Whose were they?" Morosov asked, covering his free ear in order to hear better.

"Our best guess is that they were theirs. But part of some special group."

"Copple's special security unit?"

"We'll know more in a day or two," Piligin said.

The operator came on the line and asked that additional coins be deposited.

"Give me your number," Piligin said, "and I'll call you back."

Morosov recited the numbers, then hung up. He hadn't slept and was beginning to feel hungry. He looked around him. Except for a man walking his dog in the middle of the block, the street was empty.

The phone rang.

Morosov picked it up.

"You've been checked out of the hotel and everything has been moved, including the car. You're now registered as William Johnson at the Plaza. The car is parked in the Municipal garage between Fifty-Fourth and Fifty-Fifth Streets on Eighth Avenue. It's on the third tier, section four."

"Weapons?"

"In the back of the car," Piligin said.

"Anything else?"

"An aide to the Deputy Director of the Second Directorate has vanished."

"In Moscow?"

"Yes. You might know him; his name is Boris Gargarin. He came to us by way of the army. Does the name mean anything to you?"

"Nothing," Morosov answered. "But I would check his army record and see if he ever had any connection with Gorsky. Let me know. I'll keep in touch."

"What did you do with the cab driver?" Piligin asked.

"I had to hit him on the head to knock him out," Morosov said. "He probably has a slight concussion, but he's five hundred dollars richer."

Piligin laughed.

"You're something else, as they say here," Piligin laughed. "Something else."

Morosov hung up, took a deep breath, slowly exhaled and then decided to have breakfast before he went to the Plaza.

"Our security people said he killed three of our men," Fitzhugh said, looking at Gorsky, who sat on the couch in Leon's library.

"Morosov, eh," Gorsky responded. "He's one of the best." He leaned forward slightly to pick up a cup of coffee from the table in front of him.

"He's here to kill you," Fitzhugh said.

"He must first find me," Gorsky answered, "and that will not be easy. And if he does find me, your security people should be able to kill him before he gets anywhere near me." He lifted the cup to his lips and drank.

Strogerly entered the room and closed the door behind him. "Where's Leon?"

"At church," Fitzhugh explained. "He doesn't know we're here."

Strogerly nodded. "What's this all about?"

"Three of our people were killed last night by a KGB agent sent here to kill the General," Fitzhugh said.

Strogerly's eyes widened and he took the cigar out of his mouth. "Three!"

"And we've lost the son-of-a-bitch," Fitzhugh said. "He vanished."

"Christ!" Strogerly exclaimed.

"His chances of finding me are practically non-existent," Gorsky said calmly. "He needs time and he doesn't have it. Time is on *our* side. If I am not in the least bit concerned, why should you be?" He set his cup down on the saucer. "I hope none of you were so naive as to think that someone wouldn't be sent after me."

"We realized that it would happen," Fitzhugh answered.

"Then I don't see any reason for anyone being upset," Gorsky said, standing up. "It is part of the risk. Now, if you gentlemen will excuse me, I have other matters to take care of."

Fitzhugh nodded.

"General?" Gorsky said, looking at Strogerly.

"Why yes. Of course."

Gorsky nodded and left the room, closing the door behind him.

"My God, that man has no fear!" Fitzhugh exclaimed.

"Just how dangerous is the situation?" Strogerly asked.

Fitzhugh stood up. "This man they sent is top drawer. But he's in New York and we're here and, as Gorsky pointed out, he has to find him before he can kill him."

"If he's not worried," Strogerly said, puffing on his cigar, "I don't see why we should be."

"Then we say nothing about the situation to the others?"

"Nothing," Strogerly said.

"To Leon?"

"Nothing."

"What about Mrs. Forest?" Fitzhugh asked.

"I'll tell her we met to discuss a surprise we're planning for Leon," Strogerly said. "She'll buy it."

Fitzhugh nodded.

Petorious had slept fitfully. Long before anyone was awake, he went down to the kitchen, put on a pot of coffee and as he waited for it to brew, he thought about the situation. Sometime during the night he had decided he would speak to Sally that morning about Noonan. She might be able to at least nullify Troy's latest and most bizarre accusation of Noonan being a Russian general.

"Ah, coffee!" Helen exclaimed, coming into the kitchen. "I was certain I smelled it."

"A few minutes more and it should be ready," Petorious said.

Helen sat down. "You look as if you had a bad night," she commented. "I had trouble falling asleep, but once I did, I slept well."

"Troy's statement about Noonan —"

"It bothered me, too," Helen said, straightening a fold on her pink bathrobe. "But you know Troy, don't you?"

"Only as a student," Petorious said, taking two mugs from the cupboard and setting them down on the counter.

"Well, is he the kind to make rash statements?" Helen asked.

"Dramatic ones for effect," Petorious said. "But not rash. That's the problem. If he says Noonan and this Russian general look exactly alike, they probably do, but that doesn't prove they're one and the same person. Besides, *what* would a Russian general be doing here?" Petorious started to laugh. "Why would a Russian general want to become a member of the college's Board of Directors?"

"But Troy thinks that's a ruse," Helen said.

"I know, I know," Petorious responded, taking hold of the coffee pot and pouring coffee into one of the mugs. "But he can't explain why. As soon as it's a reasonable hour, I'm going to speak to Sally. She went out with Noonan the other night and maybe, just maybe she'll be able to shed some light on who Noonan really is."

"You've been asked to leave here, haven't you, Jamie?" Helen asked.

He handed the steaming mug to her. "Not in so many words," he said, going back to the counter for his coffee.

"Nothing in all of this makes much sense," Helen said. "I mean, even if you assume that Noonan is just plain Noonan and not some Russian general, that doesn't explain why Troy was blamed for a fire he didn't start and it certainly doesn't explain why Noonan's membership to the Board is so important."

Petorious nodded, and then he said, "I bet Troy and Elly slept like babies."

Helen smiled.

"What's that supposed to mean?" he asked.

"They slept together."

"Here?"

"Come on, Jamie, don't behave like an old fuddy dud. They're young and they're in love."

"What am I supposed to say to that?" he asked.

"Don't say anything," Helen said. "Just accept it."

"I don't suppose I have much choice," Petorious answered, lifting the mug from the table.

"None."

Petorious nodded and drank.

In late December, darkness came early to Moscow. Gargarin prowled the streets and rode the metro until it was dark enough for him to approach the American Embassy on Tchaikovsky Street. His only hope for survival was to reach it and ask for political asylum. In return he'd tell them that something strange was happening, something that involved General Gorsky and several units of the Red Army.

Several times during the day, he had tried to phone Palovich, but each time the click of the automatic tracing unit warned him to immediately hang up. The unit needed a full ten seconds before it could begin to function. There was no way for him to know whether Palovich was in any way involved with Gorsky, or whether Gorsky's people put the tracer on the phone without Palovich knowing.

Gargarin started across the street. He was sweating, and his heart was beating so fast he could hardly breathe. To save his life, he was going to become a traitor. Tears filled his eyes and blurred his vision.

Suddenly a half a block down the street, a black sedan roared away from the curb.

Gargarin froze. The lights blinded him. Then he began to run. "Help," he shouted in English. "Help!"

Three Marine guards ran out in front of the gate. "Go for it, go for it, man!" they shouted.

Gargarin reached the curb, tripped over it and struggled to keep his footing.

The car slammed into him, threw him face down on the sidewalk, came to a screeching halt and backed over the screaming man before it made a U-turn and sped away.

"Dead!" exclaimed the Marine who reached Gargarin first.

The other two Marines came up to him, looked down at the broken, blood-soaked body and shook their heads.

His breath steaming the air, Petorious stood at Sally's front door, waiting for her to open it. It was cold and though he was wearing corduroy pants, a flannel shirt, a wool sweater and his duffel coat, he still felt the cold. He stamped his feet and beat his arms. Maybe having to leave Broom wouldn't be so bad after all. Maybe he'd find a place that wasn't located in the snow belt. Someplace where the winters were tolerable.

He rang Sally's bell again. This wasn't the first time he had visited her. Every term she'd invite a few members of the faculty over for a Sunday breakfast. Since his first term at Broom, he had always been among those chosen. This term she had her breakfast gathering the Sunday before Thanksgiving and —

Petorious heard footsteps, then the sound of the lock being worked and finally the door opened. "Hello, Sally," he said. She wore a red plaid bathrobe over a set of blue lounging pajamas. A white towel was wrapped like a turban on her head. She was too surprised to speak. "May I come in?" Petorious asked.

She nodded. "Yes . . . yes . . . of course," she said, stepping back to allow him in.

"It's very cold out there," he said.

"I was washing my hair when I heard the bell," she said. "I'm sorry it took me so long to get to the door."

"I should have phoned before —"

"Not necessary," she answered, then said, "Let me take your hat and coat."

Petorious nodded, slipped off his gloves and put them in his coat pocket before he handed the coat and his hat to her.

She put them in the hall closet and said, "Come into the living room. I have a fire going and it's warm there. These old houses are charming but hard to heat."

"I have the same problem," he said, following her into the living room, where a good fire was going in the gray stone fireplace.

"Please sit down," Sally sad.

Petorious chose a club chair with a lace antimacassar on the back. "Would you care for a cup of coffee?" she asked.

"No thanks," he answered. "I had breakfast a short time ago."

She sat down on the wing chair opposite him.

"Sally, I would not have disturbed your Sunday," Petorious said, "if I didn't think it was important. What I mean is, certain things have been happening around here that —"

"If you mean the fire," she told him, "I am almost too upset over it to even talk about it. I never thought Troy would do something like that."

"He didn't do it, Sally," Petorious said. He started to stand, then changed his mind. "The whole thing was rigged to make it look as if he did it." He paused. "Troy can be a problem. No one knows that better than I do. But he's not an arsonist."

"Would you care for a drink?" she asked.

He shook his head. "Sally, Troy spoke to you about Mr. Noonan, didn't he?"

She was on her feet. "Yes, he did," she declared. "And he was all wrong about that man. All wrong." She went to the fireplace, looked down at the flames and then faced him, "In my opinion, Mr. Noonan *should* become a member of the

Board. He's a wonderful, caring man." Color came into her cheeks.

Petorious suppressed a sigh. Her quick defense of Noonan said it all and he was surprised at his own feelings of disappointment. "I'm not against that happening," he told her. "Not against it at all *if* he's the right man for the position. Troy —" he was going to say, has nothing personal against Noonan, but now that he was positive that Noonan and a Russian general were one and the same person, he couldn't say that.

"Troy is doing what he's doing because he thinks it's the thing to do. 'The good fight,' as he told me," Sally said.

Petorious wished he had his pipe. "Troy thinks the Board is too heavily weighted with certain types of —"

"He's totally wrong about Mr. Noonan," she said vehemently. "He only sees what he wants to see."

"Don't we all?" Petorious responded.

Sally went to one of the end tables and picked up a pack of cigarettes.

"May I have one, too?" Petorious asked. This meeting wasn't going exactly the way he thought it would, though he really hadn't any idea of what would happen.

She gave him the pack and held a lighter for him.

"Thanks," he said, blowing smoke toward the ceiling.

Sally handed him an ashtray and then sat down again. "I know all about your Christmas invitation to Troy and Elly. He even asked me to join him before Mr. Noonan — I really don't understand what he's up to, or why."

Petorious took a deep drag on the cigarette and held the smoke for a few moments before releasing it. "I think its more than just 'the good fight,'" he said. "I think in some strange way he's picking up the fight where professors Giddeon and Platz left off."

She stood up and went back to the fireplace. "So he told you about them," she said.

"Yes."

"About me and —"

Petorious shook his head. "That doesn't matter, Sally. Troy wants to make the Board aware of its responsibilities."

She faced him and challenged, "Beside Troy and you, tell me, who else cares?"

Petorious shrugged. "Leon offered to create a department for me," he said, "if I would disassociate myself from Troy."

"And you refused?"

"I didn't see that I had much choice," he said with a slight smile on his lips. "A bribe is a bribe, even if it comes in the form of a department chairmanship."

Sally nodded. "Leon told Martin he'd eventually become head of the history department," she said.

"Then you understand the situation," he said, squashing the cigarette in the ashtray.

She returned to the chair. "I'm not going to do anything to stop Noonan from becoming a member of the Board. I already did more than I should have, but that was before I got to know —"

Petorious held up his hand. "I didn't come here to ask you to do anything," he said.

"Then why did you come here?" Sally asked.

"I want to know something more about Noonan before I make up my mind about certain things."

"I'll arrange a meeting between the two of you," she offered. "Then you can ask him."

Petorious shifted his position. He didn't really want to meet with Noonan, but he didn't see any way of gracefully declining the offer. "All right," he agreed, "you arrange it. Leave the time up to him. I'll make myself available. But —"

"I knew there would be a *but*," she said. "Tell me."

"If you know the name and address of Noonan's company, please tell me," Petorious asked, suddenly remembering that Troy said that information wasn't on the man's biog sheet.

"Troy asked me to ask him about his company," she said.

Petorious leaned forward. "Did you?"

She nodded. "He doesn't own the company any longer. He sold it to North Atlantic Industries."

"Do you know where they're located?"

"No. I was too embarrassed to ask."

"Did he happen to mention the name of his company?"

"No."

"I don't imagine there are too many companies named North Atlantic Industries," Petorious said. "I need a corporate directory. Something that would give the phone number of North Atlantic Industries."

"Thomas's Register would probably have it," she said.

"Where —"

"I have last year's edition," she said, leaving the chair. "I'll get it for you."

"I'll need a pencil and paper, too," Petorious called after Sally, as she left the room. He suddenly felt cramped so he walked over to the fireplace. The logs on the andirons were almost burnt through. He was just about to use the poker to break them apart, when Sally returned.

"I copied the phone number for you," she said, holding out a piece of yellow notepaper to him. "I also listed their address. They're in Plainview, New York. That's out on Long Island."

Petorious took the piece of paper, folded it and placed it in his pocket. "What does North Atlantic Industries manufacture?"

"Electronic measuring devices."

Petorious made no comment.

"I'm sure you'll find that he sold the company," she said.

"That would please me," he answered. "Especially since I know how much it would please you."

"I'm all mixed up about this," she said. "On the one hand, I want to do what Martin would have wanted me to do; and on the other, I like Noonan. I like him a lot and what I'm doing makes me feel like a traitor."

Petorious took hold of her hands. "Don't you want to know the truth about him?" he asked gently.

She raised her face. "He's the first man in a very, very long time who has made me feel complete, made me feel like a woman. Can you understand what that means to me?"

Petorious nodded, then he pulled her close to him and in a low, intense tone, he said, "I am sorry that I wasn't there first. I mean that, Sally. I really mean it."

Her eyes misted over.

He let go of her hands, cleared his throat and asked for his coat and hat.

"I'll get them," she said, her voice unsteady.

Before he opened the door, Petorious said, "I'd be glad to have you join us on Christmas Day, if you have nothing else going."

"Mr. Noonan and —"

Petorious held up his hand. "In that case, have a very merry Christmas and a happy New Year." He leaned toward her and kissed her on the forehead.

"A merry Christmas and happy New Year to you, your sister, Troy and Elly," Sally responded.

Petorious smiled at her, turned and walked down the steps to his car, suddenly aware that he felt sad.

Troy was waiting for Petorious. "Helen told me that you went over to see Sally," he said as soon as Petorious was in the house.

"Will you give me a chance to a least get my coat off before you jump at me?" Petorious said.

Troy raised his eyebrows. "We don't have fucking time for the niceties," he said. "My ass is pinned on the fire."

Petorious glared at him. "Spare me your dramatics and your obscenities."

Troy was going to answer, but there was something about the way Petorious looked that made him change his mind. "Are you all right?" he asked, softening his tone.

"I could use a drink," Petorious said, heading for the library.

Troy followed him.

"Close the door," Petorious told him. He took a bottle of scotch and two shot glasses out of the bottom drawer of his desk. "Noonan sold his company to North Atlantic Industries," he said, filling each glass almost to the top. "They manufacture electronic measuring devices."

"So?"

"Wasn't Noonan's company in electronics?"

"Yes."

Petorious lifted his glass. "To Sally Cooms," he toasted.

"Okay," Troy said, "I'll drink to her, but tell me why?"

"Because, my young turk, she's fallen in love with Noonan and I was too late," he said; then he drank.

Troy took a long swallow before he asked, "There must be dozens of companies with that name."

Petorious took out the yellow slip of paper Sally had given him. "Only one with this phone number."

"There are two numbers," Troy said, picking up the piece of paper.

"The second one is an emergency number."

Troy reached for the phone.

"What are you going to do?" Petorious questioned.

"Call the emergency number and try and get to the president of the company or some other officer who can tell us if they bought Noonan's company."

"On the Sunday before Christmas?"

"Christmas is on Tuesday," Troy said. "And even on Christmas the world continues to function." He dialed the emergency number.

Petorious poured himself half again as much scotch and then sat down behind the desk. "You'll be lucky if someone answers," he said.

"I'm going to stay on until someone does," Troy answered, settling himself on the edge of the desk.

"You know," Petorious commented, "she's really a very nice person."

Troy nodded. "You know, I figured Noonan for a smooth operator with the women. Sally is making a big mistake if she thinks he cares —" He broke off and held up his hand.

"North Atlantic Industries Emergency Service," a man on the other end said.

"This is Dr. Troy Sims," Troy said. "I'm calling from . . . from White Sands and it is absolutely imperative that I speak with the company's president, or an officer who has an understanding of your company's last bid."

"My God," Petorious exclaimed, "have you got a set of balls!"

Troy grinned at him and speaking into the telephone, he said, "This cannot wait. Your company stands to lose a ten-million-dollar contract."

"Just a minute," the man said.

Troy put his hand over the mouthpiece. "The guy's on the verge of cardiac arrest. He's on again."

"You can reach Mr. Wilder, the company's president, at the Blake in San Francisco. The number is —"

"Please wait while I get a pen and piece of paper," Troy said, taking Petorious's pen out of the holder and placing the yellow paper in front of him. "Now please give me the number." He wrote the number out and as soon as the man finished, he hung up. "You want to speak to the president?" he asked, moving the phone across the desk.

"Give me the number," Petorious said.

Troy slid the piece of paper toward him.

"You don't think I can do it, do you?" Petorious asked.

"That kind of thing comes easier to me than it does to you," Troy said.

Petorious didn't answer but began dialling. "It's only nine o'clock in the morning there," he said.

Troy shrugged.

"Mr. Wilder?" Petorious questioned. He looked up at Troy and whispered, "A woman answered."

"That meets with my approval," Troy whispered back.

"Mr. Wilder, I apologize for disturbing you on a Sunday morning," Petorious said, "but I have in front of me a statement from a Mr. Edward Noonan that you have agreed to purchase his company for some twenty million dollars." He jerked the phone away from his ear and pointed it toward Troy.

"What are you talking about," Wilder shouted. "What twenty million dollars. I never heard of any Noonan!"

"Better let him go back to sleep, or whatever else he was doing," Troy said.

"Thank you," Petorious said and hung up.

Troy grinned at him. "I would have been willing to bet that was a blind alley."

"And I was hoping for Sally's sake that it wasn't," Petorious answered.

"I'm telling you," Troy said, getting to his feet, "that the fucker is a Russian general."

"Even if the photograph turns out to be an exact duplicate of the man, it still could be —"

"C'mon Petorious, just what is it going to take to make you see that something very, very big is going on, or is about to go down, and we just happen to be in the center of it."

"Proof," Petorious shouted, unable to control himself any longer. "Proof that we're not making the proverbial mountain out of the molehill."

"By that time," Troy answered, "we might be dead, or the fucking world blown apart."

"What we don't need," Petorious roared back, "is your vivid imagination running amok." Then taking a deep breath, he said in a lower voice. "Try to keep calm. With any luck we will find out what's really happening."

[12]

Palovich squashed another cigarette in the already full ashtray. "None of this makes sense," he complained to Komarov. "Boris was no more an American agent than you or I." His shirt collar was open. He was tieless and unshaved. His eyes burned from lack of sleep.

Komarov nodded.

"Now all of us are under suspicion," Palovich said, "unless we find out what really happened, or we go along with the Director and create the evidence necessary to satisfy everyone that Boris was either an American or British agent."

"He was a loyal —"

"Yes, yes. You and I know that, and so do several other people," Palovich said. "But we need something to explain what happened." He lit another cigarette and asked, "What do the Americans say?"

"They have video tapes of the incident," Komarov answered. "Their ambassador intends to bring the incident to the attention of his government with a strong recommendation that it be presented to the United Nations' Human Rights Committee."

Palovich blew smoke to one side. He was seated at the head of the conference table and Komarov was on his right.

"I checked on the woman with whom he was living," Komarov said. "She's gone."

"Gone?"

"The neighbors said she left sometime in the late morning in the company of two men."

Palovich raised his eyebrows and pulled a piece of tobacco from his lip.

"The police know nothing about it. I checked our people and they know nothing."

Palovich rubbed the side of his face. It was two o'clock in the morning. He had been called back to the office at eight o'clock the previous night and the way things were going, he probably would not be able to go home for several more hours. "Not our people and not the police," he said finally.

"Foreign agents?" Komarov volunteered.

"Certainly a possibility," Palovich answered.

"Why would they take the woman?"

"Why? Why this? Why that?" Palovich exploded. "How do I know *why*? I only know that we must come up with some answers."

"The Marine Captain in charge of security at the American Embassy said that the car's license plate was covered."

"So?"

"The car was the same kind we use."

Again Palovich rubbed the side of his face. He was about to ask if the embassy guards could describe the driver, or anyone else in the car, when the phone rang. He shook his head and with the cigarette dangling out of his mouth, he went back into his office. "Comrade Palovich here," he said, picking up the phone.

"Piligin," the voice on the other end said.

Palovich immediately recognized the name.

Without preliminaries, Piligin said, "Check Comrade Gargarin's army record for any association with Gorsky."

Palovich removed the cigarette from his mouth. Piligin wasn't the kind of man whom even he, a deputy director, questioned. "When do you want the information?" he asked.

"As soon as possible," Piligin answered.

There was a click on other end of the line.

Palovich put the phone down. That Piligin already had word of Gargarin's death surprised, even shocked him. He put the cigarette back in his mouth and was about to return to the conference table, when the phone rang again. He picked it up and before he could answer, a man said, "The woman is dead."

"What!" Palovich exclaimed. The cigarette dropped to the floor. The line went dead.

He put the phone down, stooped to pick up the cigarette and shouted, "Alexei, get in here."

"Coming."

Palovich was already behind his desk. "The woman is dead. That was the second call. The first was from Comrade Piligin telling me to check Boris's army career for any ties to Gorsky." He switched on his desktop terminal and quickly typed in Gargarin's ID, followed by his own, and asked for "All military service giving units, dates and unit commanders."

"Who called about the woman?" Komarov asked.

"Anonymous," Palovich growled, waiting impatiently for the information to come up on the screen. Then suddenly it was there.

Data not available.

"What the fuck does that mean?" Palovich shouted. "I know for a fact he was in the Two Forty-Fifth Armored Infantry Division." He quickly typed in the division's number, followed by his own ID and a request to check Gargarin's name against an officer's roster for the previous five years.

"Where's the woman's body?" Komarov asked.

"The caller never said," Palovich answered, "but I'm sure it will turn up in the next few days."

"She was a beautiful woman," Komarov said.

"You never mentioned that you knew her."

"Boris introduced us two weeks ago."

The message came up.

DATA NOT AVAILABLE.

"Something is wrong," he said, picking up the phone and punching out the phone number of the KGB's central computer office. The moment someone came on the line, Palovich identified himself and said, "I want to speak with the Comrade Director now."

Within moments a woman said, "Comrade Helena Krosk speaking. How may I help you, Comrade Director Palovich?"

"I cannot access any information on either Comrade Boris Gargarin or the Two Forty-Fifth Armored Infantry Division."

"Please wait a moment," she said, "and I will check."

Palovich put his hand over the mouthpiece. "I'm beginning to hate these damn computers."

"Can't do without them now," Alexei responded.

"Comrade Director," Krosk said, "request for information about the status of the Two Forty-Fifth Division was made at zero eight ten yesterday by Comrade Boris Gargarin."

"Was he able to access the information?"

"I cannot answer that," Krosk said, "but immediately after his request we had a system crash."

"A system crash!" Palovich exclaimed, almost getting to his feet. "You mean all the information on the system is —"

"Nothing like that," she said, cutting him off. "We lost some information and we are in the process of putting that information back on the mainframe."

"Ah, then you can access the information from a back-up system," Palovich responded, somewhat relieved.

"It's not quite as simple as that."

"I need that information, Comrade," Palovich suddenly shouted. "I need that information now. Have your people stop whatever they're doing and get that information for me. Do you understand, Comrade? I am not asking, I am *giving* you an order."

"Yes, I understand," she answered in a tremulous voice.

Palovich slammed the phone into its cradle. "Gargarin requested information on the Two Forty-Fifth before he went off duty," Palovich said, rubbing his temples. He felt a migraine coming on. "Now why the hell would he do that?"

"I'm sure he told me that it was the last unit —"

Palovich stood up, walked across the room to a bookshelf and took down a red book. "We've been going at this from Boris's service. Let's try it from Gorsky's." He dropped the book on the desk and opened it to the index. "Page eighty-two," he said, flipping through the pages. "Gorsky, complete with a photograph. Units commanded: the Two Forty-Fifth, the Twenty-First Assault Team, the Sixty-Sixth Tank Division, the Eighty-Second Infantry, the Forty-Fourth Air Assault Division, the Twenty-Seventh Infantry and his last command in Afghanistan." He looked at Komarov. "Well, we have the connection between them, don't we?"

"It seems tenuous, at best."

With a nod, Palovich agreed, then he said, "We also have more questions. Was Boris killed because he knew something about Gorsky and the Two Forty-Fifth that he wasn't supposed to know? If that was why he was killed, then it was done by people who are still protecting Gorsky. Or was he killed by foreign agents because he was no longer of any use to them?"

"I don't think foreign agents were involved," Komarov responded.

"I don't think so either," Palovich said. He lit another cigarette and leaned back in his chair. "Alexei, we have to be very, very careful with this one, or we'll wind up like Boris."

Morosov entered the atrium-like lobby of the building on York Avenue where Helen Peters lived and was stopped by the doorman. "Who are you visiting?"

"Detective Callahan," Morosov responded, flashing his gold badge. "Just tell me the number of Miss Peters's apartment."

"Is she in trouble?"

"The apartment number," Morosov demanded.

"Fourteen ten," the man answered.

"Don't pick up that phone and warn her," Morosov said, "or I'll bust you for interfering with the law."

The doorman shook his head.

"The door," Morosov said.

The doorman pressed the control button and the door to the inner hallway opened.

Morosov rode the elevator to the fourteenth floor. He wasn't exactly sure what he expected to get from Peters. He hoped she might be able to tell him where Gorsky was in Albany. If he knew that, he'd be able to be on his way into Canada within forty-eight to seventy-two hours.

The elevator doors opened and he stepped into the brown carpeted hallway. Number fourteen ten was to his right. From the way the numbers went, he guessed it was probably in the corner. He reached the door and rang the bell. Chimes sounded inside.

He heard footsteps; then the door opened to the three- or four-centimeter length of the safety chain. The young woman behind it was blond, with gray eyes. She wore a white terrycloth bathrobe. From the way it hugged the contours of her body, he was reasonably certain there was nothing under it. "Lieutenant Callahan," he said, showing her the badge and his ID. "I have a few questions to ask you." He didn't know whether he was speaking to Miss Peters or her roommate, but he wanted to get out of the hallway and into the apartment.

"Is that why you weren't announced?" she asked.

Morosov nodded. "May I come in?"

She undid the safety chain and opened the door. "We can talk in the living room," she said.

Morosov opened his coat and sat down. "Ms. Peters —"

"I'm not Helen Peters," the woman said, settling on the sofa and drawing her legs under her. "My name is Kari Hanson. Helen is my roommate. Did anyone ever tell you, Detective Callahan, that you have bedroom eyes?"

"Will Ms. Peters —"

"She's visiting her brother for the holidays," Hanson said.

"Would you know where?"

Hanson shrugged. "Listen, honey, I don't ask her what she does, or where she goes and she doesn't ask me. But I know her brother is some sort of brain and teaches in a small college near Kingston." She changed her position. The top of the robe opened, baring her left breast to its nipple.

"Did she leave a telephone number, or an address?" Morosov asked, trying not to look at her breast.

She pointed to a desk just visible through an open door. "It's probably there in that mess of papers. But I can't really stop and look for it now. If you come back after Christmas, Helen will be here and you won't have to worry about having her brother's phone number."

"I really would appreciate it if you looked," Morosov said.

She shook her head. "I hate bothering with papers."

"Did she happen to mention someone named Noonan?" Morosov questioned. "Edward Noonan?"

"Nah. We just share this place. We don't share anything else." She giggled. "Now take you, for instance. I wouldn't share you with her. No way."

Morosov stood up. The way she slowly untangled her legs gave him a full view of her crotch. "I'm sorry I bothered you," he said.

"Hey, I wouldn't be sorry if you bothered me even more," she told him. "I mean, I'm totally alone and —"

"I must return to the precinct," Morosov said, beginning to feel the slow ignition in his groin.

"Afterwards. Tell me when."

Morosov shook his head.

"Hey man, I'm not asking you to marry me. All I want is a good bang. I give as good as I get "

"I don't think I'd be —"

She pointed her finger at him. "You swing the other way? Christ, every time I meet a guy that I really go for, he turns out to be married, gay, or some other goddamn thing."

"I'm sorry," Morosov said, heading for the door.

"Listen, man, just to see if you like it, try it. I mean, I've been told that I really give good head."

Morosov put his hand on the knob, twisted it and opened the door. "You sure that Ms. Peters's brother lives somewhere near Albany?"

"Yeah, yeah and I'm sure his name is James Petorious. But where does that leave us?"

"Nowhere, I'm afraid," Morosov said, stepping into the hallway.

She followed him to the door. "Hey man, look at me!" And she opened her robe, then touched herself. "When was the last time you saw a real blond pussy?"

"A long, long time ago," Morosov answered

quietly and walking slowly back to the elevator, he found himself thinking about Tatyana.

"Let me help, Mom," Nathan said, coming into the kitchen just as his mother was taking a large rib roast out of the oven.

She gave him the padded blue gloves. "Put it on the counter," she directed.

He inhaled deeply, closed his eyes and said, "Someday I'm going to learn how to make these wonderful things."

She laughed, "Well, you always used to help me cook when you were a boy. I bet you remember more than you think you do."

He put the roast on the counter and stepping back, he said, "Now that's worth a full-color spread in *Gourmet*."

"Have you thought about the party I want to give?" his mother asked.

"Yes."

"Well, is it all right?"

He put his arms around her. "It's all right. Deirdre and I have gotten to know each other somewhat better."

She gave him a quizzical look.

He grinned at her. "Mom, you're blushing," he chided.

"I knew there was something different about you, but I couldn't put my finger on it," she said, gently pushing him away.

He twisted himself into an absurd position. "Now if you told me it showed," he laughed, "I'd believe you."

"I —"

The phone rang.

"I'll get it," he said, already at the phone. He said nothing.

"Commander Brian Scott," the voice on the other end said.

"I just wanted to be sure," Nathan answered, noticing that his mother suddenly looked worried.

"There's a packet waiting for you with the duty officer at Fort Hamilton in Brooklyn. I couldn't get a courier, but I have a friend who needed some air time in a chopper."

"Thanks."

"Before the DO gives you the packet," Scott said, "he'll ask if you were ever a Boy Scout and you will answer that you made Eagle."

Nathan smiled. "Do I sign for it?" he asked.

"No way," Scott answered. "Just take it and go."

"Anything else out of Moscow?" Nathan asked, turning away from his mother and lowering his voice.

"Strange things are happening there. Ever hear of an agent named Boris Gargarin? He came up through the army and was working as an aide to Palovich, the Deputy Director of the Second Directorate."

"Name doesn't ring a bell."

"I didn't think it would. The poor bastard was strictly internal."

"What the hell is so strange about that?"

"He was missing for almost twelve hours, then he tries to make it into our Embassy and is run down by a car. Now get this, the car not only jumped the curb to hit him, but then it backed over him to finish the job. The Embassy has tapes of the incident."

"Was he one of ours?"

"No way," Scott answered. "Our people have no idea why he was coming to the Embassy. The best guess is that he had gotten involved in something he couldn't handle and by coming over to us, he'd get out from under it. He was living with a woman, but she's missing too."

"He might have killed her."

"Might have," Scott said.

"Listen, do you have a number where I can reach you when you're not on duty?" Nathan asked, motioning to his mother that he needed paper and pencil.

Scott hesitated.

"Something real big —" he started to say, taking the pencil and piece of paper from his mother.

"You know the area code. My home number is 624-2727 and when I'm not there, or in the office, you can reach me at 843-1066. If a woman answers, tell her who you are."

"Got it." He folded the piece of paper into quarters and placed it in his wallet.

"I don't know what you're into," Scott said, "but whatever it is, be careful."

"Thanks, I will. Like I said, I owe you a big one." Nathan put the phone back in its cradle, then announced, "I have to go out for a few hours. I'll be back in time for dinner."

"Where are you going?" his mother asked, following him into the hallway.

Deirdre came down the stairs.

"He's going out," his mother said, looking at her.

"I have to go," he told them as he put on his shoulder holster.

"I'll go with you," Deirdre said.

He was about to say no, but changed his mind. The less he made of it, the calmer everyone else would be. "Okay," he replied. "I'm only going over to Brooklyn to pick up something."

"Good, I'll get to see something of Brooklyn," Deirdre said cheerfully.

Still holding the *New York Times Book Review*, his father came up from his study. "Is everyone going out?" he asked innocently.

"Dad, I have to go to Fort Hamilton to get something," Steve explained. "I'll be back at the very most in a couple of hours."

"I'm going with him," Deirdre said.

Mr. Nathan nodded and looking at his wife, he asked, "You're not going, are you?"

She shook her head.

"Well now, I'm glad everyone has something to do." He turned and went down the stairs to his study.

Steve found himself smiling. "Dad gets like that when he's working," he said. "He's in another world."

His mother went to the door with them. "Take care."

Steve kissed her on the forehead. "Just have dinner ready when we come home," he said.

"It'll be on the table," his mother answered.

Deirdre kissed his mother. "I'll take care of him," she promised.

"The car is at the bottom of the hill," he said, taking hold of Deirdre's hand.

"My God, it's cold!" she said.

"A bit colder than it usually is this time of year," he answered. Then suddenly it occurred to him that he knew absolutely nothing about Deirdre. He had no idea where she was born and raised, where she went to school, or anything about her family.

They settled in the car.

"This, I know, is a telephone," she said, pointing to it, "but what's the other thing?"

"A special radio," Nathan said, moving away from the curb.

"I'm impressed."

"I told Mom it's okay to have that party on Christmas Day," he said, attempting to keep conversation between them light. He eased the car into the center lane on the service roadway that ran parallel to the highway.

Deirdre nodded. "If you think it's all right, then it's all right.

He put his hand on her knee. "I think I could fall in love with you if you let me."

"I certainly am not going to do anything to stop you," she answered with a smile. "Besides, I like family parties. Where I come from —"

"Where *do* you come from?" Nathan asked, turning on to the highway and slowing almost to a stop before he could get into the right lane.

"Kentucky. A farm not far from Cantonville, Ohio."

"A farm girl?"

"Born and raised."

"I was born in Brooklyn," he said, "but my folks moved out to Staten Island when I was a couple of years old. I graduated from New Dorp High School and then from Wagner College."

"My God, what bridge is this?" she asked, as they approached the Verrazano Narrows Bridge.

"It's named after the Italian explorer who first sailed into the harbor." Then he said, "So tell me about your family. Any brothers or sisters?"

"A brother, William and a sister, Katharine — Kate, for short," she said. "Kate lives in New

Jersey. She's older than I. And William, or Bill, is a fighter pilot in the Navy. He's two years younger than I. But both my parents come from large families, and I have lots of aunts, uncles and cousins."

"I'm an only child," Nathan said. "My father has a brother and a sister and so has my mother. Among the four of them I have three cousins, all of whom are older than I am by at least five years."

Deirdre laughed. "Some of mine are still in diapers."

"We're in Brooklyn," Nathan announced.

Deirdre looked out of the window.

"This section is named after the fort," Nathan said. "At one time, during the Civil War, there was a chain between the fort on this side and the one in Staten Island." He turned off the highway at the 92nd Street exit. "The neighborhood around here is middle-class and there's a mixture of Scandinavian types and Italians living here. Maybe I'll take you for a short drive on the Belt Parkway."

"What's that?"

"A highway that runs along the south shore of Brooklyn," he said stopping for a red light.

"You know," she said, "some of my people are on what we call vacations."

"I wish I was on one now," Nathan answered, putting the car in motion.

"Paid for by the Federal Government," she said. "Some for two, three and as much as five years."

Realizing what she was talking about, he asked, "What are they in for?"

"Making whiskey," she answered.

He laughed. "You ever make whiskey?"

"Never," she answered. "But I sure know how."

"You don't care about —"

"Not a bit," he told her, shaking his head. "But just don't tell my folks."

"Never," she said, relieved.

Nathan turned in at the fort's main gate and, stopping for the MP, he pulled out his ID. "To see the Duty Officer," he said.

"Parking is to the right of the Headquarters Building," the young soldier said, waving him on.

"I shouldn't be long," Nathan said, as he maneuvered into an empty space and put the shift in neutral and pulled up the emergency brake.

"Aren't you going to take your keys?" Deirdre asked.

"Keep the engine running," he said, opening the car door.

She put her hand on his arm "That's for quick getaways."

"It's also to keep you warm," he said, kissing her on the nose. He got out of the car and closing the door behind him, he walked toward the entrance. Deirdre's background couldn't have been more different from his own, but he wasn't interested in her background.

Nathan entered the building and asked the first soldier he saw for the DO's office.

"Go to the end of the hallway, hang a left. It's the first office in front of the main entrance. You can't miss it. It has a sign outside on the wall."

"Thanks," Nathan said and in less than a minute he was in the office. A young captain looked up at him.

"You have a package for me from Commander Scott," Nathan said.

The captain examined him for a moment and asked, "Were you ever a Boy Scout?"

"Yes, I was an Eagle Scout," Nathan answered.

The captain nodded and opened the middle drawer. The phone rang.

"Excuse me," the Captain said, picked up the phone and identified himself, listened for a moment, then looking very puzzled, he said, "It's for you, sir."

Nathan took the hold of the phone and put it to his ear. The line was dead. He frowned.

"Anything wrong?" the Captain asked.

"No," Nathan answered, putting the phone down.

"This is yours," the Captain said, handing him the package.

Nathan thanked him and hurried out of the building to the car.

"Get what you want?" Deirdre asked.

"I haven't looked," he said tightly. "Hold this," he told her, giving her the package. He backed out of the space, made a fast turn and drove the speed limit to the gate.

The MP waved him out.

Nathan made a left turn. "We're going to make that little drive on the Belt," he said. "Not far from here there's a place to park. I want to look at what I have and then destroy it." He stopped for a light and checked the rear-view mirror and both the side-view mirrors.

"Expecting someone?" Deirdre asked.

"They know I'm here," he said.

"They?"

"I don't know who *they* are," he said.

"Just what are you into?"

Nathan didn't answer, but he reached over to the radio and switched it on. "There's nothing but Christmas carols," he commented. "After a while it's just plain boring." He turned it off.

"So now you hate Christmas carols?" she asked.

He made a left and found himself on Fort Hamilton Parkway.

"If it's that important, don't you think I should know?"

"The less you know, the safer you'll be," he said, turning on to the Belt Parkway.

"And how safe will you be?" she asked, gently touching his arm. "There can't be any chemistry between us if you're not here to make it happen."

He glanced at her. "I'll do everything I can to make sure I'm here," Nathan said and slowing, he turned into the parking area just before they reached the Bay Parkway exit. Because of the weather, it was empty. He stopped, but kept the engine running.

Without a word, Deirdre handed him the envelope.

Nathan cut the seal with his pocket knife. There were two three by five enlargements. Morosov's came from a video tape. Gorsky's picture was a photocopied blowup of a photograph in a book. He knew all of the information on Morosov's flimsy, but practically everything on Gorsky was new.

"Who are they?" Deirdre asked.

"This one," Nathan answered, showing her the picture of Morosov, "is —" He was going to say an old adversary, but instead, he said, "He's kind of a friend."

"I don't understand."

"A couple of years ago in East Berlin he had the chance to kill me but —"

"My God," she shivered, "you talk about it as if it was the most ordinary thing in the world."

"No," Nathan shook his head, "it was far from ordinary."

"Who's the other one?"

"A Russian general."

"The man you're trying to find?"

"No questions," Nathan said, tearing up the flimsies.

Deirdre looked out the rear window. "A car is coming into the parking area."

Nathan floored the accelerator and the car leaped forward.

The other car followed.

"What the hell is happening?" Deirdre screamed.

"Take everything on my lap, tear it up and throw it out the window."

She rolled down the window, tore the photographs and flimsies into small pieces and dumped them out.

Nathan checked the rear-view mirror. The car was coming up on them fast. Cutting in front of another car, he moved into the center lane. The angry driver gave him the horn.

The other car switched lanes.

Nathan saw an opening and swung back into the right lane, then he went up onto the shoulder. "The streets would be better," he said tersely and turned back onto the highway.

Deirdre looked out the rear window again. "They're almost in back of us!"

"Get hold of the wheel!"

"What?"

"Hold the wheel."

"At ninety miles an hour?" she shrieked.

"Hold it, or we'll be killed," he ordered, letting go of it.

Deirdre grabbed the wheel. "I can't hold it," she cried.

"Hold it," he yelled, easing his foot off the accelerator. "Hold it!" He yanked his gun out of the holster. Sweat was pouring down his back and soaking through his shirt.

The other car pulled closer.

"Now, you bastards!" he shouted, flicked the safety off and pointed the gun at the driver of the other car. He took a deep breath and held it for as long as it took to squeeze off two rounds.

The car veered to the left and smashed into the guard rail on the opposite side of the highway where it was hit by two oncoming cars.

Nathan put the revolver back in the holster. "I'll take it," he said heavily, putting his hands on the steering wheel.

Terrified, Deirdre didn't let go.

Nathan pried her fingers off the wheel. "It's over for now," he said.

She shook her head. "I can't believe —"

"Believe it," he said. "They would have killed us."

"But why?" she cried. "Why?"

"Because I know what Robin knew before they killed him."

"But you said he was in an accident —"

He glanced at her. "He was killed."

"I —" She turned toward the window. "That makes it even worse."

Nathan didn't answer. He turned off at the Coney Island Avenue exit and stopped for a red light.

They could hear the wail of sirens from the Belt. The light went green. Nathan turned right, switched on the radio and worked the dial.

"My God, he's talking about what just happened!" Deirdre exclaimed, looking at him.

"I tuned it to the police frequency," he said. "So far no one identified this car. I have to warn my parents and arrange to meet my father with our clothes."

"Will your dad be able to —"

"He'll handle it," Nathan said, looking for a telephone booth. He drove several more blocks before he spotted one and stopped next to it. "Keep listening to the radio," he told her, as he got out of the car. He deposited a quarter, then dialed his home number. After two rings his mother answered. "Mom, put Dad on. I have to speak to him."

"Are you coming home for dinner?" she asked.

"Something has come up. Dad will tell you about it."

After a few seconds, his father said, "I'm here."

"Dad, I want you to pack my clothes and whatever Deirdre has and meet me somewhere in Manhattan."

"What's going on?"

"No questions," he told him. "Just do what I ask."

"Where do you want to meet?"

"Where would be a good place for you?"

"I'll go any place you want me to," his father said.

"B. Dalton's, in the Village. It's on Eighth Street and Sixth Avenue."

"I know it."

"Good. Don't use your car. Have a neighbor drive you. That's very important, Dad. I don't want anyone to ID the car. Put our luggage in his car as soon as possible."

"Is the house being watched?" his father questioned.

"Please deposit another ten cents for three minutes," a computerized voice said.

Steve shoved the coin into the slot, "I don't know. Maybe. But if it's not, it will be very soon."

"The telephones?"

"They're clean; I checked when I came back from Washington the second time."

"Do you need any money?"

"A hundred or two would do fine," Steve answered.

"I'll see you at ten in front of the bookstore," his father said.

"And Dad, tell Mom I'm sorry about the dinner," Steve said. "Tell her I'll probably miss Christmas, too."

"I think she knows that by now," his father answered.

"Probably," Steve said. "Kiss her for me." He put the phone on the hook and returned to the car.

"Everything all right?" Deirdre asked.

Nathan pulled away from the curb. "Yeah. My father will meet us tonight. But I could tell the two of them are badly shaken."

"You didn't think they wouldn't be?" she asked.

He didn't answer.

"So what do we do?" Deirdre asked.

"I'm going to take you to a hotel for the night. In the morning you'll fly back to Washington. I'll call you when this is over."

"No way," she answered.

He looked at her. "What do mean, 'No way'?"

"I'm not going back to Washington," she said. "I came here not to be alone and I'm not going to be alone."

Nathan eased over to the curb and stopped. "Deirdre, you saw what happened on the highway —"

She shook her head. "Yes, and I was scared shit-less, but how do you think I'd be in Washington knowing you were here? I'll tell you how I'd be: a basket case, that's how."

"Better that than dead."

"Either I stay with you," she said defiantly, "or we end whatever we have between us here and now. I'm not going spend the next few days being a basket case for you or for them. I want to be with you. Whoever *they* are, by now they know who I am. How safe do you think I'd be in Washington? *They* probably think I know everything you know."

"I don't —"

"I mean it, Steve," Deirdre said firmly. "If you make me go back to Washington, it will be over between us."

Nathan put the car into neutral and pulled up the emergency brake. "I can't let that happen," he said, putting his arm around her shoulders and drawing her to him. "You know I can't." He kissed her.

"I don't want it to."

"After we meet my father, we'll drive up to Alba-ny," he said.

"As long as I'm with you, I don't care where we go."

Nathan kissed her again. "Let's go to a hotel for a few hours," he said.

"That's the best idea you've had since we turned off the highway."

"For now, it's the *only* idea I have," he said.

"I always put weight on over the holiday season," Helen commented. "And in a place like this I just pig out."

Elly laughed. "This is the first time I've been to a family-style restaurant."

"This one is on me," Troy said, looking at Petorious.

"I won't argue with that," Petorious said, lighting his pipe. He looked around. "The last restaurant I went to that was anything like this was in the Pennsylvania Dutch country, around Lancaster."

"You know," Troy began, "I was thinking about the telephone call."

"Troy, not now!" Elly said.

"Better let him have his say," Petorious said, "or he'll feel deprived of his right to free speech."

"I don't know about you people," Troy said, "but I have this feeling that something terrible is going to happen."

"First," Petorious responded, "what is this catastrophe that you see coming?"

"I don't know."

"Second, what would you have us do to prevent it?" Petorious asked.

Troy looked down at the table and made a furrow with his thumbnail in the red checked table cloth.

"Surely, you must have some idea," Petorious pressed.

Troy nodded and said, "None of you have to do anything. I'll do it."

"All right, tell us. I can't wait to hear."

"Somehow, I'm going to get into that conference room and see for myself exactly what the Board has been doing," Troy said.

"You're not serious!" Elly asked.

"Don't any of you understand what's happening?"

Petorious took the pipe out of his mouth. "None of us do," he said, "and from the way you're talking neither do you."

"Something —"

"Elly, do you realize your friend might be certifiably insane? He's already charged with arson and now he wants to add the charge of breaking and entering to his record."

"He's right, Troy," Elly said.

"I'll tell you this, young man," Petorious warned, "if you go through with your harebrained scheme, I'll have nothing more to do with you. Do you understand what I just said?"

"What's the matter, Professor, are you suddenly turning chicken?" Troy challenged.

"Goddamn you!" Petorious exclaimed. "How dare you say that to me? I went out on a limb — Christ, you're just a spoiled, snotnosed kid who still thinks he's playing some kind of game."

"What the hell do *you* think it is? Go ahead, tell me."

Petorious's face was very red. He shook his head. "Listen, I don't know any more than you do, but I know enough not to go off half-cocked."

"Jamie," Helen said, touching her brother's arm, "please. People are looking at us."

"You were released into my custody," Petorious said. "You go anywhere near that conference room and I personally will bring you back to the jail."

"Oh, that's just great!" Troy snorted, leaping to his feet and rushing away from the table.

"Go after him," Helen ordered Elly, "and bring him back."

Elly nodded and left the table.

"Both of you are behaving badly," Helen admonished her brother.

"He wants to rush in and knock Noonan over the head," Petorious protested. "I don't have any patience for his craziness. He's a menace to himself and to all of us."

"He knows something is wrong and wants to know what it is," Helen said.

"So do I. But breaking into the conference room won't give us the answer, it simply will put him into more trouble."

"Elly is coming back with him," Helen said.

Petorious uttered a deep sigh. "I don't want him to get into any more trouble."

"I'm sure he knows that," Helen replied.

Troy sat down. "I'm sorry," he said. "I —"

Petorious offered his hand. "You don't have to say any more." They shook hands.

"Tomorrow, if you can identify Noonan, we'll begin to think about what our next move should be. Agreed?"

"Agreed," Troy answered reluctantly.

[13]

"Mr. Callahan, you have room twenty-three," the desk clerk said, handing Morosov his key. "It's the last room in the rear. Have a nice stay."

Morosov smiled and asked, "Could you tell me how to get to the National Car Rental office on Pine Street?"

The young man pursed his lips, then said, "When you go out of the parking lot, turn left, go to the next traffic light, make a right turn and just keep on going until you hit Pine Street. It's about four miles from where you make the turn."

"Thanks." Morosov left the office and drove around to the far side of the motel, where his room was located. He unlocked the door, opened it and carried a small, soft bag and a brown leather attaché case into the room. He switched on the lights, closed the door and drew the curtains before he removed his gloves, coat, hat and jacket.

Then he put the attaché case on the bed, dialed in the combination that opened it and took out the 9mm automatic, its shoulder holster and two clips of ammunition. He closed the attaché case, scrambled the setting and placed the case on the shelf in the closet.

Morosov looked around the room. The rooms in the Howard Johnson motels were all identical, even to the orange and blue color scheme. But this one, because of the holiday season, had a plastic holly wreath on one of the walls. He smiled and went into the bathroom to wash his face. The drive from the city had taken just under four hours. He'd had very little sleep and was beginning to feel extremely weary. "Another couple of hours," he said aloud, looking at himself in the mirror, "and then something to eat and a good night's sleep."

He walked back into the room, slipped into the shoulder holster, put his jacket, coat and hat on. He left the room, locked it and went to his car.

In minutes Morosov was at the desk of the rental agency. The young woman behind the desk wore a blue skirt, a white shirt blouse with a blue jacket over it and a small white cap with a blue bill. The name of the company was stitched in gold-colored thread across her right breast. Under it was a name tag with *Maria* printed on it.

"May I help you?" Maria asked.

"Yes, perhaps you can," Morosov said, taking out his police badge and ID.

Maria stopped smiling.

"Were you on duty here last Wednesday?" Morosov asked.

"Yes."

Morosov took out a picture of Gorsky. "Did you see this man?"

Maria looked at the picture.

"This is very important," Morosov said.

She shook her head. "I don't really remember. So many people come here every day. Maybe Victor did."

"Who's Victor?"

"He was here part of the day."

"Where does he live?"

The door to the office opened and a well-dressed man in his thirties walked out. The name on his tag was Harris.

"This man wants to see Vic," Maria said.

Harris came straight to the desk. "I'm the manager. What seems to be the problem here?"

"Detective Lieutenant Callahan, New York Police Department," Morosov said. "Mr. Harris, I'm looking for this man," he said, showing him Gorsky's picture. "I understand from this young woman that Victor was on duty with her part of last Wednesday."

"Is Victor in any kind of trouble?" Harris asked.

"Absolutely not. The man I want is the one in the photograph," Morosov said.

Harris nodded, handed the photo of Gorsky back to Morosov and said, "Victor has gone skiing for a few days. He won't be back until after New Year's."

Morosov pocketed the photograph and asked, "Would it be too much trouble to check Wednesday's records for the names of all of the people who returned cars that originally came from New York?"

Harris nodded. "Maria can run it up on the

computer," he said and looking intently at Morosov, he asked, "What did the man do?"

"He killed someone," Morosov answered.

Harris paled and looking toward Maria, he asked, "Do you have it on the screen yet?"

"Two," she answered. "A Mr. Downs and a Mr. Noonan."

"Downs and Noonan," Morosov repeated, then he smiled at Harris. "Thanks for your help."

"No problem," Harris said. "Which one was it?"

"Downs," he lied and returned to his car. He drove back in the direction of the motel. He decided to stop at a diner he'd seen on the way over.

He pulled into the parking area behind the diner. It was crowded with cars and at the far end he could see a half-dozen very large rigs. He found an empty space, eased into it and putting the car in *park*, he switched off the ignition.

Inside, the diner was crowded, hot, noisy and full of delicious smells.

"A table or the counter?" a dark-eyed, raven-haired hostess asked brightly.

"A table," Morosov said, then suddenly changed his mind. "Ah, I'll sit at the counter."

She nodded and walked away

Morosov sat down. The place was already set with a napkin, fork, knife, teaspoon and a glass of water.

"Menu?" the waiter asked.

"Yes."

The waiter handed him a large, blue, plastic-covered menu. "I'll be back in a few minutes to take your order. Do you want coffee while you're waiting?"

"Yes, thank you," Morosov answered, his eyes taking in the waiter's slight build, black moustache. He watched him go to the coffee urn and fill a cup and put four small plastic containers of cream in the saucer.

The waiter returned with the coffee, "Has it started to snow again?"

"No," said Morosov. He thought the man looked to be about forty.

The waiter smiled at him and then suddenly speaking Russian, he said, "Do you understand what I'm saying?"

Morosov's heart skipped a beat and started to race. He could feel the sweat start on his back. He opened the menu and pretended to study it. The man was either an emigré or, like himself, KGB. If he was an emigré, he was probably a Jew. If he was KGB —

The man tried again and said, "I came here five years ago from Kiev."

Morosov looked straight at him. "I'll decide in a few minutes," he said, controlling a sigh of relief. If he'd come from Kiev, he was certain to be one of the Jews allowed to leave. If he was KGB, Piligin would have told him.

Disappointed, the man moved away to wait on another customer.

Morosov opened the menu, which ran to six pages. He settled for a bowl of mushroom and barley soup and broiled filet of salmon with carrots and peas and a baked potato.

He ate slowly, trying not think about Gorsky. Now and then he'd hear the high-pitched laughter of a woman, or the deeper sound of a man's and he'd glance in the direction of the sound just to look at a happy face. As he ate, Morosov reflected that this would be his last assignment. When he returned, he was going to resign and do something else. He'd move south and, perhaps, become a tourist guide. After all, he was fluent in several languages.

Two truckers sat down on the empty stools on his left. The taller of the two said, "That makes two shootings in Brooklyn in less than twenty-four hours. But this one happened on the Belt. Besides the guy in the car that got wasted, the man next to him was killed and four other people were critically injured."

"I heard about it on the radio," the other man said. "Cops say dere's no connection between the two. Dey got somein' on the gunman, though. He was wid a broad and drivin' a car wid Washington plates."

The conversation stopped when the waiter asked them if they wanted coffee.

Morosov looked down at his plate. He had only eaten about half of the salmon, some of the carrots and peas and very little of the baked potato, but he was no longer hungry. "Check," he told the waiter when the man passed him.

"Dessert?" the waiter asked.

"No, just the check," Morosov said and asked, "Where are the telephones?"

"Two before you get to the rest rooms, and there's a booth outside to the left of the door," the waiter said, putting a check face down on the counter.

Picking it up, Morosov looked at it, then doubled the tax and left slightly more than that on the counter for the waiter. As soon as he was outside, he telephoned Piligin.

"I just heard about the shooting on the Belt Parkway," he said, as soon as Piligin was on the line.

"Could be the same people who came after you," Piligin said.

"Who was it?"

"No idea."

"Any educated guesses?"

"None. What do you think?"

"I don't know. I don't even know who tried to get me."

"Where are you now?"

"Albany," Morosov said, hung up and went to the car. By the time he turned into the motel's parking area, he remembered Kari Hanson mentioning that Helen's brother taught at a small college near Kingston. He recalled having seen the exit sign for Kingston about an hour before he reached Albany.

Morosov parked, went to the desk and asked the clerk, "Would you happen to know if there were any small colleges around Kingston?"

"Broom is the only one I can think of," the clerk answered.

Morosov repeated the name; then with a smile, he asked, "Is it near Kingston?"

The man shook his head. "It's on the other side of the Hudson, just outside the town of Red Hook."

"You wouldn't happen to have a phone book for Red Hook?" Morosov asked.

"You should be able to find Broom's number in this directory," the clerk said, handing him a directory.

Morosov nodded, took the directory and sat down in a chair next to the window. In a matter of moments, he found Petorious's phone number and address. He quickly memorized both and returned the directory to the desk.

"Find what you wanted?" the clerk asked, coming out of the office.

"Yes, thank you."

"Calling there from here is a toll call. It would be cheaper to make it from the outside than from your room."

"Thank you again," Morosov said. "And I'd appreciate it if you would tell me where the nearest booth is."

"Go out of the parking lot and make a right turn. About five miles down the road there's a shopping mall. There are booths there."

Morosov thought for a moment, "I've had enough driving for one day. I'll use the phone in my room. And again, thanks for the help."

Before he even considered making the call, Morosov showered, smoked his pipe and watched the seven o'clock news, which covered the shooting on the Belt Parkway. There was a picture of the wrecked car and the announcer said, "This latest shooting occurred not more than five hundred feet from Bay Parkway and in sight of the Verrazano Bridge. The police have been told by various witnesses that a man and a woman were in the car from which the shots were fired. This is Chester B. Howard, for CBS, New York."

Having seen what he wanted to, Morosov continued to change channels until he found a western and then he tried to relax. But there was something about the location of the shooting that gnawed away at him . . . something he should know.

For no particular reason, Morosov waited until nine o'clock to phone Helen Peters.

The phone rang four times before a man answered.

"Is Ms. Helen Peters there?" Morosov asked.

"Helen, you have a phone call," the man called out. Then he said, "Please wait a few moments. She'll be right down."

"Yes," Morosov answered, hoping he had finally located someone who might be able to tell him something about Gorsky.

"Hello," Helen said.

"Thank you," Morosov said and hung up. Tomorrow, he intended to pay Ms. Peters a visit. But now he wanted to sleep.

Cradling his head in his arms on the top of the desk, Palovich managed a few minutes of sleep before the ringing of the phone disturbed the dream he was having. He'd been transported back into his childhood. Then, suddenly, the phone turned into the terrifying shrieks of the Stuka dive bombers. He awoke abruptly and for a fraction of an instant, before he realized the phone was ringing, he remembered his mother screaming.

"Comrade Director Palovich," he growled into the phone, looking at his watch. It was 0630 hours.

"I have the information you requested," a man said.

"I'm listening." Palovich said, instantly recognizing the voice as belonging to Comrade Sergeant Brodavitch, an undercover operator assigned to Army Headquarters.

"All of the numbers you gave me are currently involved in the training exercise code named Hammer Strike. They are not operating together. By that, I mean, in one single geographic area."

Palovich made a brief humming sound.

"The original exercise was planned by Comrade General Gorsky some two years ago and approved eighteen months ago."

"Why the time lag?"

"Changes were made on the original plan."

"Did he make the changes?"

"That's not clear," Brodavitch said.

"Can you obtain a copy of the exercises?" Palovich asked.

"Negative."

"Where are the numbers?"

"A major part of the plan is to maintain absolute secrecy of operation, and it is being kept."

"But where are we talking about —" Palovich started to say.

"Each number is self-sustaining for the entire period of the exercise, which is due to end on the first of January."

"When does it begin?"

"It has begun," Brodavitch answered.

Palovich rubbed the stubble on his chin and said, "I'm here when you need me." It was his way of saying thank you and assuring the man that in the future, should the situation be reversed, he would be the one to help. He put the phone down, cut a fresh cigar, lit it and walked to the window. The sky was already gray with the coming of dawn. Now he was faced with the question of whether to go to the Comrade Director with what he knew, or did he wait to see if, as he was certain, the coup would take place. Now, if he went, he could become a national hero. But, depending on whether the Comrade Director was involved, he might be dead.

After several minutes, Palovich opted to wait a while longer before he made up his mind.

Though it was nine o'clock at night, the entire Board was assembled in the board room. As soon as the doors were closed, Leon asked for silence. When he got it, he said, "Gentlemen, this is an emergency meeting." He paused to allow his statement to register.

The members looked at each other.

"Mr. Fitzhugh will explain the exact nature of the emergency," Leon told them. "Please, Mr. Fitzhugh."

Fitzhugh removed the pipe from his mouth, cleared his throat and said, "Mr. Nathan has become a much more severe problem than we had previously thought he would be."

"Just give us the facts, Mr. Fitzhugh," one of the members urged. "I have dinner and friends waiting for me at a local restaurant."

Fitzhugh was not going to allow himself to be rushed. He nodded politely and then took time to pour and drink a half a glass of water before he continued. "Mr. Nathan has taken out two of our people who were sent to take *him* out."

"That has to mean he's on to something," Strogerly said gruffly.

"We must assume," Fitzhugh told them, "that he has by now made several connections, the first of which would be my connection to Robin's murder and from that to the connection between myself and General Gorsky." His eyes moved to the general.

Blowing smoke from his cigarette, De Ville asked, "Just exactly what does that mean to our plans, Fitzhugh?"

"I can answer that," Strogerly said, then looked at Fitzhugh.

"Please do," Fitzhugh invited.

"Granted that Mr. Nathan has made certain connections, these connections are still only connections. He can't go to any of the company's deputy directors and tell them about the connections he has made because he doesn't know which one might be part of the connection. And he can't go to the director because he doesn't really have anything concrete. He can't even go to any other agency involved in intelligence work because he'd be afraid to trust them for the reason I have just given. His connections are just too tenuous to be believed, especially since Fitzhugh is at the center of them."

"Thank you," Fitzhugh said.

"All of that does not answer my question," De Ville persisted.

"I'd say we have at least another twenty-four to thirty-six hours before we switch to an earlier attack date," Strogerly said, holding his cigar in front of his mouth.

"So now I have two people who are trying to find and kill me," Gorsky commented. "Two could quickly become five, then ten and —"

"General, there's only Mr. Nathan," Leon said. "No one here said a word about anyone else."

"There's Morosov," Strogerly answered darkly.

"Morosov?" Leon repeated, looking first at Fitzhugh then at Strogerly.

"He's KGB," Strogerly explained. "He's here to find and kill the General."

"*Here?*" Mr. Schmidt asked.

Strogerly shook his head.

Suddenly Gorsky was on his feet. "You don't know where he is and you say he's not here. And now this Mr. Nathan is on the loose, and you don't know where he is either."

"General, please," Leon said, nodding. "We all understand and appreciate your . . . your concern."

Gorsky pointed his finger at Strogerly, then at Fitzhugh. "You could not stop Morosov from coming and I was willing to play the odds that he would not find me in time to do anything after your people failed to take him out, but this blunder with your Mr. Nathan is inexcusable."

Strogerly's face flushed, while Fitzhugh's paled.

"Please, General," Leon said again. "Please, sit down."

"Fools!" Gorsky growled but sat down.

"Why wasn't the Board informed about the arrival of a KGB agent?" Leon asked.

"When we told the General about it," Fitzhugh answered, "he was totally unconcerned; therefore, we did not think —"

"Exactly," Gorsky snapped. "You didn't think."

"At the time," Fitzhugh continued, his eyes riveted on Gorsky, "the general was cavalier in his attitude toward the possible danger to the point where both myself and General Strogerly were full of admiration for —"

Gorsky was on his feet again. "I don't need your fucking admiration. I need your ability to do what must be done. I am not afraid of Morosov, or of Mr. Nathan. I *am* afraid that your bungling will cause this operation to fail. What did you expect me to do when you told me Morosov had come to kill me? What kind of man do you think I am?"

"I think you're a very angry man who has said things that were out of line," Fitzhugh answered very slowly, "and certainly beneath your dignity and the dignity of this table."

"General," Leon said, "please sit down."

Gorsky glared at him, but he sat down.

For several moments, the only sound in the room was of men breathing. Then Mr. Lau said, "If the attack date is switched, will everything be ready to accomplish our goal?"

Mr. Lau's question brought an audible sigh of relief from several members.

"Our plane will be ready," Strogerly answered, putting the cigar back in his mouth. He rolled it to the right side, before he said, "But the President's plane will not be in the air when ours is, should we have to move the date up."

"That would mean killing the President while he's in California," Mr. Schmidt commented.

"That can be arranged," Fitzhugh said, calmly relighting his pipe.

Strogerly looked across the table. "General Gorsky, will your people be able to seize the missile sites should the date have to be moved up?"

"They must have at least twelve hours' notice," Gorsky said. "I made contingency plans to accommodate an earlier launch date and a later one. But my division commanders must be notified twelve hours before the actual change takes place."

Strogerly nodded.

"Then," Leon said, "we all agree to wait another thirty-six hours before we make the decision to change to an earlier launch date?" He moved his eyes from man to man.

Each one nodded.

"Very good," Leon commented. "Very good indeed!" Then he added, "We are truly sorry for whatever inconvenience this special session might have caused you." He was about to stand up to signal the end of the meeting, when Gorsky challenged, "I want to know exactly what Mr. Fitzhugh is going to do about Mr. Nathan?"

"That, General," Fitzhugh answered, making no attempt to mask his anger, "is my concern."

"My concern —"

"I don't want to know about your concern," Fitzhugh said. "Mr. Nathan will not be a problem."

Gorsky uttered an exclamation of disgust!

"Gentlemen," Leon said quietly, "this meeting is adjourned."

As everyone stood up and began to move toward the door, Fitzhugh and Strogerly hung back. By the time they were in the hallway, they walked alongside of each other. Neither one spoke until they paused to get their coats and hats from the closet halfway between the conference room and the building's main entrance. Then Strogerly said, "Nathan must be stopped, if for no other reason than it would satisfy Gorsky."

"Nathan will be here soon," Fitzhugh said, putting on his tan cashmere coat.

"What do you mean, *here*?"

"We are supposed to go to Robin's funeral together," Fitzhugh answered. "*Here* means Albany. That was the way it was left. He'd drive up to Albany. I'd meet him there and we'd go to Boston together."

Strogerly eased into his shearling lined ranch coat. "You don't really expect him to show, do you?"

"He'll come," Fitzhugh said confidently. "He's too good a field man not to know he's on to something big. He'll come because I'm here."

"We don't have sufficient men to check out all the motels in the Albany area," Strogerly said. "He'll probably use a false name, so checking by phone won't turn him up."

"He'll call me," Fitzhugh said, as they walked toward the door.

"You've got to get him someplace where our people can get him," Strogerly said as they left the building and walked down the steps.

"Count on it," Fitzhugh answered, his breath steaming in the cold night air. "Count on it. . . ."

Driving a rented car, Nathan and Deirdre were just outside of Kingston at one o'clock in the morning.

"We still have at least a half-hour more before we reach Albany," he said, then added, "This is as good a place to stop as any. Besides, I'm tired of driving."

"It doesn't really make any difference to me, Deirdre answered, "as long as the place is clean."

Nathan moved into the right lane and in less than a minute, he exited the highway and came to a stop at the toll booth. "Would you know a good motel close by?" he asked, handing the man a five dollar bill and the toll ticket.

"Just continue the way you're going," the officer said, "and when you get to the flashing red light, make a right turn. The Kingston Motel is about five hundred yards up the road from there, on your right. You can't miss it."

"Thanks," Nathan said, taking his change.

"At least we don't have to go a long distance," Deirdre commented, as they reached the red flashing light, stopped and then turned right. The motel was on a hill.

Nathan stopped in front of the office.

"I'll stay in the car," Deirdre told him.

Nathan opened the car door. "I'll tell the clerk you're my wife."

"He won't believe you."

"Probably not," Nathan said. "You don't look like a wife."

Deirdre stuck out her tongue.

Nathan entered the office and said to a middle-aged man behind the desk, "I'd like a room for the night."

The man nodded and handed him a registration card.

Hesitating a moment, Nathan decided not to use his real name. He wrote Mr. and Mrs. Smith, turned the card toward the clerk and asked, "Do you need anything more?"

"For a few hours or the whole night?" the man asked.

"The whole night."

"That'll be fifty-five dollars."

Nathan fished his wallet out of his pants pocket, took out a fifty and a five dollar bill and put them on the green formica counter.

"Room twenty-nine. It's the last one around the back," he said, handing Nathan the key. "Check-out time is twelve noon."

Nathan took the key, turned and started out of the office, when he caught sight of a local newspaper on a table. The headline *"Fire At Broom College"* made him stop. He looked back at the clerk. "Mind if I take that newspaper?" he asked.

"Not in the least," the man answered.

Nathan picked up the newspaper, folded it and placing it under his arm, he left the office. "There was a fire at Broom College," he said, handing the newspaper to Deirdre, as if that would explain why he was giving her the paper.

"Is that supposed to mean something to me?" she asked.

Without answering, he drove the car around to the back of the motel and stopped directly in front of the room.

"What I like about you," Deirdre said, as she waited for him to unlock and open the door, "is the talent you have for isolation."

The door opened and Nathan reached inside for a light switch.

"My God, what the hell is this?" Deirdre asked, shocked by the room.

"Just go inside," Nathan said. He set their two bags down on the floor and then closed the door.

"This must be either Mafia, or Renaissance brothel," Deirdre commented. "The whole damn place is red. Even the lights are red!"

"Look up at the ceiling," Nathan said.

"A mirror!" she exclaimed and taking several steps into the room, she peered behind a screen. "There's a heart-shaped tub big enough to hold two people." She faced him. "I just don't believe this place!"

"Well, it's home for a night," Nathan laughed.

Deirdre looked up at the mirror. "I've never watched myself make love. Have you?"

"All the time," Nathan answered, taking off his coat. "And if I can't do it because there isn't a mirror on the ceiling, I take my pocket mirror and tape it just above my penis so I can see where it's going."

"You're perverted," she answered giggling.

"We'll discuss the pros and cons of the mirror

tomorrow," Nathan said. "Now, if you don't want to shower, I will."

"I'll shower first," she said, beginning to undress.

Nathan picked up the newspaper, sat down on the bed and after a few moments, he said, "I'll tell you this, red light isn't the best light to use when you want to read."

Deirdre went into the bathroom. "There's regular lighting here," she called. "You can stand in the doorway and read it."

"That's exactly what I'm going to do," Nathan said, leaving the bed. The newspaper story mentioned a Troy Sims as the prime suspect, and Professor James Petorious who put up the bail for Mr. Sims. Nathan immediately recognized Petorious's name. The story continued, "The library's entire military collection and part of its newspaper file were destroyed. Sims claims he is innocent. But Dr. Leon Hale, president of Broom, said that Sims had a history of agitation on campus and it would be difficult for him, or anyone else, to dispute the fact that fire-causing substances were found by the fire marshal in Sims's house."

Nathan reread, "The library's entire military collection . . . destroyed —" He lowered the newspaper.

"Your turn," Deirdre said, stepping out of the shower.

Nathan walked away.

"Are you all right?" Deirdre asked, wrapping a towel around her.

"That fire at Broom —"

"What about it?"

"It was set to prevent someone from recognizing Gorsky," he said. "The library's military collection was completely destroyed. That's just too damn coincidental, and some college kid by the name of Troy Sims is being blamed for having started the fire."

"That doesn't prove that Gorsky is here. Besides, why would he be here?"

"Because Fitzhugh is here."

"Who's he?"

"My boss. The man who had Frank killed."

"You never told me that," she said quietly.

"That college kid —" He stopped. "The military collection must have had a book with Gorsky's picture in it. The information on Gorsky came from a book. There's probably a picture of him in that book."

"You're guessing," she said.

"No, I think I'm putting it together," Nathan answered. "Gorsky wouldn't be using his own name. He'd use another name. But the kid recognized him. That's why he's been set up on an arson charge. That *has* to be the reason."

Deirdre took the newspaper and went into the bathroom to read it. "The fire marshal found the chemicals in Sims's house," she said.

"Planted," Nathan said.

"You're still guessing," she answered, coming back to where Nathan was standing.

"If I am, I'm not too far off the mark," he said. "That fire had to be set to protect Gorsky from being discovered."

"You still haven't been able to come up with one good reason why your Russian general would be here," she said.

"Whatever it is," Nathan said, "it has to be very, very big. A lot of people have died trying to kill me and my Russian counterpart." He reached for the phone.

"Who are you going to call at one-thirty in the morning?" she asked.

"Petorious and Sims and warn —" He stopped and put the phone down. "That's not the way to go. Nothing must be rash. Whatever has to be done, must be done calmly, very calmly, or several innocent people will wind up dead."

Sally took it for granted that after dinner she and Noonan would go back to the McKittrick Motel, which was why, when they neared it, she said, "Better slow down. The motel is off to the right."

"We're not going there," Noonan answered sharply. "I found a different place." He glanced at her, then shifted his eyes back to the road.

"Where is it?" Sally asked, annoyed he hadn't bothered to mention anything about it at dinner.

"As long as it has a bed, does it matter?"

His response jolted her. She tried to remember if she had done or said anything to make him angry. But even during dinner, he seemed to be preoccupied.

"Isn't that the truth?" he asked, glancing at her again.

Sally turned her head away.

He laughed. "Now you're insulted, aren't you?"

"Hurt would be more accurate," she said, facing him. "I don't know why you're angry at me, but I know you are and if you are angry, I'd just as soon have you take me home now."

Holding the wheel with one hand, Noonan reached under the seat with the other and took out a bottle of vodka. "Here," he said, "open it and have some, then I'll have some. After you have enough, you won't feel 'hurt' and I won't, as you put it, feel 'angry.'" And thrusting the bottle between her thighs, he ordered her to open it.

"I want to go home," Sally told him.

"I want to go home," he mimicked. Grabbing the bottle from her, he used his teeth to pull the cork, spat it on the floor and drank.

Sally shrank into the corner.

"Angry," Noonan said. "Angry doesn't begin to describe what I feel." He glanced at her again. "But how the fuck would you know?"

"I know that you're drunk," she managed to say.

"Drunk? Listen, you cunt, I'm beyond being drunk." And he took another swig from the bottle.

Sally crossed her arms over her breasts. This was not the Noonan who had made such delicious love to her; this was not the man who so gallantly kissed the back of her hand and made her feel like a woman.

"Fools!" he exclaimed. "Fools."

"Take me home, please," Sally pleaded.

"I want to make love," Noonan said with a smirk. "I want to make love. Isn't that what you want to do?" He drank again, put the bottle between his legs and grabbing hold of her arm, he pulled her close to him.

"No, don't!" she cried and tried to get away, but his fingers were talons that held her fast.

"Drink!" Noonan demanded, suddenly letting go of her arm and grabbing hold of her hair. "Drink, bitch, or you won't have any hair on that stupid head of yours."

She took the bottle and brought it to her lips.

"Down," he said, releasing her hair and jamming the bottle into her mouth.

The car swerved to the other side of the road. Sally screamed.

Noonan fought to get the car back in the lane and when it finally was, he eased it on to the shoulder, then stopped it altogether. He switched off the ignition and the lights.

"We could have been killed." Sally wept. The front of her dress was wet with vodka. The empty bottle lay in her lap.

Noonan picked up the bottle, looked at it and shaking his head, he tossed it into the rear of the car.

"Take me home," Sally whimpered.

"Now we make love," Noonan said, pulling her to him and jamming his lips against hers.

She twisted her face away. "I don't want —"

"I don't care what you want," he roared. He took hold of the top part of her dress and with a single movement, he tore it away from her.

She screamed.

He ripped her bra off, then he pushed her back on the seat.

"Please don't!"

Noonan pulled the bottom of her dress up and grabbed hold of her panties. "Can't fuck . . . make love with these on." He started to pull them off.

Sally fought his hands.

Noonan began to shout, but not in English.

"Oh, my God," Sally cried, "You're not —"

He brought his hand down on her face. "I'm Gorsky," he yelled. "General Anatole Gorsky." He slapped her again.

Blood suddenly poured out of Sally's nose. "Oh God, don't! Don't!" she cried. "Don't . . . " She spit out two of her teeth.

Gorsky grabbed hold of her neck and began to squeeze.

Sally tried to claw his face, but it was too far away. Too far away. She knew he was strangling her.

Breathing hard, Gorsky let go of Sally. Her body sagged back on the seat. He took several deep breaths and looked at her, then he took a cigarette out of his gold case, lit it and blew smoke at the body. Within moments a plan took shape in his mind. He started the car, switched on the lights and began to drive. By the time the police or anyone else figured out what really had happened to Sally, it would too late to do anything about it.

"Tell me that again," Fitzhugh said. He was standing in front of the fireplace in Leon's library, where now only cold ash served as a reminder of the previous evening's fire. Strogerly was there, looking considerably less than happy; Leon and General Gorsky, to whom he'd just spoken, were also there.

"I just killed Sally Cooms, a librarian —"

"Yes, I know who she is," Fitzhugh snapped, looking at Leon.

"As soon as he told me, I called you and General Strogerly," Leon said. He was seated in one of the club chairs. Strogerly was in the other and Gorsky occupied the wing chair. The drapes were drawn and the room was illuminated by two small table lamps that gave off only enough light to create two small yellow circles, leaving the greater part of the room filled with dark shadows.

Fitzhugh ran his hand across his face. He'd left his pipe in the bedroom and sorely missed it. "Perhaps, General, an explanation might enable us to better understand the situation and to help you."

"She discovered who I was," he answered. "There wasn't any other choice."

Taking the cigar out of his mouth, Strogerly asked, "Just how did she manage to do that?"

"While we were fucking."

Strogerly wasn't ready for that answer. But Fitzhugh nodded and said, "You mean you argued and —"

"No. While fucking in the car, I became so emotional that I lapsed into Russian."

"Sally, in a car!" Leon exclaimed.

"A volcano of passion in a car or a bed," Gorsky said, glancing over at Leon. He shifted his attention back to Fitzhugh. "Under the circumstances I couldn't run the risk of jeopardizing our effort, could I?"

"No . . . no, you did the right thing," Fitzhugh assured him.

"Absolutely," Leon said.

"No doubt of it," Strogerly added, putting the cigar back in his mouth.

"Did you dispose of the body?" Fitzhugh asked.

Gorsky pointed to the window on the other side of the drapes. "It's out there, in the trunk of Leon's car," he said without any emotion.

Leon was on his feet. "In the trunk of my car!" he yelled.

"It was really the best place for her — I mean, for

the body — until you decide how to handle the situation."

Fitzhugh told Leon to sit down. This was Gorsky's way of making him sweat, of putting him to the test, so to speak, because his men weren't able to neutralize Morosov or Nathan. "The problem will be dealt with," he said.

"I would like specifics," Gorsky said, taking out a cigarette and lighting it.

"The body will be gotten rid of and the car burned," Fitzhugh answered.

"Excellent," Gorsky responded, "but certainly there should be more."

"More what?" Fitzhugh asked.

Gorsky blew smoke out of his mouth, pointed the burning tip at Fitzhugh and said, "You have the opportunity to be creative so why not be?"

"Your actions, General, could hardly be called 'creative,'" Fitzhugh retorted angrily.

Gorsky took a deep drag on the cigarette, held the smoke for several moments and as he let it flow out of his nostrils in a thick stream, he said, "That is a matter of opinion, Mr. Fitzhugh. My actions certainly protected our enterprise. Now the effectiveness of your actions must achieve the same purpose. It is not enough to dispose of the body and burn the car."

"What else would you suggest?" Leon questioned, adjusting his eyeglasses on the bridge of his nose.

"I am hoping that our Mr. Fitzhugh will supply the necessary answers," Gorsky said.

Fitzhugh was in a rage, but he managed to keep his voice from betraying his feelings. "The body will be thrown into the river," he said.

"Naked, I hope," Gorsky added.

"Is that necessary?" Leon asked.

"Mr. Fitzhugh, what do you think?" Gorsky asked, then added, "Remember, be *creative*."

"If our intent is to show that she had been sexually assaulted, then she must be naked," Fitzhugh answered, glaring at Gorsky.

"You see, it is not all that difficult, gentlemen, to be *creative* if you put your mind to it," Gorsky commented. "So far we have the car burned and Miss Coom's naked body in the river. Now what do we do with me?"

Suddenly Fitzhugh realized that Gorsky had completely thought out the steps that should be taken and was, up to that moment, playing a game in which he was the only player and the only winner. Fitzhugh smiled.

"From the look on your face," Gorsky said, "you must have an idea."

"I want to hear yours," Fitzhugh responded. "I'm certain you have more than one, and if they are usable, we will certainly use them."

Gorsky hesitated.

Fitzhugh smiled again. He'd caught him. The feeling was delicious.

"I go to the police," Gorsky said, "and tell them two men stopped me on the road and at gunpoint took Sally and the car; then I give the cops a description of Morosov and your Mr. Nathan. That way, not only will your people be looking for them, but so will the police."

"Brilliant!" Strogerly exclaimed. "The local police will, of course, notify the state police."

"Excellent," Leon responded. "It certainly gives us additional protection."

"I salute you, General," Fitzhugh said and he did. "Your plan is worthless."

Gorsky frowned.

"You would have to make the police believe you," Fitzhugh said, "and if you just walked into the police station and told them that two men took Sally and the car at gunpoint, they might accept your story. But as soon as they find Sally's body — well, your story might not be so believable."

"I don't understand," Gorsky said.

"Something must also happen to you," Fitzhugh said. "The men you claim you encountered would not have left you without having beaten and robbed you."

"Fitzhugh is right," Strogerly said, rolling his cigar from the left side of his mouth to the right.

"If you want to play the role," Fitzhugh continued, "the way it must be played to make it believable to the police, then you must dress the part. By that I mean, you must be badly bruised. Your clothes must show evidence of what happened to you, and when you finally tell your story to the police, you must be distraught to the point where you are almost incoherent."

"That makes sense," Leon said approvingly.

Strogerly agreed.

"Are you up to taking the necessary physical punishment?" Fitzhugh asked.

"I don't see that I have much choice," Gorsky answered.

"None," Fitzhugh said, then with a smile he added, "especially if you want to be *creative*."

[14]

At eight o'clock in the morning, Morosov drove to the shopping center to phone Piligin. There was very little traffic on the road and the parking lot was almost empty.

There were four telephone booths and all of them were in front of the Radley supermarket. Morosov settled for the middle one, deposited a dollar's worth of quarters and dialed.

After two rings, a voice on a tape said, "Please leave your name and phone number."

Morosov gave the name he was using and his ID number, followed by the area code and the number of the phone from which he was calling.

"Yes," Piligin said.

"I've located the singer who Gorsky tried to date," Morosov told him.

"Be very careful, Igor," Piligin said. "Strange things are happening here and at home. We have it from a very good source that Nathan was involved in the shooting on the Belt Parkway yesterday afternoon. He had a woman with him."

"And the other people involved, who were they?" Morosov asked, aware of the fact that a man had stepped into the booth on his left.

"From Copple's Special Security force," Piligin answered. "We don't know why he's involved."

"Were you able to get the information on Gargarin?" Morosov asked.

"Gorsky commanded the Two Hundred and Forty-Fifth Armored Division when Gargarin served in it," Piligin said.

"So there might be a connection?"

"Possibly, but there's more and it's very, very interesting. Shortly after I asked Palovich for the information, he requested the present status of the Two Forty-Fifth and several other units that Gorsky had commanded at one time or another. All of those units are involved in a special winter exercise. No other information is available."

"That's something to think about," Morosov answered, wondering why those particular units were selected for the special exercise.

"Some of the people here seem to think that some political change is in the wind," Piligin said.

"A possibility, but I doubt it."

"Then what else could it be?"

"I don't know," Morosov said. "But right now I'd be suspicious of anything and anyone connected with Gorsky, past or present."

Piligin agreed and then hung up.

Morosov put the phone down, dug into his pocket for more change, deposited a quarter and dialed Petorious's number.

The operator asked him for another thirty cents before she would allow the call to go through.

After two rings, a woman answered the phone.

Though Morosov immediately recognized her voice, he said, "May I please speak to Helen Peters?"

"This is she," Helen said.

"I'm Detective Callahan," he said, moving around to see where the man who made the telephone call had gone.

"Is anything wrong?" she asked, her voice rising in alarm. "My brother —"

"I'd appreciate a few minutes of your time," Morosov said, watching the man walk across the parking area and get into a powder blue, late-model Chevy. "I've come all the way up from New York to speak to you," he continued.

"From the city?"

"Yes, I'm with the New York City Police Department," he told her.

She hesitated.

"I assure you it has nothing to do with you personally," Morosov said. "But it's a matter that I can't discuss on the phone."

"How did you know where to find me?" she asked.

"Miss Hanson —"

"She told you?"

Afraid that he might give the wrong answer, Morosov hesitated.

"Well, did she?"

"Not exactly," he finally answered. "I will tell you —"

The operator interrupted and asked for an additional thirty-five cents.

"Where are you calling from?" Helen asked.

"I'm about an hour away," he answered, unwilling to reveal his location. "I still haven't had any breakfast and —"

Again the operator interrupted.

"May I come?" Morosov asked.

"I'd much prefer to have my brother here."

"I promise not to take up much of your time," Morosov persisted. He preferred to question her alone.

"All right," she said without enthusiasm.

"Thank you," Morosov said. "I'll be there" — he looked at his watch — "say between nine-thirty and ten. Will that be a good time for you?"

"Yes."

"Thank you," he answered.

"Good bye," Helen said.

"Good bye," Morosov answered. He put the phone down and leaned against the side of the booth. He was sweating.

Nathan was dreaming. He held a woman's breast. He squeezed it gently. His finger curled around a trigger. The car was coming up fast. The face behind the wheel had a moustache. The car suddenly veered away. Nathan bolted into a sitting position. For a fraction of a second, he was disoriented. But when he saw the blond hair spread out over the pillow, he instantly came to grips with reality.

Deirdre stirred and moved herself closer to him. "What time is it?" she asked.

He took his watch off the night table. "Nine."

"Come back down here," Deirdre purred, caressing his penis.

He forced himself to take hold of her hand. "Maybe, if we're lucky, we'll have time for fun and games later," he said, swinging his feet on to the floor and standing. "But now we've got things to do."

Shaking her head, Deirdre sat up. "All right, what's Super Agent going to do now?"

He grinned. "First, I'm going to do this," he said and bending over her he kissed her on the tip of her nose. "Then this." And he kissed each of her nipples, made erect by the chill in the room. "Those things done, I'm going to get dressed and check the radio in the car. And while I'm doing that, you can shower."

Deirdre got out of bed. "I don't usually like to be told what to do."

"Sorry about that," Nathan grinned. He slipped on his underwear, his pants and the blue jacket his father had brought him the previous evening. "See you," he said and left the room.

There were ten cars in the parking area. Two were close to his, and one of them was the same make and model. He looked at it, then back at his. Something was different. "The damn license plates!" he exclaimed. His had federal plates. "That has to be changed and fast."

He considered making the switch then and there, but it was too risky. He'd be better off finding a shopping mall and making the switch there.

Nathan unlocked the car door, sat down in the driver's seat, turned on the ignition and then switched on the radio, tuning it until he found the frequency used by the local police. There was the usual kind of announcements: a fire in Kingston, an accident on 9W and then the dispatcher said: "Attention all units . . . . This is an APB . . . . Attention all units . . . . This is an APB . . . . Be on the lookout for two white males . . . . Possibly driving a nineteen eighty-eight, gray Ford Tempo with US Government plates . . . G dash nineteen forty-four dash twenty-two. . . ."

"Holy Christ!" Nathan exclaimed; then he heard the dispatcher give a description of him and Morosov. . . "These men are wanted for questioning in connection with the abduction and killing of a Red Hook woman. They are armed and very dangerous. Use extreme caution. Repeat, they are armed and very dangerous. Use extreme caution."

Nathan switched off the radio. He couldn't risk leaving the motel parking lot with the federal plates on the car. He took a deep breath. Regardless of the risk, he had to make the switch now.

His plates came off quickly, and so did the front plate on the car that was the same model and year as his. But the bottom left bolt on the rear plate was frozen. He abandoned it, went to another car and exchanged its plates for his; then he replaced the front plate on the car from which he had taken it.

"I was beginning to worry," Deirdre said when he came back into the room. She was wearing blue slacks and a red woolen turtleneck sweater.

"Lucky you didn't know what was happening, or you really would have been worried," he said, taking off his coat and stripping down.

She followed him to the bathroom door.

"I've been linked to the Russian agent, and the two of us are wanted in connection with the abduction and murder of a woman in Red Hook," Nathan explained. "Now if you'll excuse me, there are some things that I can't share even with you." And he started to close the door.

"Wait a minute," Deirdre said.

Nathan stopped.

"What does all that mean?" she asked.

"They have their police looking for us."

"But who are *they*?" she asked.

Nathan shook his head. "Fitzhugh, Copple, probably Gorsky — I don't know the others. Now may I close the door?"

"Wait!" she exclaimed, putting her hand on the door. "What are we going to do?"

"You're going to rent a car from two different rental agencies; then I'll get rid of the car I have. After that we'll check in at two different motels; then we'll pay a visit to Petorious and warn him and that kid, Troy Sims. They're into something and they don't know what they're into."

"Do you?" she asked.

"Not completely," he answered honestly. "But you'll have to trust me that I know enough to know what I'm doing."

"This is a hell of a time to ask me to trust you," she answered, "especially after I've been sleeping with you."

"I mean really trust me, Deirdre," he said with sudden seriousness. "The police are looking for me and so are Copple's men."

"I trust you," Deirdre answered quietly. "I trust you with my heart and my life."

Nathan leaned over, kissed her gently on the forehead and then he closed the bathroom door.

Morosov pulled on to the shoulder of the road across from the Petorious house and checked his watch. It was 9:50. Except for the police detour when he came off the bridge, he'd made very good time.

He looked at the house. It was a large, rambling wooden structure, with a porch and two graceful Doric columns at the top of the steps. Smoke was coming out of two chimneys.

He left the car, but did not lock the door. For a moment a huge trailer truck came between him and the house. When it was gone, he saw a woman standing in the doorway with a Mexican shawl draped around her shoulders.

Morosov was half inclined to wave to her, but instead he hurried across the road and up the three steps that led to the porch.

"I saw you from the window," she said, stepping aside to let him into the house.

"Detective Lieutenant Callahan, New York City Police Department," he said, reaching for his ID.

"I believe you," she said, closing the door.

Morosov removed his hat and gloves. The house was warm and smelled clean.

"Would you like some coffee?" she asked, moving in front of him.

"Yes," he answered, looking at her. She was a very attractive woman, with long dark red hair, blue eyes and a few freckles scattered on her nose and on her cheeks, just below her eyes.

"Some terrible news has just come over the radio," she said, leading the way into the kitchen. "The nude body of one of the librarians at the college was found in the river just a few hours ago."

"I saw the police cars and an ambulance when I came across the river," Morosov responded.

Helen removed the shawl from her shoulders and put it over the back of a chair. She went to the refrigerator and took out a jar of coffee.

"If it's too much trouble —"

"No trouble at all," she said. "The water is

already boiled. I was about to make a pot when I heard you pull up. You could have come into the driveway."

"I didn't want to block it," he lied. He never would have risked being blocked by another car.

"My brother won't be back until well after noon," she said, measuring the coffee out into the coffee pot. "Please sit down. Take off your coat."

Morosov nodded, removed his coat and found himself watching her. She moved gracefully and he liked the soft huskiness of her voice. He was sure he would enjoy the way she sang.

Finished at the stove, Helen sat down opposite Morosov. "First, before you ask your questions, tell me how you found me?"

"Miss Hanson said your brother taught at a small college, somewhere close to Albany. I asked around and found that Broom was just across the river from Kingston. I found your brother's name in the phone book."

"So you were the one who called and hung up when I answered," she said, almost accusingly.

Morosov nodded. The woman was incredibly attractive, so much so that he couldn't stop himself from staring at her.

Helen flushed and cleared her throat.

"I'm sorry," he said, "I didn't mean to make you uncomfortable."

She smiled at him. "I'm ready for your questions now."

"Only one question," Morosov said digging into his breast pocket and taking out Gorsky's photograph. "Do you recognize this man?" he asked, handing the picture to her.

Helen picked up the photograph and studied it

for a moment. "He wanted me to go out with him after I finished working. I'm a singer in a hotel —"

"Yes, I know," Morosov answered. "That was how I was able to track you down."

"That sounds ominous," Helen commented. She left the table and took two mugs out of the closet. "Cream, milk and sugar?" she asked, pouring the coffee.

"Black, no sugar," Morosov said, studying the flare of her hip.

"Is it ominous?" Helen asked, returning to the table with two steaming cups of coffee.

"Not for you," Morosov answered.

"For him then?" she asked, sliding Gorsky's photograph across the table to him.

Morosov hesitated.

"He's German, isn't he?" she asked over the rim of the mug. "He spoke with an accent."

"Did he give you his name?" Morosov asked. There was a light in her eyes that reminded him of the light in Tatyana's eyes before she became ill. . . .

"Never got that far," Helen answered. "I didn't like the way he looked at me."

Morosov's cheeks turned red. "I apologize for —"

"Two different looks," Helen said with a smile. "His I definitely didn't like, while yours — well, I'm still trying to make up my mind."

Morosov pulled himself back to the business at hand. "Did he say anything about himself, or where he was going?"

"Nothing. But you haven't told me why the police want him."

"For crimes against the state," Morosov snapped; then seeing a mixture of confusion and surprise move quickly across Helen's face and finally turn into a worried frown, he said in a much softer tone, "He heads a narcotics smuggling ring."

"Would you like more coffee?" Helen asked and before he could answer, she added, "I have blueberry muffins —"

"Just a bit more coffee would be fine," Morosov said.

Helen took his cup and went to the stove.

Morosov followed her with his eyes, turning slightly in his chair to watch her pour the coffee. Even more than before, he was aware of the curves of her body.

"Now what will you do?" she asked, returning to the table.

"Find him," Morosov said, lifting the mug. "We have reason to believe he's somewhere in this area."

She shrugged. "This is a college town. Nothing much happens around here."

Morosov smiled. "And who would expect something extraordinary to happen at college?" he asked

Again Helen frowned.

"*Has* something extraordinary happened?" Morosov asked, suddenly aware of Helen's uneasiness.

"It has nothing to do with narcotics," she said.

Morosov put his mug down on the table. "Would you tell me about it?"

"It started, from what I was told, when one of my brother's students objected to Edward Noonan becoming a member of the Board of Directors."

"Why?"

"Troy says the Board as it is now has only retired generals, admirals and industrialists and financiers. He claims it should have at least one member of the faculty. Are you sure you want to hear this?"

"Please go on," Morosov urged.

"Troy was sure he saw Noonan before, but he could not remember where . . . To make this very long and involved story shorter, Troy is now sure that Noonan isn't Noonan at all but is some Russian general."

Morosov almost blurted out *what* in Russian, but instead, he forced himself to cough.

"He and my brother are at the library now," Helen explained, "to see if they can find the book with the photograph Troy remembered having seen."

"Broom's library?"

Helen shook her head. "The entire military section was destroyed two nights ago by a mysterious fire. They went to Albany State."

"And this young man was blamed for it?" Morosov asked.

"Why yes. But how did you know?"

Morosov ignored her question and asked one of his own. "Does your brother's student remember the name of the Russian general?"

Helen shook her head.

"Have you ever seen this Noonan?"

"No, I've only been here a short time," Helen answered.

"Do you know where I could find Noonan?" Morosov asked.

"I —" She stopped.

Their eyes locked.

"You're not a detective, are you?" she asked, her voice tight with fear.

Morosov stood up and walked around to where she sat.

Wide eyed, she looked up at him.

"I didn't kill the librarian," he said, guessing what was going through her mind.

She nodded.

"No harm will come to you," Morosov said, then he added, "The man who tried to get you to go out with him is a Russian general. That same man is Noonan."

"Oh, my God, Troy is right!" Helen exclaimed.

"Yes, he is right," Morosov said. "The man is General Gorsky. He is not a defector. He is here for a reason. My government wants him back."

"And if you can't take him back, you have orders to kill him?"

"But why has he come here?" Morosov asked, ignoring her question again. "Why is it important for him to be on the Board of Directors?"

"I don't know," Helen said, "but Troy thinks it's a ruse."

"A ruse?"

Helen shook her head. "Troy doesn't know why . . . he just thinks so."

Morosov moved away from the table and looked out the kitchen window. The yard was covered with snow and there were bird tracks all over the white surface. "A ruse to do what?" he said, then he faced Helen. "He's here under an assumed name and an assumed identity, which was why your young friend got himself into difficulties when he started to object to the new appointment and ask questions. Gorsky becoming Noonan is certainly a ruse."

"Troy didn't mean that," Helen said. "Troy said that everyone was supposed to think that Noonan, or General Gorsky, if that's who he really is, was here to become a member of the Board, but that wasn't the real reason for him being here."

Morosov nodded. "He's right. He's absolutely right."

"If he's not a defector and he's not here to become a member of the Board, then why is he here?" Helen asked.

Morosov shook his head. "I don't know," he answered and walked back to where she was. "Listen," he said, taking hold of her hands, "you know what I am and you know that the minute I leave here you can go to the phone and call the authorities and have me arrested —"

"I —"

"I'm asking you not to do that. I'm asking you to help me. Something must be very important about that Board of Directors —"

"I already told you," Helen said. "All the members are retired admirals, generals, or presidents of international companies."

"I need your help," Morosov responded. "I need you for a cover."

"What? Are you crazy?"

Morosov gently lifted Helen to her feet. "If I came here as your friend," he said, "then no one would question my presence. You could tell your brother that I called from the city and you invited me up for a couple of days."

"But —"

"Gorsky must have come here for a very important reason," Morosov said. "That man was slated to command the entire Russian army. That's right, the entire army. For him to have given that up means that whatever is here is more important to him. And because it's more important to him, it must be more important to my government and to yours."

After a few moments, Helen nodded. "But don't you think I should know your real name?" she asked.

Morosov took a deep breath. He liked the way she smelled.

"Well, don't you?"

He exhaled slowly. "It would only complicate matters," he said. "Use the one you know."

"The detective part too?" she asked.

He shrugged. "That's up to you," he said, looking at his watch. "I'll be back at one o'clock."

"Yes," she responded.

He was going to thank her, but instead, he took her in his arms and kissed her warm lips.

"What was that for?" Helen asked, amazed.

"For me and I hope for you," he answered, letting go of her and walking around the table for his coat and hat.

She followed him to the door.

He stopped, turned around and cupping the side of her face in his hand, he said in Russian, "You're a beautiful woman."

"What did you say?" Helen asked.

Morosov smiled. "Thanks for the coffee."

Besides Petorious and Troy, there were exactly four other people in the library — two librarians behind the desk and two other people at the tables. One was obviously a member of the faculty and the other a student.

"That table there," Petorious said, pointing to the table closest to the door.

Troy nodded. "I'll be back with the book in a few minutes."

"That's assuming they have it," Petorious answered. He wasn't in the best of humor. Since he'd become involved with Troy, he hadn't really slept well.

"Any bets?"

"Get the bloody book!" Petorious snapped.

Troy threw up his hands. "Touchy this morning, aren't we?"

"Go!" Petorious ordered, pointing to the desk, where a librarian was looking questioningly at them.

"Going," Troy responded, backing away; then turning and walking to the call desk.

Petorious opened his coat and sat down. He had to admire Troy's ebullience. The fact that he was facing an arson charge seemed to have little, or no affect on him.

Suddenly Troy was on his way back to the table. "They have it," he said excitedly. "I told you they would."

"For God's sake," Petorious hissed, "quiet down! You're in a library."

"Okay, okay, I just wanted you to know."

Embarrassed, Petorious stood up. "I'm going out for a smoke," he said. "I'll be back in a few minutes."

"I thought you'd want to find it," Troy said.

"You find it," Petorious said. "It's sufficient for me to just look at it."

"My God, you are in a grouchy mood," Troy remarked.

"I'll be back."

"Yeah, hopefully in a better mood."

Without answering, Petorious left the reading room and walked out into the main lobby. He was just about go through the automatic door, when he saw a dark green sedan parked directly across the street, with two men sitting in it. He did a quick about-face, only to see Troy coming toward him.

"Now tell me if I'm crazy," Troy yelled. He was waving a piece of paper and smiling broadly.

Petorious grabbed hold of him. "Get into the men's room," he said sharply, "and stop shouting."

"What?"

"Goddamn it, Troy, why can't you do something without asking questions or making comments," Petorious fumed.

"Okay, okay, we'll go into the men's room."

Petorious pushed the door open. "Check the stalls," he whispered.

"You're kidding!"

"Check the fucking stalls," Petorious ordered, losing his temper.

Troy grinned. "Sooner or later, the ol' Marine had to come out," he said, looking into the first stall.

Petorious stepped into the lavatory and let the door close behind.

"Five stalls," Troy said, "and five empties. Now will you look at this." And he waved a page of a book in front of Petorious.

Appalled, Petorious asked, "You cut it out?"

"I'll buy them a new copy," Troy answered. "This is evidence."

Petorious took the page and looked at it.

"Well, if that's not our Mr. Noonan, who is it?" Troy asked.

"General Anatole Gorsky," Petorious said.

"Yeah, that's him," Troy said. "I just couldn't remember the name. All right, we know who he is. Now what do we do?"

"Think clearly," Petorious answered. "Think very clearly. But whatever we do, our first job is to get out of here."

Frowning, Troy cocked his head to one side. "Out of the men's room or out of the library?"

"Out of the library. There's a car with two men sitting in it just across the street from the main entrance. We have to go out that way to get to the parking lot."

"There must be another way out," Troy said.

"But I don't want to look for it," Petorious snapped. "Besides, you can bet they know my car and will follow it the moment they see it leaving the parking lot."

"Well, we sure as hell can't stay here," Troy said.

Petorious nodded. "Put that page away," he said as they left the men's room and started back to the reading room.

"I see the car," Troy said, hanging back. "Definitely not professorial types."

"Can you see the license plate number?" Petorious asked.

"Not completely. Why?"

They were back in the reading room. "We could phone college security and tell them that there are two suspicious men in a car across from the library. My guess is that the two of them are armed and —"

"You don't have to go into detail," Troy said. "You make the call. Your voice sounds older."

Petorious made a face, turned around and walked back into the lobby with Troy alongside of him. "As soon as the security car stops, we move. And for God's sake, don't run."

Troy shook his head. "There are the phones," he said.

Petorious deposited a quarter, dialed information and asked for the number of the college's security office. A computerized voice gave him the number. He repeated each digit immediately after he heard it. Then he hung up, waited for his coin to be returned, redeposited it and dialed the number.

On the first ring, a man answered, "Security Office, Sergeant Dixon here."

"This is Professor Grenville," Petorious said.

"Yes, professor?"

"There is a green car across from the library," he said, "with two men in it. One of them has a gun."

"Did you say that one of them has a gun?"

"Yes."

"Are you sure?"

"Absolutely, I saw it," Petorious said. "It's either a three seventy-five or a nine millimeter. Used the same in Nam."

"We'll get right on it," Dixon said. "And thanks, professor, for the tip."

Petorious hung up.

"You lie like a trooper," Troy laughed. "Who's Professor Grenville?"

"I have no idea," Petorious answered. "Now let's go where we can see what's happening."

Even as they moved back to the central lobby, two security cars came into view.

"Okay," Petorious said, "let's get the hell out of here." He went through the revolving door with Troy at his heels. As they crossed the street, his heart raced. Out of the corner of his eye, he saw the security guards opening the door of the car.

"They're searching them," Troy said.

"Keep walking!"

"One of the men spotted us," Troy said.

Petorious grabbed hold of his arm. "Walk!. They have their own problems."

They reached the car. Petorious unlocked the door, slid behind the wheel, leaned over and opened the door for Troy; then he switched on the ignition.

"Go, man. Go!"

Petorious eased the car out of the parking space, turned to the left, drove to the end of the lot and then made another left to gain the roadway.

"Why the hell are you crawling?" Troy fumed, looking back through the rear window.

Petorious didn't answer.

"Those two guys are up against the car," Troy said.

Petorious nodded and continued to drive at the same speed.

"Christ, I didn't even know we were being followed," Troy said, facing front and settling into the seat.

"Neither did I," Petorious said.

"Okay," Troy said, "we know that something very big is in the works."

"We don't know that at all," Petorious countered.

"C'mon, Professor!"

"My friend Frank Robin is in the CIA," Petorious said. "I'll phone him when we get back to the house. He'll know exactly what to do."

"What we should do is get into the board room and find out what the hell is really going on," Troy said.

"We'll do nothing until I speak to Frank," Petorious said in a hard voice. "And I mean absolutely nothing. Do you understand?'

Troy didn't answer.

"Troy, this isn't a game."

"I fucking well know that," Troy answered. "I've been saying that all along."

"Then stop acting as if it were!"

All of the Board members were present. Leon nodded to Fitzhugh, who stood up and without any preliminary statement, said, "We have been informed that Mr. Sims and Professor Petorious made a successful visit to the library at Albany State College."

"What does the word *successful* mean?" Mr. Lau asked.

"Without going into details, they now have in their possession a picture of General Gorsky," Fitzhugh said.

An excited murmur rippled around the table.

"We must assume they will try to use it," Strogerly said.

Gorsky was on his feet. "I want those two killed," he shouted, his face turning red.

"We have two cars waiting for them," Fitzhugh said. "Our plan is to take them alive if possible. Once we have them, there's no need to kill them."

Gorsky sat down.

"General," Leon asked, looking at Gorsky, "can you alert your divisions?"

"Yes, of course," Gorsky answered.

Leon moved his eyes from Gorsky to Strogerly, then to Fitzhugh, "Then I suggest we have the general order his commanders to take control of the missile bases and prepare to launch a preemptive strike at fourteen hundred hours tomorrow, Christmas Day."

Strogerly rolled the cigar to the right side of his

mouth. "That means the President must be dead sometime before that."

"He will be," Strogerly said. "His stand-in will confuse his people and since some our men are on his staff, they will see to it that a news black-out occurs. We want the killing to go unreported for as long as possible."

"What about the President's family?" Schmidt asked.

"None of them must be left alive," Gorsky said.

Strogerly said, "General Gorsky must stay out of sight until it's time for you to board Air Force One."

"That's going to call attention to him," Leon said. "Remember, he was beaten up by the men who took Sally. Reporters and people from the local radio and TV stations are going to want to speak to him."

"He can't go on TV," Lau said.

And Schmidt added, "Even having his picture in the newspaper is a considerable risk. There are still an American and a Russian agent looking for him."

Fitzhugh held up his hands. "Then, General, you must remain indisposed." He looked at his watch. "It's almost noon. You must stay out of sight for the next twenty-six hours. After that, the people around here will have more to think about than the murder of one woman."

All of the men around the table nodded.

"General Gorsky, put your divisions into posi-tion," Strogerly said.

[15]

Petorious chose to cross over to the eastern side of the Hudson on the Mid-Hudson Bridge rather than wait until they reached Kingston.

"Do you think they'll be waiting for us?" Troy asked.

"I like driving down the Nine better than the thruway," Petorious answered and switched on the radio. The wonderfully spritely scherzo movement of Mendelssohn's Octet filled the car.

Petorious cranked down his window and let the cold air wash over his face.

"But do you really think they'll be waiting?" Troy pressed.

"For both our sakes, I hope not."

"Those guys in the car —"

"Forget about them," Petorious said, knowing that Troy would rather talk about them than anything else.

"I really don't understand you," Troy said. "I really don't."

Petorious laughed. "Sometimes neither do I."

"You're supposed to be a big Marine hero. You have all sorts of decorations to prove it."

"So what are you getting at?" Petorious asked. He didn't like what Troy said, but decided to ignore it.

"So maybe like Gorsky, there are two of you," Troy tried. "Because one of you sure as shit doesn't want to go where the action is."

Petorious glanced at him, but remained silent. He wasn't going to let himself be taunted into anger.

"We're in a crisis situation that calls for action and all you can think of doing is calling your CIA friend."

"Maybe that's because I've been in a dozen different actions in places that you don't even know exist," Petorious answered quietly.

The Octet was over. The announcer identified it and the Public Broadcasting station by its call letters; then he said, "And now we have a few news items for you. . . . Another tanker has been sunk in the Persian Gulf by an Iranian gunboat. . . . The Pope has asked the United States to give a large portion of its surplus crops to the starving of the Third World Nations. . . . And closer to home, the nude body of a young women identified as Ms. Sally Cooms has been recovered from the Hudson River. For the last six years Ms. Cooms has been a librarian at Broom College. Ms. Cooms was abducted last night while in the company of Mr. Edward Noonan, a candidate for the college Board of Directors. Though severely beaten, Mr. Noonan was able to give the police complete descriptions of the two men. And now a sports item."

Troy reached over and switched off the radio. "He killed her," he said in low, choked voice, "Gorsky killed her." Then he shouted, "The son-of-a-bitch killed her. Doesn't that mean anything to you?"

Shaken, Petorious pulled on to the shoulder of the road and came to a stop. "It means more to me than you realize," he answered, forcing himself to keep his voice level.

"Then do something, man! Do something! We've got to get into the Board room."

"We do nothing until I speak to Frank."

"The hell with that!" Troy answered. "Gorsky killed Sally! You know that — or don't you?"

"He probably did," Petorious said.

"There's no *probably* about it."

"You have no proof."

Troy pulled out Gorsky's picture. "What the fuck is this?" he challenged. "Tell me, what the fuck is it?"

"People look alike," Petorious said, putting the car in motion again and hoping to calm Troy down.

"'People look alike!' That's one hell of a fucking answer," he growled and turned his face toward the window.

Petorious switched the radio on again. This time it was the overture from Bernstein's Candide. "'They also serve who only stand and wait,'" he said, just above the sound of the music.

"Don't quote Milton to me," Troy said, facing him. "I know what I have to do, and with or without you I'm going to do it."

"Then it will have to be without me," Petorious answered.

Troy shrugged and turned to the window again.

For the next three-quarters of an hour, neither Petorious or Troy spoke. And despite the various musical selections, Petorious was very much aware of the silence in the car.

"Check your rear view-mirror," Troy said suddenly.

Petorious looked. Two cars were behind them, one red, one green.

"I saw them in the side-view mirror," Troy explained.

"I was hoping it wouldn't happen," Petorious said, pushing his foot to the floor.

"They're coming up fast," Troy reported, looking back through the rear window.

"There's another car," Petorious shouted, suddenly spying a third car coming at them in their lane. "Hold on!" He slammed his foot on he brake. The car fishtailed, swerved to the side of the road and plunged into a drainage ditch, throwing Petorious hard against the wheel.

The doors on either side were pulled open.

"Get out! Get the fuck out of there," a man commanded.

Petorious nodded and found himself looking at the muzzle of a .357. "Do whatever they tell you to," he said, hoping that Troy wouldn't let his fighting spirit get the better of his desire to live. He hadn't any doubt at all that, given the slightest provocation, these men would kill them. He eased himself out of the car.

"Okay, the two of you in the back of the green car," the man ordered, waving the gun at them. Then to two of his own men, he said, "Burn the car."

Petorious, Troy and the man with the gun were in the rear of one car, the second car followed.

"Listen to me," Troy said, speaking in French.

"Shut up," the man commanded.

Petorious nodded. "I'm listening," he answered in French.

Then in German, Troy said, "Keep them busy. I'm going to leap from the car."

"I said 'shut up!'" The man back handed Troy across the face.

"You'll be killed," Petorious answered in German.

The man jabbed the barrel into Petorious's chest.

He gritted his teeth; he had endured physical pain before. His vision blurred.

"I'll break everyone of your fucking ribs," the man threatened.

"Now!" Troy shouted in English. He threw himself at the man with the gun.

Petorious grabbed the man's hand and twisted it. The gun went off, filling the car with the sharp smell of burnt powder.

The driver hit the brakes.

"Go," Petorious yelled. "Go!"

Troy opened the door and jumped free of the car.

Petorious pushed the man to the floor and delivered a chop to his neck.

He screamed and dropped the gun.

Petorious grabbed it and smashed it down on the side of the man's head, making a long bloody gash.

The car jerked to a stop.

Petorious put the muzzle against the back of the driver's head. "You're dead if you move," he said, breathing hard.

The second car came to a screeching halt directly behind them and the third car pulled up in front of them.

Two of the men headed into the woods after Troy and two, their guns drawn, came up to the car. "It's over," one of the men said. "You kill him and you'll die. Throw the gun down."

"Time to negotiate," Petorious answered, knowing he had nothing to negotiate with.

"Throw the gun down, Professor," the second man said.

The two men who chased Troy returned. "The bastard got away," one of them said.

The man who called Petorious Professor, said, "We'll get him later. His footprints will take us right to him. " Then he looked into the car again. "What's it going to be?"

Petorious lowered the gun and tossed it into the snow. An instant later, he was pulled from the car and thrown to the ground. Moments before the pain exploded in his head, he saw the revolver arcing down toward him.

It was almost one o'clock when Nathan drove up to Petorious's house in one car and Deirdre, following in another car, parked some distance away.

Nathan left his car and walked to where Deirdre was.

She rolled down the window.

"Keep the motor running," he said. "If anyone else comes, blow the horn twice."

She nodded. "I like you better with a beard," she commented, reaching out to touch his clean-shaven face.

"I'll grow it back as soon as I'm not wanted by the police," he said, stepping away from the car.

He looked both ways before he crossed the road and went up the front steps.

The door opened after the first ring.

"I'm Steven Nathan," he said, looking at Helen. "We met before. My partner Frank Robin —"

"Yes . . . yes, I remember," she said, looking past him.

"One car is mine," Nathan explained, "and the other belongs to my friend, Deirdre O'Keefe."

Helen nodded.

"Is your brother home?" he asked, aware that the woman was nervous.

"No, but he should be home shortly. Is there anything I can do?"

"I have something important to tell him," Nathan said. "But —"

"Please, I'm really not myself this morning," she said. "One of the college librarians has been murdered."

Nathan nodded. "I heard it on the radio."

"Come in," Helen said, "and have your friend come in too."

Nathan hesitated. He wanted Deirdre to be his lookout. But then he realized if she didn't come in, Helen might become suspicious. She was already jumpy over the murder and jumpy people are often able to pick up on things that other people can't. He motioned to Deirdre to join them. "She's coming," he said, as soon as he saw the vapor from the tail pipe vanish.

"Deirdre O'Keefe, Helen Peters," Nathan said.

They shook hands and Helen invited them into the house.

"The kitchen is the warmest room," Helen said and led them into it. "I'm baking some pies for the holidays," she said, gesturing to them to sit down.

"I came here to warn your brother and Mr. Sims, they're in great danger," Nathan said.

She paled, moistened her lips and asked, "Did Frank send you?"

Nathan looked at Deirdre; then back at Helen. "Frank was murdered," he said in a low voice.

"Oh no!" Helen cried, shaking her head. "No."

"I'm sorry," Nathan said, reaching for Deirdre's hand. "I know you were friends —"

"Almost all our lives," Helen said, the tears streaming down her face.

"Helen, there's a man at Broom —"

The bell rang.

"Oh, my God!" Helen exclaimed.

"Who is it?" Nathan asked.

The tears stopped. Now her eyes were wide with fear. She shook her head.

"Answer it," Nathan said.

The bell rang again.

"Answer it," Nathan said again, his voice harder than before.

Helen pulled herself to her feet and walked slowly to the door.

Nathan drew his gun and followed.

When she reached the door, she looked back at him.

"Open it!" Nathan ordered, positioning himself to fire.

The door swung open.

"Morosov!" Nathan exclaimed.

For several seconds, the two men stared at each other. Then Morosov said calmly, "We want the same man, Mr. Nathan."

Nathan lowered his weapon. "I knew you were in the States."

"Then you also had to know I've come for him," Morosov responded, stepping into the house. He glanced at Helen. "Close the door."

Nathan reset the safety on his gun and returned it to its holster.

"I think we should go back into the kitchen," Helen suggested.

Nathan and Morosov followed her.

"This is Igor Morosov," Nathan said to Deirdre.

Morosov nodded.

"We're both wanted by the police for the murder of Sally Cooms," Nathan said.

"I knew about the murder," Morosov said, settling in the chair Helen had previously used. "But I didn't know we were responsible for it."

"Not by name," Nathan said, "by description."

"In East Berlin you had a beard," Morosov observed.

"I got rid of it this morning," Nathan explained. "It was included in the description."

"So," Morosov said, "what do we do now?"

Before Nathan could answer, the phone began to ring.

Helen answered it. "Oh my God," she cried, "they got Jamie."

Nathan leaped to his feet, went to Helen and took the phone from her. "Sims, where are you?" he asked.

"Who are you?" Troy demanded.

"A friend. Tell me where you are."

"Put Helen back on the phone," Troy shouted.

Nathan handed the phone back to Helen. "Tell him we're friends," he said. "Tell him not to panic, and for God's sake, find out where he is."

Morosov stood up.

"He's in a gas station about five miles from here," Helen said. "I know where it is."

"Tell him to wait there," Nathan said. "We'll pick him up in a few minutes.

Helen related the message. "He'll wait," she said, putting down the phone.

Deirdre put her arm around Helen's shoulders and led her to a chair.

"Jamie is all the family I have," Helen wept.

"They'll kill him," Morosov said, "if we don't —"

"Why is Gorsky here?" Nathan asked.

"I don't know," Morosov answered. "But it has to be for something bigger, more important than becoming the commander of the Russian army."

Nathan sighed, "I'll tell you what I know."

"I'll do the same," Morosov answered, offering his hand.

Troy was waiting for them inside the gas station. As soon as he squeezed into the front of the car, he pulled out the page he had taken from the book and showed it Helen. "This is the man who calls himself Noonan," he said.

Nathan pulled away from the station. "The women will go to a motel," he said.

Helen passed the page to Morosov.

"Gorsky," he said.

"What about Elly?" Troy asked.

"I'll call her from the motel," Helen said, "and tell her to take a cab to the motel."

"No," Morosov said. "They might follow her. Have her take a cab to the bus terminal in Kingston, take a bus to another town, then come back and take a cab to the motel."

"Who are you?" Troy asked, directing the question at Morosov, who was sitting between him and Nathan.

"Major Igor Morosov," Morosov answered.

"A Russian?"

"KGB," Nathan said.

Troy whistled.

"Steve Nathan, CIA," Nathan said, identifying himself and slowing down to pay the toll on the bridge.

"You know Gorsky killed Sally Cooms," Troy said.

"We know," Morosov answered.

A few minutes later, Nathan turned into the parking area of one of the motels where he and Deirde had registered earlier.

"Where are you going?" Deirdre asked before she left the car.

"Not far," he answered.

She walked around to the driver's side.

Nathan rolled down the window. "I'll be all right," he said. "Take care of Helen and make sure that girl Elly gets here."

"Any other orders?"

Nathan shook his head.

"Take care," Helen told Morosov, as she started out of the car.

"Yes," he responded, kissing the back of her hand.

"It's too dangerous to drive around," Nathan said, after he turned out of the motel parking area.

"There's a bowling alley a few miles from here. It has a bar and serves hotdogs and hamburgers," Troy said.

"Do you bowl?' Nathan asked, glancing at Morosov.

"Only when I have to," he answered.

"You have to," Nathan told him.

It took them five minutes to drive to the Highway Bowling Lane. Inside, to the right, a senior citizens' group was holding a tournament.

The three of them rented shoes and Nathan paid for one game.

"Take the last lane on the left," Morosov said.

"Our main objective," Troy said, picking up one of the balls with three fingers, "is to get Petorious back. And the only way we're going to do that is to get Gorsky and trade him for Petorious." He launched the ball; it struck two pins on the right side.

Morosov waited until the pins were automatically reset; then he sent a ball down the middle. All of the pins went down. "You'll never get near Gorsky," he said. "You'll be killed as soon as you're spotted on campus.

Nathan held the ball. "Before we do anything, we've got to find out why Gorsky's here." He looked at Morosov. "He's the reason why we're here, why several people have already been killed."

"The only way to find that out," Troy said, "is to find out what the Board is really doing and to do that we must get into the board room. Everything that happens there is recorded."

"Are you sure?" Nathan asked, finally sending his ball down the center of the alley. All the pins went down.

Morosov nodded approvingly.

"Sure I'm sure," Troy said. "One of the guys I know helped install the equipment. He's some kind of electronics genius. He said there was even some kind of electronic projector."

Each of them took a turn before Morosov said, "We can't move until after dark." Then looking at Troy, he asked, "Do you know how to use a gun?"

"If you mean, do I know how to pull the trigger, the answer is yes. But if you mean anything else, the answer is no."

"I have a small submachine gun in the trunk of my car," Morosov told him. "All you have to do is point it and squeeze the trigger." Then to Nathan he said, "It's our version of your MK seven-sixty."

"That kind of idiot weapon, I'll be able to use," Troy answered.

"That kind of idiot weapon kills," Nathan said sharply.

They played the rest of the game, changed shoes and went into the bar.

"A table," Nathan said, leading Morosov and Troy to an empty one.

"Beer all around," Morosov called out to the barkeep, noting the couple at the bar and the small Christmas tree set up on one side of the room.

Nathan took out a notepad and a pen. "Draw the best floor plan of the administration building you can," he told Troy. "Mark all exits carefully."

Troy nodded and began to draw.

The barkeep brought the beers to the table. "Anything else?" he asked.

"Nothing," Nathan said, handing the man a five-dollar bill.

"I have to bring you change."

"Keep it," Nathan answered with a smile.

The man smiled back, thanked him and retreated behind the bar.

"This is the best I can do," Troy said, pushing the notebook toward Nathan, who studied it for several moments and then gave it to Morosov.

"The three guards on the outside will have to be neutralized," he said, looking at Nathan.

"How do you know that there will be three guards and not four, or five?" Troy asked.

Morosov glared at him. "No questions," he said. "This is not a democratic organization. You will kill one of the guards. Nathan will kill the other, and I will take care of the third. We don't want them to sound the alarm. It will take a while for their bodies to be discovered." He lifted his beer and drank.

"Just how will we kill the guards without making any noise?" Troy asked.

Morosov put the glass down. "Poison darts. It will take ten seconds for the poison to work. I have one gun. That means each of us will have to work very quickly and pass the gun to the next man."

"When do we go?" Nathan asks.

Morosov looked at his watch. "It's already fifteen hundred. Let's say at twenty-two hundred."

"Twenty-two hundred," Nathan repeated.

Morosov looked at Troy, but spoke to Nathan. "Does he understand that our chances for survival are damn close to zero?"

"I know that," Troy said.

Morosov glared at him.

"Troy, the Major —"

"Igor or Morosov," Morosov said.

"Morosov wants you to know what the reality is," Nathan said.

"I want in. I've come this far —"

"You're going to have to kill a man, perhaps several men. Are you sure —"

After a pause, Troy looked at Morosov and nodded.

"You men return to the motel," Morosov said. "I'll meet you at twenty one forty-five."

"No," Nathan said resolutely.

"But the two of you have women there," Morosov responded.

"I'm sorry," Nathan said, "but if the situation was reversed, you'd insist, as I am doing, that we stay together. Come back to the motel. All of us will have dinner together. Besides, you look as if you can use the rest."

"As you said," Morosov answered, "I'd insist that you do the same."

Morosov was alone in the motel room. Earlier, Elly and Helen had gone out for Chinese food. He dropped down on the bed and smiled at the ceiling. He had spent four months in the border area between China and the Soviet Union and had the opportunity to sample real Chinese food. "Everyone is entitled to their illusions," he said to himself. He left the bed and began to pace.

The room was nine paces in one direction and twelve in the other. He paused at the window, pushed back the heavy plastic drape and looked out. It was snowing.

He let go of the curtain, but did not move. "This is going to be my last assignment," he whispered. "I want —" He turned away and looked at the wall opposite. Centered above the bed was a cheap reproduction, a bucolic scene, complete with a river and in the distance a view of mountains whose tops were touched by the yellow light of the sun. He went to the foot of the bed and looked hard at the painting. "I want to escape," he said. "To escape."

A knock at the door caused him to whirl around. "Yes, who is it?"

"Helen."

Morosov went to the door and opened it. There was snow on her hair and on her eyebrows. He stepped back.

"I thought you'd like someone to talk to," she said, walking into the room.

He closed the door.

"I'll go if you want me to," Helen said. "But it's Christmas Eve and most people want to be with someone."

"This isn't the way you or your brother planned to spend Christmas, is it?"

"No. We were going to have dinner out with Troy and Elly."

Suddenly the phone rang. Their eyes locked. The phone rang again. Morosov picked it up.

"Turn on the TV," Nathan said. "Channel eighteen."

"Yes." Morosov put the telephone down. "It was Nathan," he said, "telling me to watch channel eighteen." He switched on the TV.

The newsman said, "The authorities have reason to believe that Troy Sims and James Petorious were connected with the brutal sex slaying of Miss Sally Cooms. One unidentified source said that the Broom College student and professor are linked to the two men who abducted Miss Cooms early this morning while she was in the company of Edward Noonan. Mr. Noonan is indisposed after having been severely beaten by the two abductors. And now an unrelated story. The police are seeking a relationship to a shooting that took place yesterday afternoon on the Belt parkway in Brooklyn to the murder of Frank Robin, who was shot to death on the New Jersey Turnpike three days ago."

Morosov switched off the TV. "They're certainly trying to keep us from Gorsky," he said, looking at Helen.

"Yes," she answered.

Morosov went to the bed, propped up the pillow and settled himself against it.

"This is the first time I've been in a room with a man I don't even know," Helen said. She sat down at the foot of the bed.

"I can't make the same claim," Morosov said, smiling, "I've been with many different women in many different hotel rooms." The snow on her hair and eyebrows had melted, leaving small beads of water in its place.

"Yes, I somehow thought you'd have been," Helen answered. Then, looking straight at him, she asked, "Are you —"

Morosov frowned. "You want to know if I'm married?"

"I'm sorry, I shouldn't have asked," Helen said quickly. "I apologize."

"An apology isn't necessary," Morosov said. "For the past five years my wife has been in an institution. She is catatonic and before that, when we were living here in the States, she was an alcoholic."

"I'm sorry," she said in low voice. "I'm really sorry." And she put her hand on his.

Morosov looked down at it and then at her.

She nodded.

He took hold of Helen's hand and gently pulled her to him. "Are you sure it's what you want?"

"Is it what you want?" she responded.

"It's what I have wanted from the moment I saw you," Morosov answered and taking her into his arms, he kissed her passionately.

Nathan, Morosov and Troy entered the Administration Building through a window in the registrar's office and with Troy guiding them, they made their way through the halls to the central corridor where the conference room was located.

"I only see one guard," Nathan whispered, peeking out of a small alcove where the three of them had paused before their final assault.

"The door is open," Morosov said. "The other two must be inside."

"Troy, are you ready?" Nathan asked.

Troy cleared his throat. "Ready."

Nathan looked at Morosov. "It has to be done this way."

Morosov nodded.

"All safeties off," Nathan said, flicking his to the "off" position. "You'll only have one shot, Troy. Go fast, hit the deck and fire at the chest area."

"Okay."

Nathan sucked in his breath and slowly exhaled. His heart raced. "Go!" he ordered.

The three of them ran toward the room. The guard drew his revolver. Troy dropped to the floor and fired. The guard looked at his chest and sagged against the wall.

Nathan and Morosov charged into the conference room. The two guards there started to go for their weapons, but Nathan picked his target and squeezed off two shots.

The guard was thrown backwards, and the second guard dropped his weapon and threw up his hands.

"Tapes," Nathan said, looking at the box on the floor.

Troy came into the room. "The control panel is at the head of the table."

Morosov moved close to the second guard. "Operate it."

"I don't know how," the man said.

"We don't have time for games," Morosov said, smashing his gun across the bridge of the man's nose.

The man staggered. Blood poured from his nose.

"*Operate* it," Morosov repeated.

The man moved to the head of the table, and activated the control system, which lowered the panel in front of the screen.

Suddenly a map of the Soviet Union was on the screen, showing four geographic positions and next to them a series of numbers circled in red.

"Mean anything?" Nathan asked.

"Gorsky commanded units with those numbers," Morosov answered.

Suddenly a klaxon began to sound and a series of red lights on the equipment begin to blink.

"The bastard tripped a warning switch!" Nathan exclaimed.

"You won't make it out of here," the guard told them.

"Troy, kill him!" Morosov ordered.

Troy hesitated.

Morosov jammed his revolver against the man's chest and squeezed the trigger. "Get the tapes!" he yelled.

Nathan grabbed the box and the three of them ran down the hall.

"This way," Troy said. "The door to the basement is at the end of the hallway, on the right."

"There they are," a man yelled behind them. Four explosions followed.

Morosov dug into his pocket, pulled out a metal cartridge, bit the top off and threw it over his shoulder.

Thunder roared through the hallway, and chunks of the walls and ceiling rained down on them.

Troy led them down the steps and into the basement. "There's a tunnel that goes from here to the powerhouse," he explained, breathing hard.

"How far?" Morosov asked.

"A thousand feet."

The three of them ran until they hit fresh air.

"Christ, the whole campus is lit up!" Nathan exclaimed.

"We can get back to the car," Troy told them, "by going around the dorms and the woods in back of them."

"Move!" Nathan said. "We'll follow."

They moved slowly, cautiously, and silently through the snow-covered woods. Now and then they heard the security guards calling to one another and stopped until the sound of the voices drifted away. It took them more than an hour to reach the car, which had been left in an abandoned barn two miles north of the college.

"I'll drive," Nathan said, sliding behind the wheel.

Morosov sat down next to Nathan. He turned to Troy. "Next time I tell you to kill someone," he said in a flat voice, "and you don't do it, I'll kill you."

"But —"

"There aren't any fucking *buts*," Nathan growled.

Troy sighed, but remained silent.

"I've got to get to a phone," Morosov said, "and warn my people to expect a preemptive missile strike."

"*What?*"

"Give me another reason why he's here," Morosov challenged. "You saw those areas."

Nathan turned the ignition on, but only switched on the parking lights before he started to back out. "Why those four areas and why are those units listed?" he asked as he turned north on the road.

"I don't know," Morosov answered. "I don't know where those four units are. No one does."

"What do you mean, no one does?" Nathan asked.

Morosov was sorry now that he'd mentioned it; it somehow made his people look stupid. But he said, "They're part of a special operation and —" Suddenly he remembered the piece of foolscap he'd found in Gorsky's room. HS stood for *Hammer Strike*, the code name for a preemptive strike against the bases and the units. "I *must* get to a phone." He put his hand on Nathan's arm. "Trust me," he said.

Nathan nodded. "But before we do anything else, we should hear the tapes."

"Certainly. But where?" Morosov answered.

"I have a tape deck, and so does Petorious," Troy responded.

"We'll try your place," Nathan answered, slowing to make the U-turn.

Fitzhugh was the first one to enter the board room. "Guards," he shouted, "get these bodies out of here."

Leon arrived breathless and was immediately followed by Strogerly, Gorsky and the other members.

Leon took his place at the head of table. There was blood everywhere.

Fitzhugh didn't wait until Leon nodded to him but stood up and said, "Gentlemen, the situation is critical. They have the tapes and will shortly — if they do not already — know our plans."

Gorsky was on his feet. "Stop them!" he cried. "Stop them!"

"My men are trying to do just that," Fitzhugh answered, "but so far the three of them have not been very lucky."

Leon fitted a cigarette into a holder and began to smoke before he said, "The question now facing us is whether we abort, take our losses and try another time, or do we let the hammer strike the anvil?"

"If we abort —" Schmidt started to say.

"The consequences will destroy all of us," Strogerly said, holding his cigar in front of him. "I for one can't see that happening to us or our plans. My vote is to let the hammer strike the anvil. All in favor?"

Every man raised his hand.

Strogerly nodded, then looked at Gorsky, who was still standing. "Can you launch, General?"

"With less than fifty percent capacity," Gorsky growled. "At any one time only fifty percent of the missiles are actually ready to fire. The other fifty percent must be brought up to firing status, and that takes about six hours."

"We don't have six hours," Strogerly said, putting the cigar back in his mouth.

"Can you confirm how many missiles will be fired?" Fitzhugh asked.

Gorsky shook his head. "The only message my commanders will respond to is, 'Let the hammer strike the anvil.' "

"We'll just have to take what we can get," Strogerly said. "It's a twenty-minute drive to the plane. The plane will be ready to take off when we arrive. It's four hours' flying time to the command point. That's four hours and twenty minutes from now . . . say five hours. It's twenty-three thirty now . . . say twenty-four hundred. That will make it oh five hundred tomorrow morning."

"My divisions will take control as soon as I give the final command. They'll certainly be able to launch."

"Good," Strogerly responded. "I'll accompany General Gorsky. Leon, stay by your radio. The rest of you follow the plan. We'll be needing all of you shortly after the first missile strikes."

"Have the President and his family been taken out?" Lau asked.

"I should be notified about that within the next hour or two," Fitzhugh said.

Strogerly nodded to Gorsky. "General, we'll leave in a half-hour."

"Yes, in a half an hour," Gorsky answered tersely.

"They really did a job!" Troy exclaimed, looking at the wreckage that had been his living room. Everything had been smashed or slashed.

Nathan put his hand on Troy's shoulder. "The upstairs will be the same," he said.

"We're wasting time," Morosov warned. "We don't know how much time we have." He was already at the door and once they were in the car, he said, "It could have been worse; they could have burned it."

"Yeah," Troy responded, "the bastards could have burned it." Then in a softer voice, he said, "Some of those books belonged to my grandfather."

Morosov didn't answer. His grandparents left nothing. They had nothing to leave. They were shot by Kolchak's men during the civil war that followed the 1917 Revolution.

Nathan rolled past Petorious's house.

"Doesn't look like anyone's there," Troy said, eyeing the darkened house.

"Park out of sight," Morosov told Nathan. Turning to Troy, he said. "You stay at the wheel. Keep the engine running. I'm going to give you a submachine gun. Use it if you have to and that means on anyone who comes close to you, or heads for the house. The people who want us will shoot and ask questions later."

Troy nodded.

Nathan slowed, made a U-turn and pulled up on the shoulder of the road where there was just enough of a bend to conceal the car from anyone in the house.

Morosov opened the trunk, took out the submachine gun and four cartridge grenades. "These are for you," he said, handing them to Nathan. "The two marked with red dots will produce the same reaction as thermite." Before he gave the submachine gun to Troy, he took the safety off and chambered the first round. "All you have to do is point it at the target and squeeze the trigger. A short burst will do the job."

Troy started to put the gun down on the seat beside him.

"Better hold it in your hands," Nathan said.

"Will do."

Nathan and Morosov drew their weapons and leapfrogged toward the house. Nathan was the first inside, found the light switch and flicked it on. "Christ, they were here too!" he exclaimed.

Morosov stormed into the library. The books had been mutilated and thrown on the floor. The desk drawers had been pulled out and smashed. "I'll check the upstairs," he said, his face white with fury.

The mattresses had been cut and the beds overturned. Even the clothing in the closets had been torn. He lingered a few moments in Helen's room. Her scent was everywhere.

"Nothing was overlooked," Morosov said, coming down the steps.

"I'll check the basement," Nathan offered.

Morosov walked into the kitchen. Every dish had been smashed. The wooden table and chairs had been broken. He leaned against the side of the door and suddenly realized there were tears in his eyes.

"I found a tape player," Nathan called. "I found one that's battery-operated!"

Morosov pulled out a handkerchief, wiped his eyes and blew his nose before he answered, "Does it work?"

The two of them met in the foyer.

"The shaft is turning," Nathan told him.

The two of them left the hose and ran back to the car. Nathan sat down next to Troy, and Morosov got into the back seat.

"Play this one," Morosov said, taking a tape out of the small cardboard box.

"Drive," Nathan told Troy, slipping the tape into the recorder.

"Take the gun," Troy said, putting the safety on before he handed it to Morosov.

The first voice they heard was Leon's.

"My God, Gorsky plans to be the new Czar of Russia!" Nathan exclaimed as soon as the tape was finished.

"Play this," Morosov said.

"There isn't any airport around here large enough to handle a Seven Forty-seven," Troy said, after listening to the second tape.

"I've got to notify my people," Morosov told them. "They must be warned." He'd misjudged the situation. The strike would come from his own country.

"I knew there had to be more than just getting Noonan on the Board," Troy commented. "But this . . . this boggles the mind!"

"They're not going to wait," Nathan said. "They know we know their plans. They have to act. Gorsky has to send his signal soon, or he won't be able to send it at all."

"That means they must get to the airport, wherever it is," Troy said.

"That plane will be Gorsky's command center," Nathan said. "According to Strogerly, the signal will be sent in five hours from somewhere above the polar region."

"I must get to a short-wave radio," Morosov told them. "There's no time for me to call my people in New York and have them relay the message."

"Leon has one," Troy offered.

"That makes it easy," Nathan said. "We were going to pay him a visit anyway." He reached over to the dashboard and switched on the radio.

The announcer said, "Our normal broadcasting has been interrupted to keep you informed of the latest developments in the assassination attempt on the President of the United States. At this time we can tell you that his wife and son have been shot. Both have been taken to Our Sisters Of Mercy Hospital in nearby Monterey, California. We do not know if the President has been shot. We urge you to remain calm."

Troy parked a half-mile from the college.

Morosov returned the submachine gun to Troy. "The same rules apply," he said firmly.

Troy nodded. "There's a path," he explained, "that goes from the road, through the woods in front of us, and comes out on the side of Leon's house."

"We'll follow you," Nathan said.

"Wait," Morosov told them. He opened the car's trunk, took out four more cartridges and two additional ammunition clips for the submachine gun. "That's it."

Troy took the lead.

"Gorsky's units will have to fight their way into the missile bases," Morosov whispered.

"You can't count on much resistance," Nathan answered.

Morosov didn't reply. He'd learned long ago not to count on anything unless *he* made it happen and not to count on anyone but himself.

"There's the house," Troy said, stopping.

"Check it out," Nathan said to Morosov.

Morosov moved off to the left, crouching low.

"He's going away from the house!" Troy said.

"He knows what he's doing," Nathan answered.

"You two guys act as if you know one another," Troy observed.

"We do," Nathan said. "We certainly do." Then tilting his face up, he added, "The snow is coming down faster now. I don't think this is just a snow shower."

Troy shrugged.

"Look sharp," Nathan warned. "Someone's coming."

Troy clicked the safety off.

Suddenly Morosov seemed to materialize out of the woods. "There are two guards in front of the house," he said. "Each has an M-16."

"Troy, you cover us," Nathan said. "We'll take them out."

"How —" Troy started to ask.

"Cover us!" Morosov snapped.

Nathan broke off two branches, each about eighteen inches thick. He gave one to Morosov and kept the other for himself. "Ready?" he asked.

"Yes," Morosov answered.

"Shoot only if we run into trouble," Nathan told Troy. "Okay, let's go."

With Nathan in the lead, they moved in the same direction Morosov had taken and in a matter of minutes were facing the front of the house.

"Stay low," Nathan whispered to Troy.

"The guards walk back and forth and turn about the same time," Morosov said. "I'll take the one on the far side." In a few moments, he vanished.

"Work your way up about fifty feet," Nathan whispered to Troy. "Cover the door to the house."

Troy nodded and moved away.

Nathan was sweating. His breath steamed in the night air. He watched the guards. They had just separated, and one was coming toward him. He readied himself to spring. The man was almost in front of him.

Nathan held his breath. He was sure Morosov was ready. He could see the back of the other guard.

The man in front of him turned.

Nathan sprang. He pulled the branch back against the man's neck, strangling his scream.

The man dropped the rifle and tried to pull the stick away from his throat.

Nathan pulled harder.

The man began to claw at the air; suddenly he opened his mouth and vomited blood. Then he went limp.

Nathan let him slip to the ground.

The man was dead.

Breathing hard, Morosov came up to him. He was carrying the M-16. "I had to finish it with a knife," he said.

Nathan reached down and picked up the dead man's M-16.

Troy came out of the woods. "You guys fucking strangled them!" he gasped.

"It's up to you to get Petorious," Morosov said.

"You're joking," Troy answered.

"Not at a time like this," Nathan answered.

"But how —"

"I don't give a fuck how," Morosov growled. "Just get him." He started for the house.

"He's crazy," Troy whispered.

"You wanted in," Nathan answered coldly. "You're in."

Morosov reached the top of the steps and moved to the door. "Now," he shouted and kicked in the door.

Two men charged out of the living room.

Morosov gave them each a short burst.

Both fell to the floor.

Leon came running down the steps.

"Freeze!" Nathan ordered, pointing the M-16 at Leon.

Leon stopped, and his hands went up.

"The radio," Morosov said, "the short-wave radio. Where is it?"

"I don't have —"

Morosov ran up the steps and slammed the rifle butt into Leon's stomach.

He doubled up. Holding his stomach, he sank to his knees and began to retch.

"The radio," Morosov shouted, bringing the butt down on Leon's back.

He screamed and tumbled down the steps.

Morosov ran down after him and lifted the rifle again.

"No," Leon cried, raising his hand to ward off the blow. "The room at the top of the steps."

Suddenly Nathan saw something move. "Troy, to your right!" Nathan yelled.

Troy whirled around and squeezed the trigger.

A woman screamed and crumpled to the floor.

Troy swallowed. "Mrs. Forest!" he cried.

"Take care of Leon," Nathan said, running up the steps after Morosov.

Troy pulled a chair to where Leon was. "Get yourself into it," he said.

"You killed her," Leon shouted, accusingly. "You —"

"In the chair!"

Leon dragged himself up and sat down.

"Where's Petorious?" Troy demanded.

Leon shook his head.

"Don't make me do what my Russian friend did," Troy said.

"Russian?" Leon screamed.

"Petorious, where is he?" Troy pressed.

"I don't know . . . I don't know."

"No bullshit, Leon," Troy said and grabbing hold of Leon's head, he forced the submachine gun's muzzle into his mouth. "Petorious?" Tory shouted, "Where's Petorious?"

Terror filled Leon's eyes.

"I'm taking the safety off," Troy said.

Leon tried to speak.

"Where?" Troy asked, pulling the muzzle out of Leon's mouth.

"Guest house. He's being held in the guest house."

Troy jerked Leon to his feet and pushed him into the library. "Call and have Petorious brought here," he said, handing him the phone.

Leon tried to dial the number, but couldn't.

"The number?" Troy demanded, and dialed it as Leon mumbled each digit, then he handed the phone to him.

"Bring Petorious to my house. Yes, *now*," Leon said.

Troy took the phone away from him and hung up.

Nathan and Morosov came into the room.

"Petorious is being brought here," Troy told them.

"I'll take this one," Morosov said. "Get your friend. Don't leave the guards alive. Nathan, help him." Then he turned to Leon, "I want the new timetable and I want to know where the airport is."

Leon started to shake. Suddenly he began to urinate.

Morosov slapped him across he face. "I'll cut you to pieces, piece by piece," he said and taking out a knife, he slashed the left side of Leon's face.

"Strogerly and Gorsky —"

"When are they going to the airport?" Morosov shouted, pulling Leon's hand away from his bleeding cheek.

"Now!" Leon cried. "Now!"

Outside Troy suddenly shouted, "Hit the deck, Professor!"

A submachine gun sputtered, followed by a burst from an automatic rifle.

Nathan, Troy and Petorious charged into the room.

"We've got to get out of here!" Nathan said urgently.

"He goes with us," Morosov answered, dragging Leon to his feet.

"The back door," Petorious said, leading them out of the room.

The five of them crashed into the woods.

"I'm freezing," Leon whined.

"Move your ass," Troy said, jabbing him with the rifle.

"There," a guard shouted. "There they are!"

Bullets thwacked into the trees and splintered branches.

Suddenly Nathan staggered. Morosov grabbed hold of him. "I caught one in my arm," Nathan said.

"Bad?"

"A graze."

More bullets slammed into the branches above them.

"Petorious," Morosov said, "take this, bite the end off and throw it,"

Moments later the woods behind them exploded into a brilliant white light and screams.

Morosov was the first to reach the car. He took the wheel. Nathan slid in beside him.

Troy forced Leon in the rear and Petorious went around to the other side.

"Which way to the airport?" Morosov asked, starting the car.

"You'll never catch them," Leon whined.

"Tell him," Petorious roared. "Tell him, or I'll beat the shit out of you."

"Tell him," Troy said easily, "or the muzzle goes back in your mouth."

"It's not an airport, it's just a landing strip, eight miles north of here. There's a roadway on the right."

"I remember it!" Petorious said. "You put it in your model train set-up."

Morosov glanced at Nathan.

"I'll live," Nathan said. He turned to Petorious and introduced himself and Morosov.

"It's not the time for explanations," Petorious said. "In fact, I'm only going to say two things: First, I'm glad to see the three of you and second, Troy, you were right."

"You don't know how right," Nathan sighed.

"There's a car in front of us," Morosov said. "Is it Gorsky's?"

Troy pushed Leon forward. "Identify it!"

"Yes . . . yes, it's Gorsky's," Leon answered with a sob. "Yes."

Morosov floored the accelerator.

The limo increased its speed.

"It's them," Nathan said. "We won't have any trouble finding the plane now."

Morosov glanced at the rear view mirror. "We've got trouble coming up behind us."

Troy and Nathan cranked down their windows and pointed their weapons at the oncoming car.

"I'll go for the windshield," Nathan said. "Try for the tires."

Each of them fired a short burst.

The car slowed down.

Suddenly the windshield in front of Nathan splintered.

Morosov's foot went to the brake.

"Keep moving," Nathan said.

A burst from the car behind shattered the rear window.

Troy squeezed the trigger of his submachine gun.

An instant later the car behind them became a moving ball of fire and careened off the road.

Gorsky's car crashed through the gate and drove directly up to the waiting 747.

Morosov, right behind, could see the men run from the car to the plane. He brought the car to a screeching halt and ran toward the plane, which was already moving.

Nathan left the car and started after Morosov, then stopped.

Morosov ran, pulling his gun free as he did so. The sound of the engines tore into his ears. He could hardly breathe. His vision blurred. He put his right hand out and grabbed hold of the landing gear. For a few moments, he was dragged along the ground. He fought the pain that sliced across his shoulder and chest. "Hold," he shouted. "Hold!"

The next instant he was lifted into the air. The pain roared through his body. Slowly he pointed the gun at the inboard jet engine and even as his hold was beginning to loosen he squeezed the trigger once, then again. "Done!" he shouted — and let go.

As those on the ground watched, the plane became an orange ball of flames that tumbled to the ground, fracturing into hundreds of small fires.

The six of them sat at a table in John's Place. Half of the day was already over. Each of them had spent hours giving statements to the Federal authorities, local police, TV and newspaper reporters.

Acting as spokesman for all of them, Nathan had said, "The real hero was Igor Morosov, a Russian KGB agent. The people of the United States and those of the Soviet Union owe him a debt of gratitude. That's all I want to say at this time."

"Anything you want is on the house," Gretta told them.

"Russian vodka all around!" Petorious said.

Gretta brought six shot glasses to the table and a newly opened bottle of Stolichnya to the table. "You pour," she said.

"Thanks," Troy smiled broadly.

Nathan filled each glass, then lifting his, he said, "Morosov was the bravest man I ever knew. I couldn't have done what he did."

"I owe my life to him," Petorious added, "and I didn't even know him."

"All of us —" Troy began. Clearing his throat,

he said, "I don't believe in heroes, but if I did, Igor Morosov would qualify."

Then in a soft, sad voice Helen said, "And I fell in love with him. I hope I gave him a few hours of happiness. What a sad man he was."

****

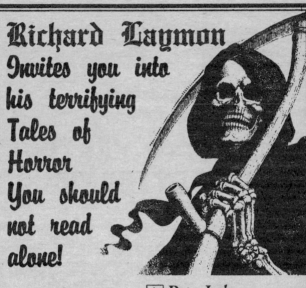

FREE!!
BOOKS BY MAIL
CATALOGUE

BOOKS BY MAIL will share with you our current bestselling books as well as hard to find specialty titles in areas that will match your interests. You will be updated on what's new in books at no cost to you. Just fill in the coupon below and discover the convenience of having books delivered to your home.

PLEASE ADD $1.00 TO COVER THE COST OF POSTAGE & HANDLING.

BOOKS BY MAIL
320 Steelcase Road E.,
Markham, Ontario L3R 2M1

IN THE U.S. -
210 5th Ave., 7th Floor
New York, N.Y., 10010

Please send Books By Mail catalogue to:

Name _____
(please print)

Address _____

City _____

Prov./State _____ P.C./Zip _____

(BBM1)